AA
NB

Naked
Love

OCT 07

CH

Naked Love

Darnella Ford

KENSINGTON PUBLISHING CORP.
http://www.kensingtonbooks.com

DAFINA BOOKS are published by

Kensington Publishing Corp.
850 Third Avenue
New York, NY 10022

All Kensington titles, imprints and distributed lines are available at special quantity discounts for bulk purchases for sales promotion, premiums, fund-raising, educational or institutional use.

Special book excerpts or customized printings can also be created to fit specific needs. For details, write or phone the office of the Kensington Special Sales Manager: Kensington Publishing Corp., 850 Third Avenue, New York, NY 10022. Attn. Special Sales Department. Phone: 1-800-221-2647.

Dafina Books and the Dafina logo Reg. U.S. Pat. & TM Off.

ISBN-13: 978-0-7582-1674-8
ISBN-10: 0-7582-1674-2

First Kensington Trade Paperback Printing: November 2007
10 9 8 7 6 5 4 3 2 1

Printed in the United States of America

I dedicate this book to every breathing thing in despair. May you ascend to the place where you truly belong, and once there, may you connect to your true peace and reunite with the authenticity *that is you.*

There is nothing on Earth more beautiful and more profound than you.

> *You are light.*
> *Love.*
> *Passion.*
> *And divinity.*
> *Keep breathing.*
> *Keep breathing.*
> *Keep breathing.*
> *Every single word I wrote for you.*

Prologue

A Suicide Note

I am a simple Midwesterner, who, on this beautiful autumn morning in downtown Chicago, made my way to the twenty-eighth floor of the Landmark II building, climbed twenty-eight flights of stairs, gained access to the roof, walked to the edge, and jumped.

This is the story of a dying woman who has twenty-eight floors, fifty-seven seconds, to tell her side of the story, and not a moment more. Time is of the essence, so let us not waste a page, a splotch of ink, or a breath.

This is not a suicide note; this is a suicide novel, and once I hit the concrete, the rest of this story will be written in my blood. But do not be alarmed—it is a fascinating story, I promise.

Chapter 28

As I plummeted toward the ground from the twenty-eighth floor, I remembered Juno and the day he lost his virginity.

The less you know about me, the better, and it's not because I'm riddled with flaws but because my life span is grossly short. From this page forward, my life expectancy is fifty-seven seconds, so I implore you to reserve judgment till the end as we return to the beginning of time.

My name is Adrian Moses. In many ways I have always felt like the biblical Moses, wandering the wilderness, waiting to be delivered from *everything* breathing.

My skin and eyes are so translucent that if by chance you blink upon meeting me, I become invisible. I have been called "painfully beautiful" by many, and even I am amazed at how well God tended to the details while putting me together. My exterior is exquisite; however, do not be fooled by that, as my interior life reflects something entirely different.

I am thirteen today, but by tomorrow I will be thirty-one years old, because all you need to change time is a pen that doesn't erase.

I grew up in Saxon, Wisconsin, a small town two hours north of Milwaukee. My mother died of cancer when I was two, leaving me to be raised by my father, Juno. That's what he insisted that I call him: Juno.

Not Papa.

Not Daddy.

Not Father.

Not friend.

"Juno to you, my dear," he would often remind me. "Juno only."

Juno was his stage name. My father was an actor, brilliant and before his time. He had a theatrical production named after him, *Juno and the Temple of Gloom*. It was the longest-running one-man show in the history of Saxon.

Juno was funny, witty, articulate, and tortured.

"Juno, may I have another piece of toast?" I would ask each morning at the breakfast table.

He would giggle like a girl. "Why certainly, daughter, you can have another piece of toast and another after that."

"Another after that," I would mimic when he turned his back. "And another after that."

Juno was different from most of the fathers on the block. He would dance around the kitchen each morning like a schoolgirl, wearing an apron and fancy hairpins.

Juno was so feminine that I was never sure if that was just part of his act. "And another after that and another after that, daughter," he would mumble incessantly, trying so hard to please me. On many occasions, he would insist that I was his daughter but never that he was my father.

"You are my daughter," said Juno on one such day.

"And you are my f—" I would begin, but he'd cut me off.

"Ah," he scolded. "Bite your tongue."

"But why can't I say the word *father*?" I always asked.

"Because I am an *actor*—more specifically, Juno," he would declare. "And performers must be free to be . . ."

"Be what?" I challenged.

"To be whatever the script dictates," he said passionately. "For I am *created*."

When he said that, my eyes would roll back in my head. I wanted to mock him so badly, it was all I could do to control myself. "Juno, isn't that make-believe?" I asked him. And when he heard those words, he grabbed his chest dramatically. "Make-believe?" he squealed. "Make-believe?"

Oh Juno, I thought, *you're such a drama queen.*

"The only make-believe things in this world," he'd whisper in my ear, "are the phony lives we try to convince the rest of the world we are living. I, on the other hand, am very realistic about my fantasy world."

Juno was a combo of Pee-wee Herman and Mr. Rogers, and if that doesn't scare you, nothing will.

He was always running late, behind, or on empty. He was always catching his breath, wiping the sweat off his brow, trying to keep up and catch up. And perhaps the fact that his sperm took it upon themselves to reproduce and deliver him an offspring was the greatest irony of all.

"What do you want to be, daughter?" he asked, usually every day.

"I want to be rich."

"That's nothing to aspire to," he said. "Who cares about riches?"

"I do," I would say. "I want to live in an ivory castle."

"Castles are overrated," he said.

"How do you know?"

"I was born in one in Milwaukee," he said. "Reva Joe Moses was the queen of the castle and I was her prince."

"Your mother was a queen?"

"Yes," he said, "so trust me when I tell you that castles are overrated."

"Okay," I said. "Then I want to be an artist."

"Oh," he would squeal with delight. "What kind?"

"I want to write the story of my life."

"But you're only a teenager," he said with a laugh. "You haven't lived enough life to make a very long story yet, eh?"

"I've lived long enough."

"Nonsense. There's a lot of living left to do," he would always say, while attaching an apron to the front of his feminine-looking pants.

After Mother died, Juno started wearing aprons, hairpins, and skirts, easing toward womanhood and a little farther away from manhood. At first, I thought he did it because he needed to protect himself from spilling biscuit flour all over him, but after a while I began to worry that it was more than that. He began to go through an identity crisis, changing from male to female in front of my eyes—at least that's what I gathered from the pre-death photos of him and my mother. As far as I was concerned, they both died back in the summer of '69. My father was never the same after my mother died. It was like he became someone else, lost in grief. It was as if he made a personal vow *never* to be normal again.

I used to have friends till the eighth grade, but then I came home early one day with playmates to find my beloved father scrambling eggs, wearing a skirt, high heels, and a pair of Hanes panty hose. He'd inserted tube socks under his shirt in place of breasts.

"Juno!" I screamed. "You're wearing a skirt!" He was so startled that he dropped a raw egg on the floor. I remember it bursting open, sunnyside out, raw and oozing.

The grits hit the fan.

The eggs hit the floor.

Juno is a boy who wants to be a girl.

Your father's posing for Cosmo *on his downtime.*

He's a girl on his off days and when no one's home, he's masturbating to the Julia Child cooking show.

Dear God, do away with me now!

He even shaved his legs and armpits. He had less body hair than I did.

Cold cream.

And mud masks.

Hair gels.

And manicures.

"Juno!" I shouted. "Why are you wearing an old lady's skirt?"

"This is not a skirt!" he insisted. "This is a kilt!" he said, trying to justify the absurdity. "And I'm wearing it for a role that I landed in the new town play!"

"What?" I asked him, horrified.

"I am a Scottish guard," he said, parading around the kitchen in front of my friends, who were giggling amongst themselves.

"Do guards wear lipstick and mascara?" I snapped, noticing his makeup.

My friends burst into laughter and ran out of our house. From that day on, I also became an absurdity, just like Juno. The world would define me in the same manner they defined him, so we *both* became outsiders.

I loved him because he was so beautifully unusual, and at the same time, I hated him because he was so ridiculously unusual.

I juggled both emotions emphatically and erratically, waiting for the moon to pull on the tide to ascertain exactly how it was that I felt about Juno.

Poignant.

That is the best description I could come up with.

I felt *poignant* about him.

"I'm having a crisis," I confided to him on the eve of my fourteenth birthday.

"Why?"

"Because I have these," I said, ripping open my shirt and exposing my breasts, which had grown rather large during the last year of my life.

Juno's eyes popped out of his head because he could not believe how gargantuan my breasts had become. Now, it may seem odd revealing my breasts to my father, but Juno was so feminine it was like showing them to a woman. No big whoop.

"Oh my," he said gently. "We'll have to upgrade your cup holders."

"My cup holders?" I asked, eyes wide.

"Yes," he replied flatly.

"You mean my *bra*?" I said loudly, pulling on the words for emphasis.

"Yes, yes," he replied briskly.

"Okay," I replied.

Tortured by reality and tormented by dreams, I often found him sitting on the bedroom floor, crying real tears for a life barely lived at all.

"Juno," I called gently. "Juno, are you unwell?" He wouldn't respond. He'd just sit with his back against the wall, eyes cast downward, spiraling out of control in silence.

"Shhh," he advised softly.

And I would stop speaking *and* breathing.

"Shhh," he would repeat. "Back up and give me space, daughter. Give me space to go."

"Where are you going?"

"Crazy," he'd say. And then water would begin to flow from his eyes.

Crazy.

I would crawl on all fours to sit beside him in silence. If he was really going crazy, I was destined to be an orphan before all was said and done.

"Why are you crying, Juno?"

"Because I am sad," he replied softly.

"Why are you sad?"

And that's where the conversation would end because Juno just stopped responding.

Why are you sad?

Why are you sad?

And why are you sad?

He never answered and I never knew. It felt like I spent my entire life reading Juno's emotional barometer. Loving and distant at the same time, he wasn't an authentic, active participant in my childhood. He was too busy chasing his own little boy *or* girl on stage three nights a week, and when the lights dropped low, Juno appeared center stage to deliver his monologue to the eager residents of Saxon and Milwaukee. He entertained the crowd with theatrics and dramatics as I sat in the front row applauding. Every night he got a standing ovation from the tiny audience of twenty people or so—we would rise to our feet to pay homage to a man who was truly one of God's unique creations.

I was human till the age of fourteen—then I became something else. I woke up one night after having a nightmare, hoping to sneak into Juno's room and steal a space on the floor for comfort. But upon entry, I found him on his knees in a submissive position, sucking a gentleman's *wee wee* like a lollipop.

Oh, dear God!

I screamed.

Juno screamed and so did his companion. All three of us sounded like adolescent girls, but in truth, only one of us was.

Me.

Not them.

Me.

I quickly tore out of the room while Juno yelled something inaudible to his male companion, some sort of indecipherable gibberish or code.

I ran back into my bedroom and locked the door. This was beyond any nightmare a fourteen-year-old girl could ever have on her own.

God, can you please take me now? I collapsed face first into my pillows and sobbed, while Juno struggled with damage control on the other side of the door.

"Daughter!" he called. "Daughter, let me in!"

I did not respond because I did not think he was worthy of a reply.

"Daughter!" he called in panic. "Daughter, let me in!"

Knock forever, Juno, but I'll never let you in.

Knock again.

And again.

But I'll never let you in.

I'll just lie here until I rot, waiting for God to deliver me, just like Moses did.

"Daughter!" he yelled.

"Daughter!"

The next day I finally unlocked my bedroom door and stepped

outside. There lay Juno, face pressed against my bedroom wall where he had fallen asleep mid-knock at midnight.

"Juno," I said, shaking his sleeping body. "It's time to get up off the floor." Slowly, he opened his eyes, which were blanketed by shame and humiliation. "It's time to get up off the floor," I repeated as I walked away. "You're not a virgin anymore."

Chapter 27

As I whisked past the twenty-seventh floor, I remembered the day I offered to switch genitals with Juno.

On the morning of the "great unveiling," Juno called an emergency meeting about his sexuality. Attendance was mandatory.

We convened on neutral grounds—the dining room table where Juno felt obligated to offer an explanation, and I felt even more obligated to accept it.

"I want to talk about last night," he began.

"I don't," I staunchly replied, but fourteen-year-olds don't have options.

"I never wanted to hurt you," he said with tears in his eyes. "I am devastated that you saw that."

"But not devastated that you did it?" I challenged.

He did not respond, only lowered his head.

"Are you ashamed?" I pressed, penetrating him with hard eyes.

"I am myself," he defended. "I am *created*."

"What does that mean?" I shouted. "Why can't you just be normal?"

His eyes widened with surprise, then his chest sank in disappointment. "Everybody else's father is normal, but you're not!" I screamed. "And because you're not normal, that means *I'm* not normal. We're both freaks! The only difference between us is you chose to be a freak and I didn't!"

"You don't think I'm normal?" he asked, rather surprised.

"You wear skirts, lipstick, panty hose, mascara, and insist that I call you Juno instead of Father! Do YOU think you're normal?"

"I am as God made me," he said softly.

"If God wanted you to be a woman, he wouldn't have given you a dick!" I shouted.

Juno burst into tears and laid his head on the table. That was the day I saw how truly fragile he was and how strong I had become. Not that I was really strong at all—I could easily have crumbled into a thousand little pieces.

But by my own good graces, I had just enough of whatever it was I needed to hold on. Juno, however, was not so contained; he cavorted all over the place, drenched in sweat, tears, and theatrics.

"Juno," I called gently. "My dear, sweet Juno. I'm right here. I'm right here. Stop crying." I bent down and kissed him on top of his head, caressing the side of his cheek.

My father was a butterfly who traded his masculinity for estrogen and fake ovaries. The only thing he was missing was a menstrual cycle, and if he could have found a way to buy a real-life period off eBay, he would have. I swear before God, every twenty-eight days, he would have been a bleeding ox.

"Juno," I said gently, but he just kept crying. "Juno," I called again.

"You're ashamed of me," he said as he raised his head from the table. I looked down at him as I towered over his weakened frame, a wilting, artificial flower dying from lack of sun.

Who would ever have thought an artificial plant would need sunlight to thrive?

Say it ain't so, Lord.

And it was in this instance that I became a full-grown woman. My interior blossomed to catch up to my overflowing breasts, which were bursting out of my training bra, otherwise referred to as "cup holders" by Juno.

I needed either a bigger bra or smaller breasts.

I needed a mother with an authentic reproductive system and a father with a real set of balls.

"You really are ashamed of me, aren't you?" he asked in disbelief. I did not answer him because I could not lie to him. And if I could not fib, then the alternative would be the truth, and the truth was *yes*, I was deeply ashamed.

And horrified.

Disgusted.

Disappointed.

And resentful of his behavior, which I perceived as selfish. It seemed as though he cared more about his perverted adulthood than he did about giving me a normal childhood.

"Why did you marry my mother?" I felt compelled to ask. "If you liked boys, how did you end up with a girl?"

He didn't answer right away, and as I stood there, I watched his eyes fill with even more tears.

"Why?" I asked again, insistent that he not negate me by refusing to reply.

"I am an actor. Taking on roles is what I do best," he declared.

"So what role have you taken on with me?"

"I've taken on the role of father," he said quietly. "And I love the part."

"This is not a play," I said, pulling on the words for emphasis. "And I am *not* created! I'm not one of your characters and this is *not* a script! You live in a fantasy, Juno. It's time to come back to the real world and be a grown-up because *I* need to be a kid again. You had your turn and now I want mine!"

With those words, Jack came out of his box and the yin separated from the yang. The bald eagle grew a head full of hair and the whole ecosystem shifted its balance.

"Pancakes or waffles?" asked Mr. Juno, jumping up from the table, changing subjects, time, and place.

I looked into his eyes and saw that he had moved on. The

topic of his sexuality was no longer up for discussion. It was as if he had become someone else, and the balance of what was left of him collapsed against his deep-seated eyes. "Make a decision quickly," he insisted.

"Huh?" I asked, dumbfounded. "Are we done?"

"Done with what?" he asked naively.

"Our talk," I said flatly.

"Yes," he said, searching for ingredients in the cupboard. "Pancakes or waffles?" he asked again.

"Waffles," I replied without thought.

"How about pancakes?" he suggested.

"Are you giving me a choice?"

"No."

"Okay," I said sarcastically, "pancakes."

"Was there something wrong with waffles?" he asked, offended.

"Juno!" I called out to him, exasperated.

"What, child?"

I stopped and really looked at him, and for the first time I saw Juno—not the man I had spent a lifetime hoping to get to know, or better yet, understand. He was a mass of feminine energy, too tired for his chronological age. He was trapped beneath a male exterior. He was an error.

Juno should have been female, and even though he was wearing "man" clothes, a plaid robe and fairly *normal* slippers, I was beginning to see him as a woman.

Oh, goodness.

What happens when you think your father should have a vagina, even more than you should, though you're the only *real* girl in the room?

Do you trade with him out of pity?

Not that I wanted a penis, mind you, but considering the severity of it all . . .

"How are your studies going?" he asked, trying to change the subject.

"Fine, Juno," I said flatly.

"And your art?"

"I don't have any yet, but I'm going to one day," I said. "Think I might take up painting. I like pictures."

"Oh," he said, delighted. "Will you go to art school?"

"Hadn't thought about it," I said. "Maybe."

"I think that would be delightful," he said with an overly gracious smile.

"Do you want to trade?" I asked him straight out, while he was deep into his own mode of disconnect, the one he was famous for: present in body only, mind far away, somewhere with Alice in his own version of Wonderland.

"Do you want to trade, Juno?" I asked again, pressing him, interrupting his journey down the Yellow Brick Road.

"Trade what?" he snapped, coming back to reality.

"Parts," I said abruptly.

"Daughter!" he exclaimed. "What are you talking about?"

"Do you want a vagina, Juno?" I asked harshly. "You know : . . a pussy?"

He was flabbergasted.

"And should I take your penis?" I asked seriously, with the implication that I should take on his "man" role around the house. Fixing broken things. Chopping wood in the winter. Changing tires.

Stuff like that.

I could let Juno be responsible for more feminine assignments, such as keeping his pedicure updated and maintaining his brow waxing on a weekly basis.

"Daughter," he said, obviously embarrassed.

"Do you want one or not?" I screamed at him.

There was a gigantic pause.

"I already have one," he mumbled.

"Have one of what?" I shouted.

"I have one on order," he said humbly.

"One of what? One of what?"

"Vagina," he said, looking at the floor.

"What the bleep?" I shouted, in place of profanity.

"When, Juno?"

"Soon," he said.

"What the hell are you talking about?"

"I've put one on reserve," he clarified. "A vagina."

"You've gone out and bought a vagina, Juno?" I shouted, well beyond the top of my lungs.

"And breasts," he quickly gasped.

My mouth dropped. "Juno, what are you saying to me?"

"I'll be changing from a man into a woman next year, daughter. I've been in the process for some time now," he said. "I've been taking estrogen injections. Don't I look smoother?"

I was on the verge of vomiting.

"That's why I never wanted you to call me Father," he said weakly. "Because I knew that at some point, I would only disappoint you."

I was silent.

The air was gone from the room. I believe it was on this day that we both began to suffocate, Juno and I. The only difference between us was that he began to die and I began to decompose. I actually preceded him in death, at least when it came to a death amongst the living.

"Do you hate me?" he asked.

"Not as much," was all I said.

"As what?" he asked, face crumpled into a frown.

"As you hate yourself," I said, before walking out of the kitchen and up to my room, where I slammed the door so hard, it cracked the window.

We never discussed it again. As a matter of fact, we never discussed anything at all.

Ever again.

The curtain closed on Juno's show two days later. It was an abrupt and dismal end to a small blaze of glory.

Juno had just become too weird for our small town, and the rumor mill was functioning full-time. Alleged homosexuality and rumors of a pending sex change didn't sit well with the locals.

I found out about Juno's cancelled performances while dozing off in the drama class he had forced me to take to "broaden my horizons."

My horizons were broad enough, or so I thought.

My instructor, Mr. Hydel, a large, rustic man with an exceptionally hairy nose, delivered the news to me. And rather insensitively, I might add. "Adrian, your crazy father has twinkle-toed himself right out of the production, with those shameless skirts and that hideous, high-fashion lip gloss. Has he gone absolutely out of his mind?"

"What?" I snapped.

"His show was cancelled last night."

"But everybody *loved* him!" I screamed in protest.

"They loved the part he played on stage, but not the role he was living in real life," said the snooty teacher with one brow raised, looking at me with great suspicion, almost as if it were I who was lining Juno's lips with gloss.

"Then to hell with ALL of them!" I shouted, leaving the class promptly, running all the way home to rescue Juno. I just knew he had splintered into itty bitty pieces, and I had to get home quickly so I could put him back together again.

Juno, I said, *please leave all of your pieces in one spot so I can put you back together again.*

I found Juno at home, just as I knew I would.

Broken.

Crumpled to the ground.

He was sleeping naked in his bed, rolled into a ball, wearing a wig and a face full of makeup.

I covered him with a blanket.

"Juno," I called to him.

He didn't answer.

"I'm sorry about your show," I said. "To hell with city hall. They don't know you very well!"

And still there was no response.

I rubbed the side of his face, kissing him on the cheek. I must have kissed him a thousand times, trying desperately to heal him.

"Good night, Juno," I said. "Sleep. Sleep well."

Somewhere between sunset and sunrise, Juno killed himself. Dying as dramatically as he had lived, he hung himself from his bedroom closet, naked, strung up by bedsheets.

I found him shattered, broken, and bruised, with a shriveled penis and blossoming breasts.

How could he kill himself when he'd always said that there "was so much life left to do"?

Juno, how could you live and die under the weight of so much hypocrisy?

I didn't come unglued.

I should have.

I didn't scream.

I could have.

I didn't wail about, throwing myself on the floor, begging God for Juno's return.

I didn't even cry.

But now I wish I had.

I wasn't angry with Juno, nor was I mad at God.

I did two things.

One, I cut him down.

And two, I extended the greatest courtesy that a daughter ever could to her father: I buried him in a dress.

Chapter 26

As I descended past the twenty-sixth floor, I remembered the day the "confused man/woman" packed me up and moved me away from my childhood.

The day after Juno's funeral, I was shipped out like a carefully packaged unit of blood.

I was stamped "fragile" on the forehead, "do not shake" on the behind, and "keep refrigerated" somewhere along the side of my heart.

I was being transported from the burbs of Saxon to the slums of Milwaukee, where I was to be delivered into the flabby arms of Reva Joe Moses, my grandmother and Juno's slightly cuckoo mother. I say *slightly* cuckoo with caution, because I didn't know her very well. She could be an all-out loon, or she could be the closest thing to sanity I've ever known. *Strike that last comment.* With the kind of luck I typically have, I wouldn't bank on her sanity.

At all.

Juno and Reva Joe weren't exactly the best of friends, and the more "girly" he became, the more distant she'd become. She did not even attend his funeral, citing hemorrhoids as the "demon that kept her away."

One of Juno's confused man/woman friends kindly offered to drive me to Milwaukee from Saxon, and it was indeed two hours of unwarranted hell.

"How do you feel?" he/she asked me in the car on the way to the big city.

"About what?" I asked him.

"About the future," he stated with great optimism.

"How am I supposed to feel?" I asked flatly.

"I would hope that you are filled to the brim with hope!" he said with a pause, flashing a gigantic smile. "Your father used to tell me that you wanted to be an artist. Paint things, pretty pictures and such."

I did not respond.

"He said you wanted to go to art school, eh?"

I did not respond.

"And," he said, desperately trying to smooth over our lack of conversation, "that you longed to be the queen of a very big castle."

Silence.

And more silence.

"Oh, Adrian," he said on the cusp of a huge burp, "things really can't get much worse, now can they? The worst of it is behind us."

I turned to him and glared, maybe even snarled.

"So much of life is captured, not by what it is, but actually by how we see it to be," he said, trying to sound overly bright. Actually, reciting the alphabet in the correct order would have been "bright" of him, considering how dumb he looked.

"Wouldn't you agree?" he asked, pushing me deep into my skin.

I shrugged my shoulders, trying hard to dismiss him, or better yet, ignore him.

"You're grandly beautiful," he said. "Do you want to be a model when you grow up?"

"No."

"What about an actor . . . like your father, perhaps?"

"No!" I blurted.

"Then *what*?"

"I don't know," I said rudely.

"You have no ideas?"

"I have ideas. Lots of them," I said to him, showing teeth. "But if I acted on *any* of them right now, they would all land me in jail!"

Juno's friend gasped, raising his hands to the sides of his face, "Oh, my!"

"Yes," I said in a low, taunting voice, "'Oh, my' is right."

"Have you had therapy?"

"And why would I need such a thing?" I snapped. "The question is, have *you* had therapy?"

He turned and looked at me, examining me from head to toe, up and down, making a slew of accusations but keeping them all to himself.

"I hope you can find some joy in Milwaukee, Adrian, and re-connect with that inner child that wants so badly to smile out loud," he said with the optimism of a high-school cheerleader.

What the . . . ?

"I just want you to be happy, child, and Juno would want the same."

As he rambled on, his words began to bleed into the background.

"You owe it to yourself to find that special place where you can let go and just be . . ."

Blah.

Blah.

Blah.

He went on and on with his nonsensical psychobabble about a bright, new future.

A bold, new world.

The exploration of endless opportunity.

Shut the hell up, man/woman!

His mouth was moving and the words were spilling out, falling all over the floor, but he wasn't really saying anything at all.

Cork it, buddy! I need a minute to reconnect with myself here.

By the time we were thirty minutes outside of Milwaukee, I think he had actually succeeded in talking me into a coma. I turned to him, motioning for him to lean close, and when he did, I screamed at the top of my lungs.

"I'm ecstatic!

Can't you tell?

Feel like I'm on my way to Disney World right now!

Milwaukee, Wisconsin, has got to be the HAPPIEST freaking place on Earth!

Wouldn't you say????

Let's stay in touch so we can do tea once a month!

Would you like that?

Thank you for driving me!

You're such a nice man.

Oops, I mean woman.

Oops, I mean man!"

This man's butt came right up off the nice leather bucket seat and his head crashed into the sunroof.

He was scared halfway to death, and this, combined with the dagger-look I had just shot him, was enough to shut him the hell up. And not just for the rest of the ride, but for *life*.

He drove the rest of the way in silence. I actually think he was frightened of me, casting small, furtive looks in my direction, but only for a beat before quickly turning away.

Now this was *funny*.

I felt like the Big Bad Wolf riding in the front seat, and he looked like Bambi on crack.

What a loser, I thought. Maybe the next time a young girl buries her last living parent, he'll know better than to try and sell her on the sunny side of life the very next day.

Ruf! I shouted again, glancing his way, before bursting into laughter. I laughed so hard I had to grab my sides with both hands. When Juno's man/woman friend came unglued from his seat and rammed his head into the sunroof, his toupee shifted. It was now lopsided, and he looked like a poorly groomed poodle.

Ruf! I barked out loud, throwing myself deeper into my own hysterics. I turned to him and shouted once again.

Ruf!

He looked at me, horrified, staring. I must have looked as though I'd gone stark, raving mad.

"Dear God," he whispered below his breath. "The child's gone mad."

I laughed till I broke even with the pain. It was nice to breathe *life* again, if only for a moment. It was a well-deserved pardon, a gap between hurts, before the pain would come gushing back into my busted heart again.

Yes.

It was so nice to have a moment, a glimpse of authentic relief.

Juno's friend, by the way, of whom I never bothered to ask his name, was more than happy to open the door and escort me to Reva Joe Moses's doorstep.

"Good-bye, child," he/she said, waving a limp wrist and disappearing into thin air, plowing his giant SUV down the wet streets, flooded with the aftermath of Mother Nature's tears.

"Good-bye, child. I hope to never see you again," I think he whispered.

Never.

Ever.

Chapter 25

*As I descended past the twenty-fifth floor, I remembered the day I had
breakfast with the giant, polka-dotted muumuu.*

When she opened the door, I felt as though I had entered a
time warp. By my last calculation and glance at the calendar, we
were well into 1985, but when Reva Joe came to the door, I took
one step backwards, which just kept taking me back about fif
teen years.

How did I end up here?

And *here?*

Reva Joe stood with both hands on her wide-load hips, wearing a polka-dot muumuu, with a set of large pink rollers in her
off-white hair. Her eyes scanned me up, down, and back up
again. Her skin was an ashy white, almost dingy, and the odor
coming from her house was a combination of pancakes, sour
milk, and rotting sulfur.

"Adrian," she said with a strong, unfriendly voice. "Don't just
stand there—bring your little country behind in here. You're
letting out all my good heat."

I entered slowly, almost reluctantly. She put one hand on the
back of my shoulder. I thought she was attempting to greet me,
but instead she pulled me roughly into the center of her living

room. When she shut the door, the air seemed to evaporate out of the room. I gasped, taking in a deep gulp of air so I could keep breathing.

Oh sweet Jesus, I thought to myself. I slipped on a banana peel and fell into poverty. She was so poor I felt we could have shot a *National Geographic* special on poverty right here. Everything was old, dingy, broken, dusty, and cracked. Nothing in the place was shiny and new. I was about the newest and shiniest thing she had probably seen in years.

There was something about poverty and being dirt, butt-ass poor that I *hated*. Not that anyone enjoyed a life of meager means, but there was something about it that I absolutely could not deal with.

I hated to wake up in poor skin. I wouldn't necessarily call myself a snob, but there was something about lack and limitation that just stunk to high heaven.

Didn't Juno say she used to be a queen?

What happened to her castle? It looked like the castle burnt to the ground and all that was left were the memories. From the looks of things, even that was generous because it didn't look like she had a thing.

I glanced around the living room, cluttered and dingy with ugly green shag carpeting and brown paneling on the walls.

The living room couch might have been decent back in '69, but it was an eyesore in 1985. It had long lost its affect and effect, and the only plausible word I could use to describe it was *disastrous*.

"Put your bags in the back bedroom," she said.

"Okay."

I walked slowly to the end of the wood-paneled hallway, where I made a sharp right turn and stepped into my room, which looked more like a jail cell.

It was primary.

Primitive.

Basic.

A full-size bed sat in the center of the floor. The walls were brick and painted with a crusty, thick coat of white gook that someone tried to pass off as paint. A putrid-looking red comforter rested lopsided on the bed.

The walls had no pictures.

The floors had no rugs.

The house had no real color.

The air had no real spirit and the room had no real *hope*.

I placed my bags on the floor and sat on the bed, almost falling off. The flimsy mattress jiggled and teetered—I could feel my butt inching its way closer to the edge by the sheer force of gravity.

When I finally grounded myself on the shaky structure, I sat and stared at the floor in disbelief. When I got tired of that, I turned my attention to the ceiling, and when I tired of them both, I fixed my attention on the wall until I was interrupted by the intrusion of the giant polka-dot muumuu.

"Breakfast is ready!" shouted Reva in a voice that was way too loud. "Come and get it!"

I do believe I'm going to have to teach her how to use her indoor voice.

"I'm not really that hungry," I said quietly.

"Two things you never do under this roof. *One* . . . you never turn down a meal," she said as she turned to walk out. "So get your little country butt up off the bed and follow me."

"What's the second thing?" I asked, following behind her crusty heels.

"What?"

"You said there were *two* things that you never do in this house."

"There are," she said flatly.

"What's the second one?"

"I'm not sure yet," she said as her big jelly butt wiggled beneath that hideous outfit. "You'll find out soon enough."

"What if I wanna know now?"

"Wanting to know and *needing* to know are two different things."

"You're the boss, Reva Joe," I replied with a hint of sarcasm.

"Just don't forget rule number one," she snapped.

I sat down in the rickety wooden seat and pulled myself up to the table. Reva Joe set a plate of runny eggs, burnt toast, and undercooked bacon in front of me. It didn't resemble anything I'd ever eaten before in my life, or would want to eat, for that matter.

Poverty can be so unappetizing.

I sat and stared at the meal without touching it. I was scared of it. Reva Joe was sitting opposite me, devouring her plate of inedibles.

"What grade are you in?" she asked between each giant bite.

"Ninth."

"You like school?"

"I like it okay."

"You a good student?" she asked, a large piece of toast hanging from her mouth.

"Good enough," I replied.

Reva Joe just grunted and continued eating. "Like boys?" she asked with one eye on her food, the other on me.

"I guess," I responded uncomfortably.

She slammed her fork down on the plate. "Oh, Jesus, Father, Mary, Virgin Lord! Don't tell me you're one of them fairies like your father!"

"Oh, Christ, Reva Joe!" I shrieked, pushing my body *and* my chair a few inches away from her.

"*That's* rule number two," she stated. "No flying fairies in this house!"

"I'm N-O-T gay, Reva Joe!" I screamed. "Just don't like any *particular* boy right now! Why are you so paranoid?"

"Paranoid, my ass!" she screamed. "I dealt with that fairy shit from the time your father was a little bitsy boy. Always tried to convince him that he was . . . you know . . . well . . . thank the Lord you ain't one of those big ole 'L's' 'cause I don't take in gays or strays," she said, turning her complete attention back to her runny eggs. "I should get a sign and hang it out front that says: *No Gays. No Strays.*"

In that moment, I looked at her so harshly that my essence pierced her, and I could feel hatred brooding.

"What?" she asked, feeling the heat of my disapproval. "What?"

"Nothing," I said, looking right through her.

"It looks like *something* to me, that look on your face. Looks like a whole lot of something."

"Nothing," I repeated.

"Why aren't you eating?" asked Reva, staring at my uneaten plate.

"Not hungry," I said flatly.

"You one of them sensitive types, ain't you? Oh boy," Reva huffed. "This is gonna be a *long* four years."

I didn't respond. Just stared.

"This house ain't big enough for you *and* your feelings. One of 'em has to stay outside. You get what I'm talking about? You understanding me, Adrian Moses?"

I could feel heat rising, swelling inside of me. I could also feel its desperate urge for release, an internal throwing up that wanted to deposit itself all over Reva Joe.

"I don't want you calling my father a fairy!" I declared emphatically. "It just doesn't sit well with me. My father was a brilliant man. He was talented and funny and he cared about people's feelings."

"That's apple pie in the sky!" scowled Reva as she set down her fork and stared at me intensely. "Your father was a loser. Nothing more. Nothing less. It's not as dramatic as you're making it sound. Now, I could sit here and gas you up, blow sunshine up your narrow little behind, but that won't do anybody any good," she said, staring at me with growing malice.

"Why are you talking to me like this?" I asked, baffled.

"I will speak as I damn well please in my own goddamned house!" said Reva, exasperated. "I will speak against fairies and faggots, niggers and extraterrestrial beings! I will stand on the rooftop or cop a squat in a ditch if I damn well please! This is MY house and YOU ain't gonna come in here and start running things like you ran your fairy, faggot father!"

Pause.

This was the first time I left my body. On the heels of Reva Joe's last spoken words, I stepped outside myself while she screamed insults in the background.

Retard.

Imbecile.

Trifling.

Loser.

But I didn't hear much more than that because I was gone, disconnected. I made a mass exit from my current frame of consciousness.

Blank.

Nothing.

White noise.

The room bled to a fuzzy disconnectedness. I was separated from its interior, lingering somewhere just outside myself. For a moment, I flew with the birds, enjoying the freedom I had always searched for and that I always knew existed.

A plop on top of the head brought me back into my body or my mind, or maybe it was a little of both. Stinking Reva Joe had rolled up the morning newspaper and popped me on the crown of my head.

"I make the rules! I *am* the rules!" she screamed. "What I say goes and if I want to run butt-ass naked down the middle of the street with my double-D breasts blowing in the wind, then I will do as I damn well please!"

My eyes widened and I reached for the top of my head. I looked at her with astonishment that my father, a gentle soul, would have killed himself and left me in the custody of a lunatic—the wicked witch of Wisconsin.

How could this be? Surely there must have been a switch at the hospital. I could not accept that the lovely, charming Juno, star of the longest-running one-man show in Saxon, Wisconsin, could be remotely related to, much less spawned by, this godawful creature who would dare to call herself a *mother*.

Dare I say horrible and vile?

I never knew Reva Joe as a child, and within five minutes of coming into her presence, I now understood why Juno had kept me away from her my whole life.

She really was a poor-white-trash lunatic.

"Rule number three—no zoning out at the breakfast table while I am talking to you . . . off in La La Land somewhere!" she screamed, "Probably running around with a bunch of La La Land fairies."

Reva stood up from the table and cleaned off the plates. She made some sort of growling sound as she stepped into the kitchen. "Hmm," she said. "The apple don't fall too far from the tree. I can certainly see the resemblance between you and Juno."

"I do wish I could say the same, Reva Joe, but you don't remind me of my father at *all*."

Those were my last words on that particular day. For that comment I was sent to the backyard to pull dead weeds for the remainder of the afternoon.

As I stood in a ditch off to the side of the house, I could see Reva Joe indoors, sweeping, laughing, and dancing about the house. Actually, all I could really see was her horrific polka-dotted muumuu. She was such a peculiar, brazen woman.

Dancing.

Spinning.

Drinking.

Twisting.

And laughing.

A muumuu without a body.

Turning on its own.

Spinning.

Drinking.

Dancing.

And laughing.

Yes, that was who I had eaten breakfast with that morning. It was my very first day in hell and I had sat down to share a meal with a muumuu.

Chapter 24

As I descended past the twenty-fourth floor, I remembered the day I got a peek at what sits just beneath Reva Joe's off-color muumuus—a solid plate of steel body armor. Not a pretty sight indeed . . .

Preparation for the first day of school was no easy chore, mentally speaking. I was a bundle of nerves that morning, starting all over again.

New teachers.

New lessons.

New friends.

New framework and mind-set as I would soon embark on a whole new series of experiences.

I was an outsider.

Orphan girl.

The one who fell prey to Mother Nature and Father Tragedy. Mother got swallowed by cancer and Father got eaten by insanity. So I was a mixed nut.

A wild-eyed outsider on the verge of puberty and menopause at the same time, body confused, mind lingering somewhere between temporary haywire and stark, raving madness.

Trapped beneath the giant polka-dotted muumuu of an eccentric, defiant fifty-five-year-old woman. The one who had a fondness for the late Sixties and a particular fancy for muumuus with various patterns, especially polka-dots. The one with the super-white skin and dirty, worn house slippers that showed off her fat, white ankles so desperately in need of lotion. Sometimes at the breakfast table, her crusty ankles would bother me just enough that I longed to grab a stick of margarine and reach down and rub it on the base of her dry, cracked skin. Not for her sake, but for my own.

I couldn't stand to look at her ankles. And they never changed. They stayed fat and dry, cracked and calloused.

Yuk!

Yuk!

Yuk!

I was up at 5:30 A.M., even though I didn't have to get out of bed till six. But I always woke up at 5:30 in Reva Joe's house because that was the precise hour that Reva would blast the controversial A.M. talk radio show, Bueford & Mitchell, throughout the house. These were obnoxious guys who took calls from locals who insisted on spilling their radical political views on the air. Sometimes the callers were mental whack jobs who simply needed airtime to work through their bizarre life situations and spread noise pollution around the city.

It was maddening.

I always felt that Bueford & Mitchell were prejudiced and small-minded, so I understood why Reva Joe was drawn to them. They were what she was, and beyond the setting on the A.M. radio, they could have been interchangeable.

She was Bueford & Mitchell, and they were Reva Joe Moses, the unkindest and most senseless woman in the midwestern United States.

Bueford & Mitchell were often harsh and unkind, but some people found their particular breed of humor gratifying, and Reva Joe was foremost among these ignoramuses.

Upon stumbling out of bed and dragging myself to the bathroom, I rolled my eyes at the sound of their obnoxious voices. I could hear them degrading people, and Reva Joe laughing, then cackling and howling. Obnoxiousness at its finest.

As I stood in the tiny, tattered bathroom with the dingy rugs and mildewed pine paneling, freezing cold from the draft, I could barely stand the misery.

I showered, dressed, and reluctantly joined Reva Joe at the rickety dining room table, where she sat over a bowl of dry oatmeal, pressed against her elongated boom box, blaring Bueford & Mitchell.

When I entered the room, neither of us spoke. She was so absorbed by them bashing a teenage gay man that she was hardly aware of me.

"So, you're a faggot?" one of them said. It was either Bueford or Mitchell. Both were disgusting to me, so I didn't bother to differentiate between them.

Reva Joe laughed. This kind of badgering was right up her alley.

"I am a homosexual male," said the young man. "And I find the word *faggot* offensive."

"What difference does it make? You're either a fag or you're not . . ." said one of the radio personalities.

This is when Reva Joe slammed her hand down on the table and howled, "That's right, Bueford! Give his faggot ass hell!"

I couldn't believe it.

I stared in awe.

This is the way I'm going to start my first day of school, with new teachers to meet, new lessons to learn, and new friends to make? This is how it begins? With howling faggots and egotistical prick personalities who entertain fat ladies with crusty ankles in giant-sized muumuus, eating dry oatmeal.

I must be at the movies.

This cannot be real life.

More urgently, this cannot be my *life. And if it is, it can't get any worse than this, can it?*

Promise me, God, that it can't.

A couple of minutes after Bueford & Mitchell pummeled this young gay man and crushed a few innocent bystanders just for the hell of it, Reva Joe came to the realization that I was sitting adjacent to her at the table.

She laughed, nodded her head, and excused her big, fat ass so she could go into the kitchen and bring me a bowl of cold, dry oatmeal.

She set it down with finality. It looked dead enough to me with those hard, cracked raisins and oats that were so bone dry, they looked like wheat.

I had been with Reva Joe almost three weeks and had already lost five pounds. Her cooking was nothing to write home about. As a matter of fact, her cooking was nothing to write *anybody* about.

It was awful.

Foul.

Poor.

Yes, that was a good description of her meals: poor. The food itself reflected her own decadence. It had no spirit.

Life.

Essence.

Breath.

The food was dead, much like Reva Joe herself.

I stared at the bowl of dead food and Reva returned to her love affair with Bueford & Mitchell.

A listener called in to the radio program and this is the conversation we heard that day while sitting at Reva Joe's wooden table, on my first day of school, on the twentieth day of my stay in hell:

Bueford: *Caller, you're on the air with Bueford & Mitchell.*
Male Caller: *I'm calling because I heard you guys giving a hard time to that young man who just called in a bit ago.*
Mitchell: *You talking about the gay teen?*
Male Caller: *Yes.*
Mitchell: *What's your name?*
Male Caller: *I'd rather not say.*
Bueford: *Then what's your beef, chief?*
Male Caller: *(hesitates) You shamed him.*
Mitchell: *(laughing) We shamed him?*
Male Caller: *Yes.*

Bueford: What are you . . . some pathetic bleeding heart who spends his whole life looking for causes to take up?

Male Caller: I just think it's wrong for people to make fun of things they don't understand.

Mitchell: In case you haven't noticed, we're not particularly interested in what you think.

Male Caller: I had a friend . . .

Bueford: Big whoop.

Male Caller: And he cared about what people thought.

Mitchell: (laughing)   And we care about him because . . . why?

Male Caller: He was tortured his whole life because he felt unaccepted by the people he loved most. He had a beautiful daughter and all he wanted to do was love her, but he never felt like he did it right. He had a wretched bitch for a mother and all she ever did was put him down and call him 'fairy' and 'faggot'. But he was brilliant . . . a creative genius who had the longest-running one-man show in Saxon. Few people could see his beauty and his brilliance because they spent the whole time judging him and in judging him they missed 'him' altogether. Two weeks ago, he hung himself and the world lost a great talent. I lost a great friend and people like you are a whole lot emptier because of it—the biggest tragedy of all is you don't even know it. I guess that makes you a little bit pathetic, wouldn't you say?

Reva Joe slammed the boom box's power button and shut the whole thing down. This was *the* most intense moment of our encounter so far. We were staring at each other, in essence naked, with no place to hide.

The irony of it all was bone-chilling.

Someone had phoned Reva Joe's favorite radio show to speak about the death of her only son, and, in the process, had shamed her into an accidental visit to her own rotten soul. The man on the radio had spoken the truth, for it was a fact that we were all a little diminished as a result of Juno's death. In this moment we were all delivered a little bit closer to ourselves, whoever we happened to be, good or bad.

There it was, staring us in the face. We couldn't avoid it.

Reva Joe shot a fierce look my direction. She looked at me

angrily, her eyes smoldering to a surly black. I do believe that for the first time since I had been with her, a chunk of pain had finally managed to float its way to the top. Reva Joe was actually beginning to show a flash of emotion that was separate from her anger, prejudice, and hatred. I stood in awe of it, for I simply had to watch.

"What are you looking at, monkey butt?" she snapped.

"*You*," I said intensely, staring back.

"Well, bug off, kid. You're bothering me!" she said, grabbing her breakfast dishes and walking into the kitchen.

"Did you hate him?"

She stopped in her tracks and stood still in silence for about a minute, her back turned to me.

"Did you hate Juno?" I repeated.

Still, there was no answer.

"Did you hate your only son?" I repeated, but this time it was louder.

I wanted her to feel it. I wanted the words to shoot through her like a flame against ice. I wanted to know her truth, but more importantly, I wanted *her* to know her truth.

She walked into the kitchen and never answered. I waited in the dining room for several beats before moving to the corner of the room, where I waited. I would wait and listen, because I knew that just around the corner there would be some evidence, no matter how brief, of her humanity.

I could feel the breeze in the air and I knew it was coming: *Humanity*. It took about three minutes to arrive and when it showed up, the great dam *broke*.

It began with soft, muffled sobs. They were so low they were barely audible to the human ear. And as I waited and listened, they began to pour in, slow at first, then quicker, and eventually torrentially.

Reva Joe stood against her sink, crumbling. Her knees fell against the base of the cupboard, and as they buckled, down she went.

Sob.

Sob.

Sobbing.

As I watched, it hurt. Through her pain, I was able to connect with my own and deal head-on with the loss of my father
and feel the rippling effect it had had. Not just on me, but on
me and Reva Joe. And not just on me and Reva Joe, but on the
rest of our community.

I slowly entered the kitchen, crying, shoulders jerking back
and forth. As I approached Reva's crumpled form down on the
kitchen floor, I could feel the heat from her skin. It was the heat
of her anger, the rise of her fear. It was many years of repressed
emotion and pain. I could feel it rising from the center of her
being, heating up the room. I could taste Reva's pain in the air
as she exhaled, breathing out all that she had held in for so long.
It was all the stuff she tried to bury beneath the "faggot" remarks and other unkind words. It was rage and fury, disappointment and devastation.

In the end it was an explanation of the unexplainable. "You
loved him, didn't you?" I declared as I stood over her, hovering
like the orphan child that I was, in need of resurrection, or at a
very minimum, an authentic moment to connect with someone
who truly felt *my* pain, the loss of my beloved father. "Didn't
you, Reva Joe?"

Reva looked up at me, her eyes bleeding with agony. She extended her flabby arms outward in my direction and I knelt
down beside her, and she grabbed hold of me, sobbing into my
chest.

The tears were hard and heavy, filled with blood and history.
I knew this because I had cried the same tears once, a long time
ago. It was probably the day I cut down a naked Juno and laid
him on the floor, staring in shock and disbelief at his stiff corpse.

"Why couldn't he just be normal?" she asked, digging her
hands deep into the base of my back. "Why couldn't he just be
normal?"

I didn't know how to respond. There were no words to soothe
the anger, and I knew it, so I was silent for a long, long time.

"Why?" she screamed aloud. "Why?"

"He was himself, Reva," I said in a deep, strong voice. "He was *himself*."

Reva let go of her death grip on me, sat up on her knees, and leaned back. Her face, red and exasperated, was depleted of all the stuff that makes life worth living. She looked empty. There was a void behind her eyes that seemed infinite, at least to my fourteen-year-old eyes.

"He was a faggot," she said angrily, pulling herself off the floor. As she rose to her feet I could see the angry armor come back to life again. The hard steel that covered her heart was in place once more. Hence, a swift return to the madness.

"What are you doing down there on the floor?" she snapped. "Get up! Get up! You're gonna be late for the school bus!"

I slowly rose to my feet, in awe of what I had observed.

"What are you staring at?" she snarled.

"Why are you so afraid to be *human*?" I asked. "You're scared to death of your feelings. You're so afraid that it took you twenty days to show a shred of emotion over the loss of your *only* son. It's easier for you to pretend that you hate him than to admit how much you loved him. I don't know, Reva Joe . . . I'm only fourteen so I don't know a whole heck of a lot about the world, but there's something about living like that that just doesn't seem right."

"What do you know about me?" she snipped. "What do you know about life? You haven't lived long enough to know anything. Get ready for school, kid. You're on my *last* nerve this morning." And with that she left the room, without further ado.

Chapter 23

As I descended past the twenty-third floor, I remembered the day I derailed and went my own way.

The school bus stopped just outside of Reva Joe's house, *directly* in front of it. As I stood on the dry, rotted porch, I was petrified, waiting in angst for the big yellow bus to pull up right in front.

It was preschool all over again, at least that's what it felt like. It also felt like the first day of spring and the last day of winter. It was a tropical storm and a blizzard all at the same time. There was so much going through my mind and so much emotion flowing through my body, I didn't know what to process first.

I was hoping—no, *praying*—that the bus would skip Reva Joe's driveway and wait up the road so the kids wouldn't see where I lived. I was embarrassed by this house. Terribly, terribly embarrassed. It was old and wilting, indicative of the life inside, or lack thereof, and I was deathly afraid to be associated with it. They would think of me as shoddy if they saw this house, or perhaps they would think of me as dirt poor.

I was the daughter of a gifted, eccentric actor who was a brilliant, loving, free spirit. I was his kid, the one people pointed to at his plays, the one who was always connected to something extraordinary, not pathetic like this.

Poor.

White.

Trash.

As I stood on the porch and held my breath, I knew the bus would stop here because Reva Joe's house was the marker for the second stop, right in front of her mailbox. And sure enough, just as I knew it would, twenty-three minutes before the eight o'clock hour, my reputation went to hell in a handbasket. The big yellow bus pulled up, slowly grinding its gigantic wheels to a stop, brakes squealing loud enough to wake the dead. Reva Joe stepped front and center outside the raggedy house onto the termite-eaten porch carrying a brown paper bag containing one fried, greasy bologna sandwich.

Shoot me NOW, Lord!

Reva's arrival on the porch was dramatic. It felt like a billion people were watching this 250-pound woman in an orange muumuu, large enough to cover a pickup truck. To top it off, her heels were not only crusty on the back side, but her feet were pure black on the bottom.

Shoot me NOW, Lord!

Shoot me NOW.

This entire transaction took all of about sixty seconds, but the slow motion in which it transpired made it seem like an all-day affair.

"*Give 'em hell,*" I think she said, handing me the greasy brown paper bag.

"Thanks," I mumbled beneath my breath, terrified to turn around and make the long journey down to the end of the driveway. Each step felt like an eternity as I looked up at the big yellow bus and saw a hundred eyes staring back at me.

Blank stares.

Empty faces.

Kids with smirks.

Not her life or his life.

Not even *their* lives.

But *my* life.

Orphan girl raised by white trash.

Mother Nature took my mother. Insanity took my father, and all that was left was the sullen beats of Midwestern inhospitality in the hostile environment of an obese woman completely disconnected from whatever it was that makes a human being whole, human, or *both*.

The driveway was only twenty feet in length, but I felt as though I were trekking from Milwaukee to Buffalo, naked and exposed.

I could see everyone who could see me, including the bus driver, a cantankerous-looking, harsh, middle-aged woman who looked so *over* the bus-driving business it wasn't even funny. She was wearing a tight, blue, unfriendly looking uniform that looked like cardboard. When the big yellow bus doors opened, I felt like a theatrical spectacle.

"Oh boy," I whispered beneath my breath, "here goes a whole lot of *nothing*." I entered the bus and saw a sea of unfriendly faces.

"New kid?" asked the butch-looking bus driver.

"Yeah," I whispered under the muffled sounds of my own insecurity.

"Take a seat in the back," she commanded. "We got one left."

Oh boy, I think I said again, as I raised my eyes just enough to catch sight of the last seat at the very back. I was greeted by the cold stares of a group of pubescent teens with raging hormones, each looking for a special reason to hate their neighbor. Love was definitely not in the stale, dry air that smelled of three-day-old socks and fungus-filled tennis shoes.

I slowly crept down the narrow aisle. It was the longest walk of my life, even longer than the twenty-foot walk to the bus.

Lord, take me now, I could feel myself screaming. *Take me now and run me over with something big.* Before I made it halfway down the narrow walkway, Butch Mama Bus Driver put the bus into drive and pulled off.

I felt as though I were on a broken amusement-park ride. I

grabbed the back of a seat and struggled to balance myself against the dips and curves of the bus.

I could hear plenty of laughter, but I dared not look up. I heard a girl on the bus whisper, "Loser . . ." I don't even think it *was* a whisper.

I think everyone on the bus heard it. The word was thundering, and the worst part was that it sounded so much like me.

Felt like me.

Loser.

I wobbled to the back and collapsed into the torn leather seat, inadvertently crashing into the kid next to me.

"Sorry," I said quickly, before catching eyes with him. When I did, what a sight it was.

Sparks.

Fireworks.

Meteors.

Hook, line, and sinker.

Hard.

I had fallen into the lap of the most beautiful specimen I'd ever had the privilege of laying eyes on. A strong confirmation of my heterosexuality, he was delicious. I hate the use of the impersonal cliché, but I cannot resist the urge to say that his skin was indeed smooth as whipped butter. He was the prettiest boy who wasn't a girl that I had ever seen.

He was a black boy. Actually, he looked like a black boy *and* a white boy. He was a mixed boy, all jumbled up into a big pot of pretty. His face was slightly oval-shaped, and everything on it— eyes, lips, nose, and cheeks—were impeccably placed. It was so perfect that I wanted to reach out and touch him just to make sure he was real.

"Sorry," I said again, quickly raising myself upright.

"No problem," he whispered.

The rest of the ride was completely silent, or maybe not. Maybe the rest of the ride was a hallucination. I could hear the idle chatter of kids around me, but I zoned out completely, enjoying the beauty of this fine young man beside me.

My heart raced.

Pulse skipped.

Palpitations.

The rest of the day was a blur.

New school.

New lessons.

New teachers.

No friends.

I ate Reva Joe's slobbering bologna sandwich alone in the school cafeteria. As I sat isolated from the rest of the world, I caught eyes with a group of students who all seemed to be connected, one to the other. They were like train tracks, each one began where the other ended. As I gazed at them, and then through them, I remembered my days in Saxon where I, too, had friends. I, too, used to be part of the track. Interconnected.

I watched them laugh, listened to them talk. I watched their giddiness, so lighthearted. I didn't wish to participate, I just wanted to watch. My first day left me with a bitter taste in my mouth.

I didn't like anyone.

Wasn't drawn to anyone.

They all felt foreign to me, these kids. And maybe it was because I didn't know their names, or their stories or it could have been because I was feeling antisocial.

I called them all "eggheads," my new word. A bunch of idiotic eggheads playing their own version of "follow the leader." I knew I didn't want to be a part of the train or the track, so I derailed and went my own way.

I felt like an outsider. An intruder.

The bus ride home was equally uneventful and lonely, till the gorgeous boy from earlier that day came and sat beside me.

I almost gasped when he took his seat. I could feel my insides jumping around as the heat rose between us. Originally, I thought it was just me, but within seconds I realized it was also coming from him. Could this beautiful young black/white boy be as drawn to my ivory-white skin as I was to his cocoa-butter complexion?

"How was your first day at this dump?" he asked.

I was shocked that he asked, and when I was able to summon the strength, I turned to him and made a ridiculous attempt at a smile.

Duh.

I feel like a dweeb.

"Fine," I said with the stupidest grin that a fourteen-year-old could muster. "Thank you for asking," I quickly added.

"No problem," he said.

"You're umm . . . " I mumbled, "the nicest person I've met today."

I looked at him and it was the first time I saw his eyes. They were the most beautiful transparent green I'd ever seen. At the same time, he looked back at me and when he did, his green eyes connected to my deep blue-eyed stare. In that moment I felt something pretty darned amazing.

Could he actually like me, too?

I felt special. It was the first time I had felt anything close to special since Juno had killed himself.

"What's your name?" he asked boldly.

"Umm," I said, having to think for a minute. "Adrian."

"You sure?" he asked with this insane, mind-blowing, heart-bending smile.

"Yeah," I said, grinning, every tooth in my mouth *literally* showing.

"Cool," he said, extending a hand. "My name is Anthem."

"What?" I asked, astounded. "Anthem?"

"Yeah," he said with a grin that was almost as goofy as the one I had just given him.

"Where did your parents get that name?"

"I was born at a baseball game while the national anthem played . . ."

"What?"

"Yeah. I guess I was in a hurry to get out and see the game . . ."

I laughed out loud. It was a cackle that should have embarrassed me, but for some reason it didn't.

"That's right on!" I said, head lowered. "How do you follow up with a last name for Anthem?"

"It's Rogers," he said. "Very simple."

"You could be a country singer with a name like that!" I laughed.

"I do play the guitar, you know."

"What grade you in?"

"Tenth."

"Cool," I said. "That makes you about fifteen?"

"Sounds about right," he said with a slight grin.

"Fifteen and never been kissed?" I asked, smiling big.

"Speak for yourself," was his reply.

"I *am* speaking for myself, silly," I said with certainty, spilling the beans—if he was quick enough to catch them.

"And you?"

"Ninth," I said shyly.

"A nubie . . ." he said teasingly. "That puts you at about fourteen."

"Fourteen is a good place to be," I said, followed by a long pause, till the bus approached Reva Joe's hideous driveway. Suddenly, I felt conscious of my life, this house, Reva Joe, my situation. I was still aware of being poverty-stricken, but for whatever reason, it all seemed okay.

"Well," I said, "guess I'll see you tomorrow."

"Yeah," he said with his big, beautiful smile. "Guess you will."

I think I floated off the school bus that day. Yeah, I floated off the bus and drifted down the driveway and up to Reva Joe's front doorstep. Funny thing, the house was still a puke-green color. The flowers were still dead in the front yard and the weeds were still growing against the side of the house. The trees still needed trimming, and Reva Joe greeted me at the door in a brown muumuu and dirty black feet. From a distance I could see she was still poor white trash, but none of that changed the fact that this was indeed one of the most beautiful days of my life. The sky was perfect, sun bright, the clouds snowy white.

Oh, what the heck. I was in great like.

Great.

Great.

Like.

"How was your first day of school with that bus full of losers?" she asked as I entered the house.

"Great," I said, floating off toward my room. "It was just *great.*"

Chapter 22

As I descended past the twenty-second floor, I remembered the war of the weeds.

The day I met Anthem, life changed. Everything else stayed the same, but it didn't matter because there was magic in the air.

Guess that's what love does—it makes you believe in stuff all over again. It makes you remember the bloom of beautiful roses smack in the dead of winter. It makes you feel filthy rich, even if you're dirt poor. It makes you feel light enough to fly even if the weight of the world rests upon your shoulders. It makes you smile.

You don't care about *anything* but love, and being in it. Now, I'm not saying that I am in love, because that would be a stretch, but it is safe to say that I am in great like, or simply that *I Am*, and for now, that is enough.

"I suggest you get your head out of your rear end and turn your attention to those weeds out in the front yard," said Reva Joe sourly as we sat at the breakfast table early one Saturday morning.

Uh-oh. Interruption of all that is good and holy. Here she is, bursting through in her usual attire and house shoes, weed-whacking my dreams to death. She caught me off guard, noticing for a moment in time that I was, in fact, *happy*.

"Weeds?" I asked, my expression bottomed out.

"Weeds," she spat, over a bowl of dry oatmeal and the morning paper. Ironically, she hadn't listened to Bueford & Mitchell since the day they reminded her that she had lost her only son and was forced to deal with the fact that she, too, was human.

"You do know what weeds are? Don't you, girl?"

"Yeah," I said with attitude. "It's that stuff growing all over the side of your house."

"That's right," she sputtered. "And you are the smart-ass that's gonna yank 'em all out."

"Great way to spend my weekend," I said sarcastically. "It's what I always dreamed of doing, pulling weeds."

The next thing I knew, it felt like the dead of summer in early spring. On the hottest day of the year, I was squatting in Reva Joe's front yard, wearing long gloves, tight shorts, a plus-size T-shirt, a wide-brimmed straw hat, and sunglasses, pulling weeds. Reva Joe was smiling, winking, and waving at me, being downright annoying.

She was reveling in my morning misery, bathing in it, and with every weed I pulled I could feel her sheer delight. She was loving it.

"What the freak?" I said to myself out loud, growing more and more agitated by her not-so-subtle amusement at my torture.

"Hey, *you!*" I heard someone shout from across the front yard. I stood up in a huff to tell off whoever was addressing me in such a manner.

You?

You?

Who the heck are you? I felt like asking, but couldn't because when I turned in the direction of the "you," I saw that it was *him*.

Anthem.

In all his star-spangled glory, he was standing at the edge of my front yard wearing a pair of sexy jeans, a casual top, some hightops, and carrying a guitar.

Doggone. Didn't look like HE was pulling weeds today. Oh no, he looked yummy . . .

"What are you doing?" he asked. And I don't know why, but

suddenly I became excruciatingly aware of the fact that I might not be at my most attractive. My legs had grass and dirt stains on them, this T-shirt was faded and holey, and my hair was a mess; if he came an inch closer, he could probably smell the stench of Reva Joe's eggs and onions on my breath.

I was pulling weeds and what difference did it make how I looked? It makes all the difference in the world, that's what difference it makes, because now I was caught off guard, exposed, and looking like a wretched mess in the presence of the most beautiful boy on the planet!

"Pulling weeds," I said, embarrassed.

His eyes did a full scan of the house, taking it all in. "Looks like you got a big job ahead of you."

"Yeah."

"How long is this gonna take you?"

"About two years," I said, looking around the property.

He burst into laughter and so did I. I always did that when he was anywhere in my presence—I gravitated, darned near levitated, toward him.

He looked at his watch.

"Two years, huh?"

"Yeah . . . about that."

The closer I got to him, the more beautiful he looked—so much so that it didn't matter what he thought of me. All that mattered was what I thought of him.

"What are you doing?" I asked, checking out his guitar.

"I'm on my way to play."

"Where do you play?"

"Down at the lake," he said. "You know the lake at the end of the road?"

"Yeah," I said, smiling. "Why do you play at the lake?"

"Nature is my best audience," he said with a beautiful smile.

"So you play for trees and bees?"

"Something like that," he said, laughing.

"How long you gonna be down there?"

"Two years and one day," he said, eyes scanning the weeds against the side of the house.

"Give me thirty minutes," I said, smiling. "I'll meet you there."
I turned around and started to walk away.

"What about the weeds?" he asked.

I didn't have a chance to answer because no sooner had he asked than Reva Joe appeared at the front door with one hand on her hip and the other pushing on the screen door. Realizing that I was closing shop for the day, she gave me an evil glare. "Now, just what do you suppose you're doing, Miss Hotsy Totsy?"

"I'm taking a break," I said boldly.

"A break!" she exclaimed. "You ain't done enough shit in the front yard yet to earn a break!"

I quickly turned around and was greatly relieved to see that Anthem had already begun his descent down to the lake. Thank goodness, because I wouldn't want him to see Reva Joe and me engage in a war of the weeds. I wasn't trying to be disrespectful, but the fact that she was expecting me to pull freaking weeds all day felt like a violation.

I don't know. Maybe I was wrong, but I would have been more apt to pull the damn weeds if Reva Joe had offered to help, or at least pretended that she appreciated my efforts instead of mocking me.

"Reva Joe . . . it's hot as Hades out here and I do not plan on spending my entire day swatting mosquitoes and pulling weeds."

"You gotta earn your keep around here, girl!" she screamed. "Ain't no free rides!"

"Juno's insurance money ought to be plenty enough to earn my keep around here!" I screamed back.

"I have rules in this house! And weed-pulling is one of my Saturday morning rules!"

"Well," I said boldly, "seems like we have a bit of conflict, Reva Joe, because *today* I plan on going down to the lake . . . I can pull doggone weeds tomorrow! Them weeds ain't going nowhere! They been here for thirty years!"

"Oh, bite your tongue, you ungrateful heathen!" she screamed, raising her hand to me as though she were about to backhand me, but then she caught herself. "You are an ungrateful thing, just like your raggedy father!" she screamed. "Lazy, lazy, lazy . . . lazy as the day is long. Couldn't get Juno to pull weeds for all the tea in China! I tried every weekend but your father wanted to run around this here city and be a faggot . . . he didn't want to mess up his manicure! Now I really see the apple don't fall too far from the tree! You're just like him . . . worthless . . . what GOOD are you? What do I need you here for, causing me trouble? Making my hemorrhoids swell! What good are you?"

She stomped through the house, ranting and raving, shoving stuff and throwing things, displaying her disgust at my decision to boycott weeds today.

She went in and out of rooms, entering, exiting, barking, and spitting. It was nasty and vile, like witnessing a temper tantrum and an exorcism, all in one.

What to do next . . .

I went into my bedroom and shut the door. I could still hear her spitting and chewing on her own hatred. She was filled with such a rage, I expected at any moment the freaking weeds would disintegrate all by themselves just because I was praying they would and that God would hear my desperate plea.

Worthless!

You ain't worth nothing!

Ain't shit!

As I listened to the abusive echoes of this gigantically disturbed woman, I thought about Juno and what life must have been like growing up with such an abusive, insensitive jerk, for lack of a better word.

I was so angry. There was a fury that grabbed hold of me, almost shaking me right out of my lily-white skin. I felt a flashback of her cruelty to my father, who was such a gentle soul, and in the light of that I flew into an unforgiving rage, the kind that was disconnected from sanity.

I felt like tearing Reva's head off.

Ripping her guts out.

Stopping her heart.

I quickly changed into something more suitable for a lake

serenade, then burst out of the room where Reva was still flinging things, throwing things, breaking things.

"I am NOT worth nothing!" I screamed, standing three feet from her puffy face in the middle of the dingy living room. My outburst stopped her dead in her tracks.

I felt vulnerable, angry, and hurt for all the years she had mistreated my father and denied him the right to be who he was—Juno, the gentle, eccentric soul. I wondered how many times she had crushed him. I pondered the number of occasions she had not only clipped his wings, but burned them off, allowing him to plunge repeatedly to his death.

How many times can you kill a living, breathing thing?

"I am NOT a nobody . . . I'm NOT a nothing . . . I'm SOMEBODY and so was my father! Don't EVER talk about either one of us again! Who do you think you are? You're a miserable old woman who's probably going to die alone! If you're lucky, you'll be asleep when you die because God knows you wouldn't want to be awake for that last look at the woman you turned out to be! Now put that in your pipe and smoke it!"

Reva's eyes widened in disbelief as I appeared to grow taller right before her eyes, ascending beyond ignorance and shame, putting her in her place, once and for all. And with that, I turned around and stomped out the front door, slamming it so hard the windows shook. That was the end of Reva Joe Moses and me, at least for that day.

By the time I made it to the lake, I had all but forgotten about the fat woman in the muumuu and was much more focused on finding Anthem. It was easy to forget Reva Joe when I thought about Anthem. All I had to do was be still and listen to the sound of the music. I could hear it coming from the bushes. I climbed down a hill, through some weeds and bushes, and there he sat, on the edge of an embankment, playing his song. It was really pretty, his song. It was so divine, in fact, that it was hard discerning which was prettier, him or the music.

I sat down beside him and let him play. I didn't recognize the tune. It was a simple melody, or seemingly so. The chords looked effortless as he glided up and down the strings. He turned to me, paused, then stopped altogether.

I started to hiccup because I was so taken by him. His beauty was breathtaking.

"Oh my God," I said out loud, laughing from the sheer pleasure of it all. "That was . . . was . . . way cool."

He smiled at me and I thought I would simply fall backwards, slide down the embankment, and slither into the lake. *That's how pretty he was.*

I could barely look at him. Barely. But he was much too beautiful to turn away.

Shoot.

I couldn't look, but yet again, I couldn't look away.

"Are you nervous?" he asked.

"No way," I lied.

"You seem nervous," he said, looking steady and calm.

"Well, I'm not," I said defensively. "Okay . . . maybe a little."

"I have a trick to get over being nervous," he said.

"What?"

He leaned into my ear and whispered gently, "Don't be." Instantly, there were chill bumps over my whole body. The air from his breath and the smell of his flesh was almost too much to take.

"What do you make of it?" he asked, lightly playing his guitar.

"What?"

"Life," he said, staring into the lake.

"Sucks pretty good so far," I said flatly.

He stopped playing his guitar and looked through me so deeply that it burned.

"Why?"

"Stuff," I said.

"What kind of stuff?" he asked, resuming his beautiful melody on the guitar.

"Just stuff," I said uncomfortably, not wanting to go there. He looked at me again with those eyes, and I felt as if he were almost violating me because they pierced so deep. But it was a beautiful violation, something wanted *and* resisted at the same time. I desperately wanted him to see me. Since Juno's death I had spent so much time hiding myself.

"Does it have to do with that lady you live with?" he asked. "Who is she?"

"A real loser," I said, chuckling. "My grandmother."

"Wow," he said, laughing. "I never heard anyone call their *grandmother* a loser."

"We come from two different worlds."

"Where are your folks?"

"They moved on," I said.

"What do you mean?"

"They're dead," I said softly.

"Oh," he said quietly. "So they started over?"

"Huh?"

"People don't die," he said. "They just start over."

"Who told you that?"

He looked at me and smiled, then started drawing circles in the dirt.

"Where do they start over?"

"I don't know," he said. "That depends."

"On what?"

"Wherever it is that they're supposed to be."

"So, you believe in reincarnation?"

"Yeah, I really do."

"Who taught you that?" I asked.

"No one taught me."

"So you think you've lived before?"

"Yeah," he said.

"Who were you before?"

"Somebody special," he said with certainty. "Somebody really important."

I laughed.

"Yeah, I know," he said. "I got ripped off this time around."

"No, you didn't," I said with sincerity. "You're somebody special and important this time around, too."

There were no words to add.

No words.

Just a smile.

A simple grin.

He laid his guitar down, accepting my words as he leaned in, kissing me softly on the cheek. The heat from his face combined with the heat from mine and met somewhere in the middle. Instinctively, I drew closer to him and him to me as we went from rubbing cheeks to touching noses to touching lips. His soft lips against mine were almost combustible. We weren't really kissing—we were feeling one another out. And once we were done with rehearsal, he kissed me.

It was the first time my lips had pressed against another person's and it was exhilarating and scary at the same time. I was a novice and uncertain if I were "doing it right," so I simply tried to follow his movement as his tongue extended, withdrew, and extended again. It was as if our tongues were playing hide-and-seek.

He reached for my hand—his was hot, and it felt like the rest of my skin: *ignited*. He squeezed tight, then gently released and started rubbing my shoulders.

My insides were going crazy, and on the outside, I only *pretended* to stay the same. But I knew I was not the same nor would I ever be. I had been touched by something much more powerful than myself. I didn't know what to call it, but it was as real as anything would ever be. Now both of his hands were placed over my arms, rubbing briskly, generating even more heat than was already there. And his kiss was deeper, his eyes more intense when they looked at me. His skin was hot, like electricity, and this energy surrounded us, practically swallowing us whole. My body followed suit and soon my hands were on his arms and I, too, began to rub vigorously.

It was an exchange, a subtle communication. Our breathing deepened. It was a struggle just to take the air into my lungs—he was consuming me.

His arm held the top of my arm before slowly sliding down. I twitched as his warm flesh pressed against my breast. He paused, then continued, gliding his fingers gently over my nipple.

Stroking.

Caressing.

I almost gasped, terrified and exhilarated at the same time as we explored the highly forbidden realm of desire.

I wanted him to know me.

I wanted him to know me fully and completely.

I wanted him to feel my breast, but I felt guilty because I knew deep down inside I probably shouldn't.

It was wrong.

Immoral.

Or maybe a little of both.

"Are you okay?" he asked.

"Yes," I said, flushed.

"I can stop," he suggested.

"Why?"

"Because I don't want you to be uncomfortable."

"I'm okay," I said. "I want you to know me naked."

I almost choked when I heard the words roll out of my mouth.

Oh, Jesus.

What did I just say?

"Wow," he said. "No one's ever said anything like that to me."

"I'm sorry," I said, overwhelmed by embarrassment. "It was sort of spontaneous."

"Don't be," he said. "It's nice. You're a real person."

"Isn't everybody?" I asked him, surprised.

"No," he said. "Most people are just *pretending* to be real people." And with that he looked so deep into my eyes, I could feel him fall in between them.

"Dove," he whispered.

"What?"

"You're as beautiful as a dove," he said.

I laughed.

"No," he said, "I'm serious."

He picked up his guitar and resumed playing. As he played, I listened, enchanted.

As he played, I watched lovingly and lustfully. What did I

know about love and lust? I wasn't an expert at giving or receiving touches. No one had ever played rub-a-dub-dub with my breasts before. I'd never wanted them to. I had the occasional crush here and there, but this was different. I longed for Anthem as though I had been waiting for him all of my life, all fourteen years of it. But this ran deeper. I felt like I'd known him all of my life, even before I came here. There was a haunting sense of familiarity. It felt as natural as an April rain for him to touch my breast. And though I was indeed a virgin, somehow we had consummated this relationship even before we met. How we had done this I was uncertain, but I knew that through time, somehow it would reveal itself.

It was the spring of my fourteenth year.

It was a spring I would never forget.

Chapter 21

As I descended past the twenty-first floor, I remembered the day I was left standing in piss, poop, and broken dreams.

From that day at the lake, Anthem and I spent every waking moment that we could together. Most of this time was spent on bus rides to and from school. We ate lunch in the cafeteria and met in between bathroom breaks. We never seemed to get enough of one another. I was always looking for him, and he was always looking for me, but the nicest thing of all is that we were always looking for each other.

I was known around school as Anthem's girl. Now, that was both good and bad. It was good because this kept the other girls away from him, but bad because a lot of the girls in our mostly Caucasian school hated me because Anthem very well could have been their national pastime. By the time spring pushed its way into summer and school ended, we were tightly bonded. Actually, it was more like human fusion.

Once school ended, our routine changed a bit. Our mornings consisted of long walks through the woods, bike rides through the trails in the afternoon, and evening meals consisting of fried bologna sandwiches down by the lake. On one such occasion on a hot summer night, I will never forget the sudden, impulsive urge to remove all of my clothing and strip down to my bare-naked butt. Right in the middle of bologna on white bread with mustard and iceberg lettuce, the "call of the wild" whispered to me. It was bizarre, yet it was one of the most exciting moments of my life.

Anthem and I were talking about women in sports. We may have even been arguing over it. We were both pretty feisty when it came to debates.

I stood and looked over both shoulders.

We were down by a corner of the lake that was pretty iso-lated and it was rare to see passersby on this side of the embank-ment because the bushes were tall and the grass wild.

I stood up and slowly removed my shirt. I had no natural in-hibitions. Contrary to the way that most girls in their fourteenth year perceived themselves, I thought my body was beautiful.

It was beautiful because it was mine.

I had eased my way into menstruation and breast develop-ment. The skinny twig I used to be was curving her way into the woman I was becoming.

I liked the curves, and I was equally attracted to my lily-white, soft and supple skin. It felt good to me and I wanted to share that feel-good place with Anthem.

As I eased out of my blouse I will never forget the look on Anthem's face. His eyes were big and distracted, trying to focus his attention on our conversation despite my hardening nipples.

"Tell me about your family," I said, gently stroking his arms. Obviously, I had grown very comfortable in his presence. He, on the other hand, was like putty, suddenly shy and distracted. Perhaps bold nudity has that effect on men. He had only felt my breasts beneath my shirt, but had not actually seen them.

"Not much to tell," he said, stumbling.

"Tell me anything," I said, allowing my bra to twist itself down my torso where I stepped out of it.

"What do you want to know?" he asked, face flushed of all copper and bronze coloring.

"Tell me about your parents."

"Not much to tell . . . Mom's a waitress in a dive close to downtown, and I have a sister who's a space cadet."

"How old is she?"

"Who? My mom or sister?"

"Your sister, silly."

"Seventeen," he said, exasperated. "She's addicted to zit cream and Kung Fu."

"Does she have a boyfriend?"

"Every Friday she gets a new one," he said. "Just in time to be taken to a new food joint for the weekend. She's been to every new restaurant in town," he said before bursting into laughter.

I laughed, too, but not because what he said was so funny, but because every time he laughed, I laughed with him.

He was so beautiful, how could I not?

"What does your mother say?" I asked.

"She wishes we could all date her boyfriends," he said, laughing more. "We'd all eat really good if we did."

I started to unzip my shorts, slowly.

"What's your mom like?" I asked.

"Cool," he said. "Stressed a lot 'cause of money. Working for tips sucks!"

"Are you guys close?" I asked, curious.

"Me and Moms," he said. "We're cool."

"Are you black, Anthem?" I asked naively.

On the edge of my words, he shot me a piercing, confused look, and suddenly, I felt obligated to clean it up.

"Oh my God," I said. "Not that it matters to me . . . at all . . . I think you're beautiful."

He turned away from me for a beat, then returned.

"Mom's white," he said. "Dad's black."

"Where is your dad?"

"Not sure," he said. "He was too busy to stick around and raise a kid. Eighteen years can feel like a lifetime to a nomad. Enough about me," he said. "I wanna know more about you."

"Not much to know," I said, dropping my shorts down to the soil, stepping out of them.

"Got any hobbies?"

"Yeah," I said. "Well, no, not really, but . . ."

He looked at me with one brow raised.

"I want to be an artist," I said.

"What kind of artist?"

"I don't know."

"Do you create art now?"

"Not really."

"So, you're not a serious artist?"

"Yeah," I insisted. "I mean, no . . . but I'm gonna be one day."

"Okay," he said. "Usually people who want to do something . . . walk in the direction of that thing."

"I want to create the story of my life using pictures," I said. "I want to make a whole wall as a tribute to my life."

"That's pretty deep," he said.

"I'm thinking about owning an art gallery someday," I said. "Not really creating the art myself, but more like selling it."

"That's cool," he said.

"I think so," I said, smiling.

"Where are your parents, Adrian?" he asked, pretending not to be so distracted by my impending nudity.

"My mom died from cancer," I said, growing uneasy.

"And your dad?"

"Suicide," I said, eyes dimming as I stared at the moist ground. He stood up and slowly inched his way toward me. When he got to me he put his arms around me and held on tight—for life, death, and for forever.

"What is your biggest passion in life, Adrian?" he whispered into my ear. "Biggest, biggest passion?"

"You," I whispered back.

He shook his head. "Your passion has to be bigger than a person."

"Why?" I asked, pulling back.

"People *leave*," he said with certainty. "Passion is forever." I nodded my head because I truly understood.

As we held each other, I felt safe and warm, as though I had returned to the womb. I held on to that moment like it was my dying breath, and in many ways it was because within seconds, the world as I knew it evaporated again for the third time in my life. The first time was when Juno woke me one early autumn morning to tell me that my mother had died as I slept. The second time was when I had to tell myself that my dear, sweet Juno really was gone, and the third time was when Reva Joe Moses, in all of her blazing, white-trash glory, stomped through the bushes screaming bloody murder because we had been *caught*!

Anthem and I had been uncovered and revealed at the most inopportune time of our lives, with him holding me and me standing in the middle of the bushes stripped down to my little white drawers.

This was the epitome of a compromised situation, and what was to follow could only be categorized as an electrical storm in the middle of a calm, sunny day.

"What in the hell?" Reva Joe screamed. "Adrian Moses! Get your clothes on!" I pulled away from Anthem immediately and he jumped back three feet in an attempt to move in the opposite direction from Reva Joe's fury.

"What are you doing down here?" screamed Reva as she stomped through the brush, surrounding me with what felt like strangulation. I immediately dropped to the ground, hunched over, as I attempted to gather my clothing.

"What are you doing, you little hussy?" she screamed. "Your mother and father would turn over in their graves if they could see you right now!"

I was shaking, horrified and frightened.

Reva didn't know about Anthem.

How could I tell her? He was black and she hated anybody who wasn't white. I was terrified at what would happen now.

"Get your clothes on, you filthy little slut!" she screamed, making such a commotion that she was drawing attention from nearby parts of the lake where curious locals wandered into our immediate area.

I was petrified, topless, hunched on the moist ground as I struggled to gather my garments, which all seemed to slip through my hands as though they were animated.

"Hurry up!" Reva screamed, towering over me, her voice projecting thunderously. "Hurry up! Hurry up!"

Out of the corner of my eye, I could see onlookers as they peeked through the bushes, staring and snickering.

I had never been so embarrassed in all of my life. Our sexuality *and* humanity had been crushed by prejudice and ignorance, right in the middle of Lake Woodsley at the back end of the world in Milwaukee, Wisconsin.

I ached to slither into the ground like an earthworm and disappear. My senses were overwhelmed by the gawking strangers and the catcalls of stupid teenage boys. Reva Joe's insults showed Anthem just how god-awful my life really was.

"I cannot believe I have a SLUT for a grandchild!" she screamed.

"Hey!" shouted Anthem. "Stop calling her names! Who do you think you are?"

Reva Joe shot him a look that felt much like the kiss of death, and as she stomped across the ground to meet him face-to-face, I feared their confrontation could have a terrible ending.

"You stay the hell away from her!" said Reva Joe to Anthem.

I scurried to dress while the two of them stared at one another. "Who do you think you are anyways, boy?" said Reva, sizing him up.

He didn't respond as she circled him, mentally inspecting as though she were judging cattle or horses. "Must be nice for you—huh, boy?" she continued. "Must be nice getting your grubby, dirty, nasty hands on that fresh white skin."

"Stop it!" I screamed at Reva Joe. "Stop it, Reva Joe!"

"I will not stop!" she screamed, turning her back to me. "Isn't it, boy?" she scowled, turning her attention back to Anthem. "What's white pussy going for these days, boy? Huh?"

I will never forget the look on Anthem's face as Reva Joe uttered those filthy, disgusting words. In that moment, she had castrated him in front of everyone. He looked ashamed and I was beyond devastated. I lowered my head, defeated.

We all were.

Life would never be the same again in Milwaukee, Wisconsin. This event was so monumental, it would never be the same again in the whole United States of America.

I remember the tears that welled in Anthem's eyes—never will I forget them. They were only visible for a brief moment but they ran deep. I have never seen pain so personified. If pain had a voice, it was Anthem's deep baritone. If pain had a face, it was the expression behind the tears in his eyes. If pain had a name, it was *Anthem* that day.

I felt it deeply. His pain was bigger and broader than mine. It was more focused and centered, springing from all the injustice of the world.

It was excruciating.

I hated Reva for what she had reduced him to, a brown-skinned boy born into a world of ignorance and prejudice where people would make him feel like much less of a man, much less of a human being.

That day, through his eyes and for the first time, I saw Juno's pain. I saw it as if it was alive and had a name, and a purpose. I saw how the world had looked at Juno and judged him, how he had fallen prey to their ignorant remarks and prejudice. I saw more than ever how they had overlooked Juno's beauty and, in the process, killed him long before he ever died.

I blacked out, and driven by fury, I lost it. I charged full speed toward Reva Joe, and somehow Anthem intercepted me, lifting me off the ground and holding me midair. My legs spun as he swung me round and round, trying to hold onto me.

"Let me go!" I screamed. "Let me go!"

Reva Joe's eyes widened and she stepped back a bit, gasping at the unfolding fury.

"I want to kill her!" I screamed. "I want to kill her!"

"Adrian!" Anthem yelled, trying to hold me in his arms.

Adrian!

Adrian!

He tried to bring me back.

He tried with all of his might and strength to bring me back from the blind rage, but it wasn't working. I didn't want to be brought back, and I didn't want to listen.

I didn't want to dismiss Reva Joe's behavior. I wanted her to be accountable and I also wanted to inflict pain upon her. That was my last conscious memory of that day. It was the worst day of my living, breathing life. The last visual impression seared upon my brain was the image of my tiny body collapsing into Anthem's strong arms.

The next day I woke up alone. I was in bed at Reva Joe's house, in the room that had been designated as my own.

I opened my eyes to see the wood paneling, appearing as though it were peeling off and falling down around me, much like the rest of my life. As the room came into focus, I saw that the door was shut and the house quiet.

There was no Bueford & Mitchell.

There was no Reva Joe blowing through the house making odd noises, talking to herself. There was no smell of rotten eggs and dead oatmeal. And the hell on earth that I can only recall as being some form of "yesterday" seemed far behind me now.

Weakly, I lifted myself out of the bed and maneuvered to the door, but when I tried to turn the knob, it was locked from the outside.

"Reva!" I yelled, banging on the door.

"Reva!" I screamed again. "Let me out!"

There was no answer.

"Let me out!" I screamed again, only to be met by silence.

"Reva Joe!" I screamed. "Let me out!"

Suddenly, there was a knock on my bedroom window. The sound scared me and I almost jumped out of my skin. I turned and saw Anthem's beautiful face. Instantly, I was soothed and humbled to see him once again. In spite of everything that had happened—the shame, the guilt, the hurt, the pain—he came back. After such a bitter encounter with Reva Joe, I feared he would think of me as poor white trash.

I ran to the window, which was locked and wouldn't open, but I was able to read his lips through the glass as we pressed our hands against the frame, which had been heated by the sun.

We had a conversation without words, relying solely upon

the contortion of our lips and tongues to portray the deeper meaning behind our words.

I'm sorry, he uttered, his mouth moving slowly to form the words.

Me, too, I said, touching my chest.

Are you okay? he asked, pointing at me.

Yes, I nodded.

Can you come out here? he asked, motioning toward the outside.

I shook my head, *no*, and he put his hands together as though he were praying. It was his way of asking, *please*.

I shook my head again, *no*, and there we stood, looking longingly into one another's eyes.

Deep.

Like a river.

We were separated by a thick glass pane, yet I knew we were still connected. There were tears in our eyes, mine and his, and no need for words. He pulled back and mouthed the words, *I love you*.

I love you, too, I mouthed, drawing closer to the window, and somewhere in the middle of that love, I lost myself. I was so lost in our love that I did not hear Reva Joe turn the lock and enter the room. And it was here that she found me, resting my face against a warm piece of glass, caressing my reflection.

I jumped and turned around. She looked ghastly, as though she had been drinking all night. It was a frightening sight indeed. I shrieked, backing away from the window, and saw that Anthem had disappeared. He had left so quickly I almost thought he had been an illusion.

"Pack your bags!" scowled Reva Joe, opening the closet and pulling out my clothes—hangers, suitcase, and all. She made her way to the dresser drawers and began throwing my undergarments onto the bed. I withered into the background, shriveling away from her.

"Where am I going?" I asked quietly.

"Year-round boarding school!"

"What?" I asked, mouth dropping to the floor. My lily-white skin turned ghastly ashen. "Boarding school?"

"I'm done, Adrian," she said. "I can't deal with you no more! I can't take no chances you laying down with that niggah boy across town and coming back home with black babies."

"What an awful thing to say!" I said out loud.

"What an awful thing it would be," was her only comment.

I got up off the ground and moved away from the window, almost relieved that I was getting the hell away from Reva Joe, but terrified as to what the future held.

"When am I leaving?"

"In the morning," she said with finality. "You'll be staying there for about three years. There'll be some trips back to my house here and there, but for the most part, that's home now."

"That's not home," I said. "It'll be just like this, a place where I lay my head down."

"It'll be good enough," she snapped.

"How are you paying for it, Reva Joe?"

"That's not your concern," she said.

"I think it is," I said boldly. "You're using Juno's money . . . the money from his house, aren't you?"

She looked down, then away, as though she could be guilty.

"Yeah," I said out loud. "You're using his money."

She was silent.

"How are you paying, Reva Joe?" I demanded. "How are you paying for it?"

"None of your busybody business!" she screamed.

"You're using the money Juno left, aren't you, Reva Joe?"

"What's it to you?"

"That's for when I graduate, Reva Joe! That's gonna pay for my art school!"

"You ain't going to no art school!" she squealed. "You think you're some kind of artist? You ain't no artist!"

"I'm gonna be an artist someday!"

"Don't waste my time with your crazy mumbo jumbo. Just get those bags packed up!"

"You can't use my college money for this, Reva Joe!"

"That money is for your education," she insisted. "And I can do as I damn well please in the name of you getting some good common sense into that little bitty, pea-sized brain of yours!"

I stood with tears swelling in my eyes.

"Where is this boarding school?" I asked.

"Tucson, Arizona," she said without emotion. "Plane leaves at 8:00 A.M. sharp."

She walked out of the room and slammed the door.

I walked back to the window where I'd last seen Anthem. He was gone now, and tomorrow I'd be gone forever. It was so unfair, an unfairness that reminded me of my mother dying and my father killing himself. It was the kind of unfairness that left me feeling as though I had no control over life and love.

Why was it that the moment I gave myself permission to love something *other* than my two dead parents, I soared, only to blossom and fall by the wayside again?

I looked out the window and searched for signs of Anthem *and* for signs of life; for what seemed like an eternity, there were no signs of either. The long, dusty street where Reva Joe's house sat was just as void of life now as it had ever been, and I had to find a way to make peace with the fact that tomorrow, I was leaving forever.

I stood at the window and stared outside, hoping I would give myself permission to cry. I knew I was waiting to be rescued, waiting to be saved. I was waiting for Anthem to ride up bareback on a white stallion wearing a brilliant white suit. I envisioned him swooping me up and us riding like hell against the wind and the fury of the city, rising above all its prejudice. Me and my white skin. Him and his beautiful bronze coat. It was enough to blend its way into perfection.

I wanted it to so bad that I stood at the window most of the day, waiting, waiting, waiting, actually believing that he would find his way to me. Isn't that the way it always went down in the movies? Surely he would come and I would be standing right here waiting.

Even if we couldn't ride off into the sunset together, I just wanted him to know that I loved him. And that even though I was only fourteen years old, I felt as though I had lived a thousand years and could possibly live at least a thousand more, but I knew I didn't want to live those thousand years without him.

I sat up in the window till the sun rose to its highest peak, then began its gradual descent. I sat there till night crept against the sky in the dark, waiting till there was nothing left to do but wait, wish, and want; and when I was done waiting, I began to pack my things.

Piece by piece I pulled myself away from the life I had known, and garment by garment, I folded myself up and packaged myself away.

I fell asleep that night by the window, but was shaken awake at 2:00 A.M., only to see the word, *Dove*, scribbled on the glass, but Anthem didn't come back.

The next morning my alarm clock woke me at 6:00 A.M.

I was still sitting by the window, waiting. I got up, showered, packed my last bag, and entered Reva Joe's grubby dining area for the last time, where she sat at the table with a bowl of dry oatmeal and the morning newspaper. Her eyebrow rose when she saw me, acknowledging my entry.

I sat.

She turned her attention away from me and back to the newspaper, where she pretended to keep all of her focus.

"Plane's leaving at eight."

"You told me yesterday," I replied flatly.

"I'm telling you again," she said with great attitude.

I stared at the oatmeal sitting on the table and the longer I looked at it, the more I hated it. It represented *everything* I hated about being here. It was cold, like Reva Joe. It was lumpy like the fat on Reva Joe's body. It was poor like Reva. It was inconsistent and erratic, also like Reva Joe.

Reva Joe is a bowl of overcooked oatmeal, I thought. The mere thought made me laugh.

"I *hate* oatmeal," I said, staring into the bowl.

Reva Joe looked up, cutting a single eye to me. "You're so ungrateful," she said under her breath.

"There's a difference," I said, exasperated by her negativity. "There's a difference between being ungrateful and being discriminating."

"Oh, yeah?" she spat sarcastically. "And what would you say that difference is?"

"I like what I like," I said. "I hate what I hate."

"Ditto," she said, shoving oatmeal into that trough of a mouth of hers.

"I don't think I'll be coming this way again, Reva Joe," I said with certainty.

"Fine by me."

"Just pay the people," I said.

"What people?"

"Boarding school," I said. "Just keep my tab current and I'll ride it out till my eighteenth birthday."

"And then what? You can't just run back here when it's all said and done," she said coldly.

"I would live in a sewer before I came back here," I said, both eyes raised. Her expression bent toward anger and I could see her take issue with my comment. "Matter of fact," I said arrogantly, "I would *be* a sewer before I came back here."

"You're the most ungrateful little bitch I've ever known," she gritted in a low voice.

I leaned across the table, speaking quietly but confidently. "And you are the saddest person I've ever met. My father did *not* belong to you. He was much too good a man to be related to you, and I think that deep down inside you're pissed off 'cause you know it."

"I oughta wash your mouth with soap!" she said. "You don't talk to a grown woman like that, you mangy little thing!"

"Yeah," I confirmed. "Deep down inside . . . you know it."

Reva glanced at me, and her eyes reflected a lifetime of hatred that was there long before my arrival on the planet. It was the kind of hate that turns inward on a person, collapsing them into themselves.

We sat the rest of the time in silence till the shuttle pulled up in front of Reva's raggedy house and the horn beeped.

I slowly got up from the table and grabbed my bags, which I had set in the middle of the floor, and headed toward the door.

"See you in hell," spat Reva Joe, who, by the way, didn't even bother to look up from her morning paper.

"You're already there," I said. And *those* were my last words.

Chapter 20

As I descended past the twentieth floor, I remembered the day I touched the ground on the hottest day in the hottest place on planet Earth.

Summer.

Tucson, Arizona.

Hell hath no fury like a 116-degree day in the desert. As the pilot set the plane down on the runway and uttered the triple-digit temperature, I thought I had misunderstood till I stepped outside and the wave of heat sucked me into its blistering essence.

I remembered the rush of heat enveloping me upon entry. It was like being shoved into an oven to be baked alive.

"What in God's name?" I mumbled as I stepped onto the concrete, feeling the heat and intensity against my face as it turned my white skin to a blistering red almost instantly.

I boarded the shuttle at the entrance of the airport and headed in the direction of the Wintergreen Boarding School for Girls.

I felt the "foreignness" of it all as the shuttle rolled through the city, making several stops along the way for the other passengers. Everyone on board was silent, not one person saying a word. I think everyone was focused on keeping cool, lest they all collapse from heat stroke. As the last passenger exited and we headed to the other end of town, I almost laughed out loud. It appeared that Reva Joe had indeed sent me to hell.

What a fucking bitch, I thought.

Please excuse my French.

Wintergreen Boarding School for Girls was the last stop, situated at the farthest end of town, removed from everything, including civilization. It was where everything and nothing existed simultaneously.

Sidewalks were barren and streets were empty with the exception of several old cars clunking their way down the road. They all looked to be on the verge of expiration from the heat, the cars *and* the people.

This was the city of the walking dead. It was just too darned hot to be anything else. When high noon temperatures cap at 119 degrees, what can one do except *hope* the next breath comes easy, if it comes at all. And it was so blazing hot it did appear that life, death, air, and breath were all open for negotiation.

What a fucking, fucking bitch, Reva Joe. When the shuttle pulled up to Wintergreen, I was pleasantly surprised. The structure looked regal on the outside. It looked like a military academy or something of great official standing. Whatever its image represented, it was a long way from Reva Joe's dump in Milwaukee, Wisconsin.

The shuttle eased to a slow stop and when he opened the door I quickly grabbed my bags and got out.

It was so quiet, it was almost eerie. I turned around in circles and for miles I saw a giant dust bowl of nothing, but there was *something*. There were the mountains beneath the backdrop of the clear blue sky; though it was hot as hell, it was still clear and very blue. There were cacti and tumbleweeds, desert lawns and graveled front yards. I also noticed this was a very weed-unfriendly climate. Maybe it was too hot for the weeds. It looked like they just said, *"To hell with it—we'll pack our bags and head to Reva Joe's for the summer."* I laughed out loud at this thought, in the middle of the street at the end of nowhere on the hottest day of the year at the edge of the hottest freaking place on planet Earth.

Bajiminity Gookbackers!

This really is the story of my life.

I eased my way to the rather imperial-looking structure and rang the bell. I had no idea what to expect from an all-year boarding school situated at the end of the world on the hottest place on planet Earth. Nevertheless, I confidently approached the big brown double doors and knocked boldly.

No one answered so I knocked again, this time much harder.

Still there was nothing, so I knocked one more time . . . and just as I did, the big brown door swung open and in that moment I thought I had fallen into an episode of *The Munsters*. A woman with pale, pale skin wearing a long, black Elvira-looking dress with equally black lengthy hair and heavily made-up eyes opened the door and stared at me so hard, I think she got an "eye bleed."

Reva Joe, you fucking, fucking bitch! I screamed inside my head as I stood on the step of this regal place that was run by monsters in the middle of nowhere on the hottest place on planet freaking Earth.

"Adrian?" she said, breaking into a smile. I was uncertain if her smile said, *Welcome,* or if it said *We are about to offer you as a child sacrifice to the Sun Gods.*

I didn't trust her, this woman. Her skin was too white and her hair too dark. Her eyes were made up and her dress was too long and creepy. She wore blue fingernail polish and I thought that was just dang crazy. After all, this appeared to be a conservative organization, at least from the architecture on the outside. And when this woman smiled, her cheeks curved upward, then down and around.

So what in God's name do you make of that when you've just left the only place you've ever known in exchange for the hottest place in hell at the edge of the world in the world's most combustible place on the planet?

I wanted to run out in the middle of the street and sob, and God only knows it's a miracle that I was able to pull myself together and go inside.

"We've been expecting you," she said in a strong accent, moving aside and motioning for me to enter. As I entered, I paused at the door and looked around one more time, realizing this very well could be the last time I was ever seen. Once I entered this structure, I was up for grabs. I could be swallowed or sacrificed or maybe *both*.

The interior was beautifully decorated with interesting, exotic-looking sketches hung on all the walls. They were exquisite, captivating enough to draw me in.

Living art.

I was sucked in first by their uniqueness. They were charcoal drawings of naked men and women, interconnected from one to the next. They held just enough of the forbidden to be soul-stirring. The more I looked at them, the more brilliant they seemed. The first sketch was that of a beautiful naked baby boy, which connected to a naked toddler, then connected to a naked boy, who was connected by way of a naked man, whose outreached hand made a complete circle of the group.

Wow!

The more I stared at the sketches, the more fascinated I became. They were meticulously hung in the center of the hallway, extending all the way to the end and winding around a corner. I responded to them in a bizarre way, almost as if I had drawn them myself. Was I experiencing some sort of connection of the past, future, and present simultaneously?

Was this some kind of paranormal bleed-through?

Was this someone's living story?

"You like?" asked the woman who had just let me in the house, standing so close behind me that it almost made me jump out of my skin.

"I *love* them," I said, turning around and moving a few inches away from her in the same breath.

"Where did you get these beautiful pictures?"

"My son, Dayglo," she said.

"Dayglo?"

"Dayglo, meaning yellow. He is my golden boy, and like the sun he is the center of the universe."

"Really?" I asked with a smile, touched by her connection to her son. "Dayglo."

"My universe," she said with a crooked smile. "You'll meet him someday. He lives in Argentina with his father, but makes his way back to his mother a couple times a year."

"Where are you from?" I asked.

"Buenos Aires," she said with a smile, seeming a little less frightening.

"How did you get here?" I asked with a frown.

"Flew," she said, flapping her arms like a bird, then she started to laugh. "You should be lighter," she said, sizing me up.

"What do you mean?" I asked. "I'm already white as a ghost . . . if I were any lighter I would be invisible to the naked eye."

"That's a good start," she laughed.

I must have looked confused because she went on to explain.

"Lighter . . . lighter," she said. "You take it all with such seriousness, huh?"

"What?"

"Life," she said. "It's such a big deal to you Americans," she said, stepping away a beat, then reappearing.

"Yeah," I said. "They don't take life seriously where you come from?"

"Not really," she said casually. "Not like here."

I paused a beat, reflecting on her words. Let's see, Mother died of cancer and Father died of crazy, sent me to live with a lunatic in Milwaukee who wore muumuus and walked around on dirty, black feet. Fell in love with a black boy, got laughed and ridiculed right out of town and sent to live at the Wintergreen Boarding School for Girls in the middle of Nowhere, USA, on the hottest day of the year in the center of the hottest place on Earth. Well, that about sums up my life. Sounds pretty freaking serious to me.

"To what do you aspire?" she asked me.

"Huh?"

"What do you want to do with your life?"

"A vacation would be nice," I said, laughing. "Is that light enough for you?"

She raised her brow.

"I want be an artist."

"You *are* an artist?" she asked.

"Not yet," I said, "but I'm gonna be."

"So, I would imagine that when you graduate from here you'll take up a study of the arts."

"Perhaps," I replied.

"Come," she said, luring me through the entryway and then further through an enclosed patio. The rest of the house was nice also, but it did not seem much like a school with pupils and teachers, textbooks and lessons, cafeterias and auditoriums. Maybe schools in Tucson were just homes that people never left because it was too freaking hot to go anywhere else.

"I am Mayan," she said, turning to me again, this time tamer, more subtle and sweet. "And this is my home. Welcome."

"Where is the school?" I asked, looking around.

"First things first," she said, disappearing into another room, then reappearing with a small cup. "You need to take a urine test."

"Urine test?" I asked. "Pee in a cup?"

"We have a zero drug policy," she said, well-spoken through the thickness of her Argentinean accent. "A lot of parents send their kids to us because we are the last stop between their kid and the street. And though I have great compassion for them, the user *and* the one who is being used, this is not a rehab program . . . it is an institution for learning and for excellence."

"Well, I'm not on drugs," I said flatly.

"Do you think any kid who ever walked through these doors would admit it if she was?"

"I'm not a liar."

"Your body speaks a stronger truth," she said, looking at me intensely, forcing the cup into my hand. "And that is why I will wait for your urine."

I stared at it without expression.

"Why are you so offended?" she asked, puzzled.

"Just feels dehumanizing," I said. "You're asking me to pee in a cup so that I can be afforded the luxury of living in the middle of a giant dust bowl? No offense, but this ain't exactly the Ritz."

"Yes," she said in a matter-of-fact manner. "Now . . . use the rest room there," she said, pointing to the bathroom. Reluctantly I went into the bathroom and did as she requested. Upon exiting, I handed her the warm cup of pee; she in turn opened the patio door and poured the pee outside onto the concrete. It splashed against the 116-degree pavement and evaporated almost immediately.

"What was that?"

"Shhh," she whispered, placing one finger over my lips.

"Why did you do that?" I asked, talking through her fingers.

"You don't do drugs," she said with conviction.

"How do you know?" I asked. "You read minds?"

"I read hearts. Come now," she said, leading me to another part of her home.

We entered a large dining area where a divine-looking plate of food sat, awaiting my arrival. It was a juicy cheeseburger with french fries and a cup of fruit. It looked like something in one of those hamburger ads that takes your breath away. It was a far cry from Reva Joe's dead oatmeal and burnt-up, tasteless burgers on stale buns.

Hallelujah! Things were finally turning around.

"Sit," she insisted. "Eat."

She didn't have to tell me twice, because after the first time she said it, my rump was in the bottom of that seat and I had already eaten half the burger and had started on the fries.

Mayan sat down beside me and chuckled. She rubbed the side of my head gently, pushing my hair out of my face.

"When was the last time you had a good meal?"

"I don't know," I said with a pause. "What year is it?"

Mayan burst into laughter. "Oh my, you are a witty American, aren't you? I had almost forgotten that they made them so witty these days. We should give your grandmother a urine test," said Mayan in jest.

"What do you mean?" I asked, actually taking a break from my food to contemplate her statement.

"Reva Joe," said Mayan with distaste. "She speaks untruths about you."

"What do you mean?" I asked, completely taken away from my food.

"She said you were the cause of great trouble," Mayan said.

I sighed.

"She said you had behavioral and emotional problems."

I didn't answer.

"But," she said confidently, "I can tell she lies. So, I need to mail her a cup to pee in. What do you say, huh?"

Now, that was funny and so I laughed. I will never forget my laugh that day. It was a gut laugh, came up from my toes, then through my belly and blew itself out in the roar of my vocal cords. My laughter was a welcome relief.

Well, I would say this was a pretty interesting introduction to the Wintergreen School for Girls. However, it was about to get even more *interesting*.

There were four other girls living in this large home that doubled as a school, and I would meet them later that evening.

I was at a loss to find that I had nothing at all to say, but worse yet, even if I had, they would be hard-pressed to understand my English.

Dear God.

Just when I thought things were taking a turn for the better. None of the other eight girls spoke English! They could make their way around a meal with simple phrases here and there but beyond that, there was a language barrier the size of the Great Wall of China.

I mean, really now. *"Como Esta?"* can only get you so far.

Reva Joe, what have you done to me now?

"You seem a little uneasy," said Mayan, observing my despair at the evening meal. Ironically, she seemed very much in control of this situation, which I was beginning to think was desperate and hopeless.

"I am," I whispered under my breath.

"Why?" she asked, poised and confident.

"Mayan," I said, trying to speak in a low voice, "no one at this table speaks English."

"I see," she said, raising a wineglass to her red lips. "Don't you speak English?"

"Yeah," I replied flippantly.

"And I speak English?" she reaffirmed.

"Yes," I said reluctantly.

"Then your hypothesis does not hold together very well. There are at least *two* people at this table who speak English."

"Wait," I said, shaking my head. "How could you open a school in America where no one speaks English? Doesn't that sound a little crazy to you?"

Mayan laughed out loud.

"Did I miss something?" I asked, perturbed.

"Only what you fail to realize," said Mayan in her typical calm manner. "Look at the girls from left to right," she instructed.

I did as she requested and Mayan began to break it down grandly, as the girls continued talking, unconscious of the fact that they were the topic of our private conversation.

"Lolita is the leader," said Mayan. "She is seventeen years old, standing at six feet; she is as brilliant as she is exotic and beautiful. She is a swan, and her beauty has a rippling effect—it extends outward. She is the girl everyone wants to know, but few will ever get that privilege. Lolita is cautious, trusts no one, and takes very few into her circle. She is fierce with her loyalty and if she takes you under her wing, she will be your friend for life. If you betray her, she will rip out your jugular with her own hands and spit on your face as you bleed to death.

"She's *not* friendly, so if you're looking for a smile or a kind word, you'll starve to death waiting for it. She doesn't want to know you. She doesn't care about you, but if by chance one fine day she should happen to take a fancy to you, consider yourself fortunate. If you ever get the chance to know her, you will have an irrevocable bond. She is the youngest and only girl of eight children. She has seven older brothers who wear very big shoes, both in size and presence, in Lolita's world. She aspires to be a nuclear physicist. She has been with me three years. She'll graduate next year and move on to a top college. Her family lives in Argentina but insists that she have an American education. It is my guess that Lolita will never say two words more to you than she absolutely has to. Truthfully, you're just not interesting enough for her."

I rolled my eyes.

"Don't take it personally," she advised. "It's just her way."

There was a brief silence between us as I processed the information Mayan had given me, and then she moved onto the girl seated next to Lolita. She was the most unusual looking of the four, fair-skinned with auburn hair and light freckles. She was every bit a Spanish-speaking Argentinean, but you wouldn't know it by looks alone. She looked more like a girl from the Midwest than Buenos Aires. This girl was very developed and shapely for a teenager. Her breasts looked like they tipped the scales somewhere around a D-cup and her hips curved and did a dip when she strutted down the hall.

"We call her Pepper," said Mayan. "Pepper because she's hot and spicy, sassy, and sometimes out of control."

"Wild child, huh?" I asked, a curious brow raised.

"The wildest of them," confirmed Mayan. "Erratic and unstable, largely unpredictable, and that is the thing that makes her a high risk. Her unsecured tendencies are what make me want to return her shapely little rump back to Argentina straightaway."

"But you don't . . . ?" I inquired.

"I will not," she states emphatically. "I am bound by a stupid and blind allegiance to that girl you see down there with the fire in her hair."

"Why?" I asked with great curiosity.

Mayan looked away, then returned her stare to me. "She's a rescue."

"What does that mean?"

"Rescued from the filth of a lower-class nation. She was sold into sexual bondage at the age of twelve because she had the body of a twenty-five-year-old woman."

I looked at her, so wild and lively and free and outspoken and glorious, then turned away and lowered my head.

"But she wasn't a twenty-five-year-old woman," continued Mayan. "She was a twelve-year-old girl in a body that spoke far louder than her own mouth and mind could."

I looked down, nauseous at her words.

"And no, those are not D-cups that sit so eloquently on her chest, they are Es."

I almost choked.

Good Nelly.

"The last two girls are twins, fraternal. And they could not be more opposite, one from the other. They are Patricia and Benita. Patricia stays because if I send her back to Argentina, she will die on the street. She is lazy and manipulative, but wise of the streets. She is a gambler, taking chances every day with her own life, breaking the rules. She will steal the shirt off her grandmother's back and slit your throat in your sleep if she gets the chance. Don't cross her. Don't look at her wrong, and if you can help it . . . don't look at her at all."

"Really?" I asked, surprised.

"Oh, yes," said Mayan. "Do not take my words with lightness . . ."

"She sounds atrocious," I said with attitude.

"Atrocity is in the eye of the beholder," said Mayan.

"Why do you put up with her?" I asked. "Someone who, as you say, would, 'cut your throat while you slept'?"

"She wouldn't cut *mine*," said Mayan with certainty. "I love her . . . or maybe it's not so much love as it is great compassion."

"Why do you have so much compassion?"

"It's not every day you meet a fifteen-year-old girl who for most of her life was tied to a pole in a basement and raped by her own father daily."

"Oh, God," I said, horrified.

"So now you understand my position in the sun with her, yes?"

"Yes," I said. "And what about her sister?"

"What about her?" said Mayan, almost with a chill and coldness about her.

"Do you have compassion for her, too?"

"Yes," she said softly. "Deep compassion. She was forced to rape her own sister for their father's pleasure."

I looked at the girls and watched their eloquent conversation and their beautiful faces and felt the energy of the dance of life. I wanted to cry but I knew that my tears would be unwelcome, and more so, they'd be resented.

I was that foreign girl in a strange land in her own country, and though my story was no great American novel, it could hardly be compared to those of these girls.

"And what of you?" asked Mayan. "What is your story?"

"I don't have one," I said.

"Foolishness," said Mayan.

"My story is different from theirs," I said. "But in a lot of ways it's not . . . I guess I'm a rescue, too . . ."

"Tell me about your mother," she said.

"Don't remember much of her," I said. "She died when I was two, almost three. I remember the shape of her head after she lost all of her hair. It's such a strange thing to remember. I remember the look in my father's eyes at the funeral when they closed the coffin for the last time."

"What kind of look?"

"It looked like he jumped in the casket with her . . . shut down, just pretended to go on living . . . you know?"

"What was your father like after your mother died?"

"Tortured," I said.

"What do you mean?"

"He got lost after she died . . . started liking boys."

"Little boys?" she asked in horror.

"No, not little boys, Mayan. He wasn't a pervert! Big boys!"

"Aaah," said Mayan, nodding. "He was a homosexual?"

I paused, taking a deep breath, absorbing the complexity of his homosexuality. "Yes . . . I guess he was," I said.

"And you were ashamed?" asked Mayan.

"I was confused. He liked dresses, so he wore them. He liked breasts, so he wanted a pair for himself. I offered to trade genitals with him because I wanted him to be happy . . ." I started, stopped, then tears began to swell in my eyes.

"It does not sound like he was so confused at all . . ." she said.

"No, maybe he wasn't. Maybe it was just me who was confused."

"I do not think you were confused," she said.

I glanced at Mayan, then quickly looked away. "Sometimes we run from the truth, calling it confusion. The truth can break you," I said, "Or make you whole, depending on what side you fall under when it finally hits the ground."

"You are wise beyond your years," said Mayan. "You speak as though you have lived a thousand years."

"I *have* lived a thousand years, lady . . . a thousand years and then some."

Mayan nodded in recognition of the truth of my statement.

"Will you tell me more about the school?" I asked, wanting desperately to change the subject.

"All of our studies are conducted in English," she said. "All of the girls here *do* speak English, perfect English, but outside of the classroom they prefer their native language."

"Oh," I said, watching them engage one another in laughter and the brisk conversation of Spanish dialogue.

"Of course," she said, raising her wineglass, chuckling.

I wondered why Mayan had not yet introduced me to the girls or them to me. And then I began to ponder why the rude girls had not introduced themselves.

"Why don't they say hello?" I asked Mayan, who completely ignored me, interrupting their conversation by announcing something poetic in Spanish. All eyes turned to me. The one they called Pepper started to giggle, and soon the others followed her lead. They made brief comments to one another in Spanish. They were short and succinct—God only knows what they were saying to one another.

How rude, I thought.

How utterly and impossibly rude.

"Hello," said each of the girls as they went around the table.

"Hi," I said, uncomfortable in my own skin. I could see them sizing me up. I saw their lips moving and a few utterances in a foreign tongue. I couldn't understand a word they said, but I could see what appeared like universal disapproval. In other words, I wouldn't be making any long-term friends in this joint. Truth is, I probably wouldn't make any short-term ones, either.

I spent the rest of the meal in silence, watching the girls of Argentina communicate eloquently with one another as they sat blind, deaf, and dumb toward me. In some ways, I couldn't believe their inhospitality, but in other ways, it seemed as though their behavior would be a given, and what possessed me to expect anything different? This was the hottest place on the planet on the hottest day of the year. Did I expect outgoing and gregariousness toward the *gringo* from Milwaukee with the lily-white skin?

As I stared at the table, the girls began to bleed into the background. They all resembled each other, and were truly beautiful with fair skin and long, flowing black hair.

It was poetic watching them converse with a lot of "r" rolling, hair twirling, and the typical catty nature of the female species. And though I did not understand the words, I could pretty much tell they were talking about empty, idle things. And oh yeah, there were several "dagger" stares thrown in my direction. Within minutes I began to shrivel, comparing myself to the glisten of their skin, the white of their teeth, and the flow of their hair.

I did not envy them, nor did I wish to be them, but I did want *something* from them. I just didn't know what it was. After all, I was beautiful, too—me in all my glory, with my lily-white, porcelain-textured American skin. This was *my* homeland, not theirs. So why did I feel like the outsider? How did the English language become secondary in the American city of Tucson?

I could feel myself shriveling at the table, sitting in deep disappointment that I had not asserted myself to make a bigger impression, to be grander than the smaller me I had become. It was obvious they were excluding me. I sat at one end of the table with Mayan and they all congregated down at the other end, huddled like a tiny Argentinean nation.

"You shouldn't," said Mayan with sincerity.

"I shouldn't what?" I asked, bitter.

"*Need,*" she said flatly.

"I don't," I said, offended, turning my attention back to the grilled chicken breasts on my plate.

"You do," she stated affirmatively. "You need their approval . . ."

"I don't *want* their approval."

"You don't want it," she stated. "You *need* it."

"I couldn't care less," I spat, trying not to make a scene, growing more and more aggravated.

"You care too much, and therein lies the problem."

Exasperated by her claims that I was seeking approval from these girls, I was ready to be excused. "I want to go to my room," I insisted.

"No," said Mayan calmly.

I looked at her, exasperated.

"You will be excused when the meal has concluded," she said, all of her attention turned to a simple glass of wine.

I was so angry I could not even look at Mayan. I just sat in my seat, boiling like a lobster dropped into hot water. I agonized on the inside and my shell hardened on the outside.

How dare she keep me here against my will, and in the midst of such rude, arrogant girls?

Who did she think she was?

Who did she think I was?

I wouldn't stand for it.

"You can stop it," she said.

"What?" I asked, with attitude.

"The mental commentary," she said. "I can hear you."

"What are you talking about?" I asked, extremely irritated.

"Your thoughts are loud," she said. "I hear them."

For the rest of the meal I sat in complete silence, turned off my brain, and simply stopped thinking. I refused to give Mayan the satisfaction of reading my mind, though if she would read it now, it would say something pretty dramatic.

She looked at me hard.

I'm sure she heard that.

Later that night, I was allowed to return to my bedroom, which, by the way, was a tiny little laboratory cubicle with only enough square footage to accommodate a large rat.

I lay down in the twin-size bed and stared at the ceiling, catching eyes with the blades of a fan twirling round and round. I counted the rotations in a trance-like state. With each rotation I could feel myself plummeting backwards through time, back to the days when I had a mother. I missed my mother so much, though I barely knew her at all. I missed Juno so much, though I was angry with him for leaving.

Damn you, Juno.

Damn you for leaving.

I missed Saxon, Wisconsin, because the town was small enough to remain unpolluted by "big city" thinking. I missed the familiarity of knowing who I was and where I was going. These were things that I used to take for granted when Juno was alive. Simple stuff, like would I wake up in the same place twice?

I didn't miss Milwaukee at all and I sure didn't miss Reva Joe and her dead bowl of oats, but I sure did miss Anthem a lot. I missed him so much because he was there and I was here, and I wanted to bridge that gap somehow. I didn't get the chance to say good-bye, but I knew someday soon he would return to my bedroom window and I just hoped Reva Joe wouldn't get hold of him if he did.

I jumped out of my bed and turned on the light where a small computer sat on a nearby desk. I got online and did an Internet search for Anthem's address.

I didn't know much, but I knew his last name was Rogers and he lived on Buckingham Lane, so I searched for any Rogers on Buckingham in Milwaukee, and sure enough, there was an Anna Rogers at 327 Buckingham Road, Milwaukee, Wisconsin.

I smiled because I felt the distance between him and me had just been shortened, and that was a big relief—a much-needed grace in the midnight hour, on a night when the world felt so big and I so small.

I sat down at the computer that night and wrote Anthem what would be the first of many letters.

Dear Anthem,

Hi . . . it's me, Adrian. First, I want to say that I hope you get this letter, and secondly, I hope you'll write me back. I did not mean to disappear right in the middle of getting to know you, but the Wicked Witch (Reva Joe Moses a/k/a "Grandma") sent me away to a year-round boarding school in Tucson, Arizona. This place got swallowed by the sun . . . it's the hottest place on planet Earth. The bargain boarding school that Reva Joe sent me to is as foreign to me as anything you could possibly imagine. The school is owned and run by a woman from Argentina . . . and all the girls here (all four of them) are from Argentina and no one speaks English. Well, actually, they do speak English but choose not to because they don't want me to understand all the mean things they are saying about me.

I miss you, Anthem.

I would say that I want to come home but I have no home to come to, so I will leave you with this: maybe someday you can come here to the hottest place on Earth. But it would be with me, the coolest chick in town (smile).

You will always have a home with me, Anthem, because I have carved out this exceptional block of space in the tiniest part of my anatomy and saved it special for you in my heart.

I'll see you soon.

I love you.

Adrian

Chapter 19

As I descended past the nineteenth floor, I remembered Dayglo and his fascination with "Snow White."

A day at the Wintergreen Boarding School for Girls turned into a week, then a month, followed by a single unit of time known as an eternity. How could a single moment last so long? During my first month at the school, the girls remained distant, each of them virtually having nothing to say to me at all.

They were consistent with their exclusion, and Mayan did nothing to override that but insisted that I find my own place with the girls. But I did nothing to fit in, and they did nothing to accept me because they were too attached to their own importance.

The rigorous routine of our everyday schedule gave life a predictability that was unbearable.

Wake up at 6:00 A.M.

Shower at 6:15 A.M.

Breakfast at 7:00 A.M.

First class at 7:45 A.M.

Lunch at noon.

Studies end at 3:00 P.M.

Homework till 5:30 P.M.

Dinner at 6:00 P.M.

7:00 P.M.—*free time at last!*

I spent my free time studying the pictures on the wall, mimicking the sketches of the naked body in my room in private where I kept them beneath my bed.

I spent my free time studying the flowers in the garden off the patio in the back of the house.

I spent free time writing letters to Anthem, all of which went unanswered.

I spent my time searching for pennies to throw into the wishing fountain in the center of the courtyard. I found a new penny every day that someone, somewhere, had discarded. Most of the girls saw pennies as worthless. I saw them as the most valuable commodity at the school. They were my link between the dream and the desperation, and that very fact made them priceless.

I always found enough time to make a new wish every day, but God never seemed to find the time to answer, and on a day when I was least expecting it, I think He heard an echo in the wind.

It was dusk in Tucson and there was a pause in the blazing heat, which was "very warm" instead of "unbearably hot."

On such a beautiful evening, I stood over the fountain with a rusted penny that I had found sticking out of the rug in the library earlier that day. I hadn't found a penny in several days, so I found myself overwhelmed with joy and couldn't wait for "free time" that evening so I could go to the fountain and make a wish.

I made the same wishes every day.

I wished for a beautiful home.

I wished for a pot of gold so that I would always have enough money to control my own destiny. I never wanted to live at the mercy of someone else.

I wished for someone to love me deeply, like a husband, and I also wished for someone to love deeply, like a son. I wanted a big, black truck, a nice one with leather insides, and a hot stereo system. And more than anything, I wanted to do what I wanted with my own life and live my days as I saw fit.

No schedules to keep.

No rules to follow.

No authority to respect.

I wanted a golden retriever and two exotic fish.

As I stood over the fountain, concentrating hard, I heard a faint male voice whisper, "It worked."

The voice startled me and I jumped.

I saw the shadow of an applauding man approach me from a distant corner.

"Congratulations," he said in the very familiar sounds of an Argentinean accent. "It worked."

"What worked?"

"Your wish came true," he said. "I am here." And as soon as he said those words, he stepped into the light of the courtyard and I almost collapsed onto the concrete.

My God!

He was divine.

A beautiful specimen, standing close to six feet, with nice, broad shoulders and a bemused expression. His eyes looked jet black against a thick mane of black hair, and it looked as though he had just stepped into manhood, because I could still see the shadows of a little boy.

"I am here," he repeated with a grin.

I looked at him and smiled, feeling that familiar rush of adrenaline intoxicating me with its dance.

"You're a boy," were the first words I uttered. So much for an intelligent conversation, I thought to myself.

I blew it.

"And so I am," he said with a laugh, his eyes doing a quick glance just below his waist, which embarrassed me tremendously.

"I didn't mean it like that," I said shyly. "Of course you're a boy . . . I mean, a man."

"And so I am," he boldly declared, pushing his testosterone out ahead of him.

"This is a school for girls," I said, eyes scanning the grounds. "I'm just not accustomed to seeing boys . . ."

"Well," he said with a smile, "this boy belongs to the girl who owns this house."

"You're Mayan's son!" I exclaimed.

"And so I am," he said again.

I quickly extended my hand, slightly embarrassed. "I'm sorry . . . I didn't know."

"Don't be sorry."

"No," I said, shaking my head. "I wasn't expecting you,"

"I am the secret who makes himself known in a big way," he said, winking.

I smiled, turning away for a beat, then focusing my attention on the fountain. "So you are the new girl that the others call 'Snow White'?" he asked, observing intently.

"I didn't know they called me anything," I said. "They barely speak at all."

"Do not give them your eyes," he said.

"Of course not," I said in jest. "I'm keeping them for myself to see with."

"Pay them none of your attention," he said firmly. "They are jealous of you."

My smile faded. "They hate me."

"They are threatened by you," he stated emphatically.

"Why?"

"Because they are small and they *know* they are small. You, however, are a giant and they see that. All small things eventually must surrender to the thing that is much greater than themselves . . . it is the way of nature."

I stared deeply into his eyes, listening to his words, losing myself in the thought of him.

"What do they call you?" he asked.

"Probably 'bitch,'" I said.

"No," he said. "Your name?"

"Oh," I said, embarrassed. "Adrian."

"So your name really is not Snow White?"

I rolled my eyes.

"She really is beautiful, you know, Snow White . . ." he said, pausing for a beat. "Adrian," he said, smiling as he took my hand into his, "I hope that all of your wishes come true."

He moved away from me and went back into the house. And out of the corner of my eye I could see the desperate, drooling expressions of every girl in the house staring at me.

"Small," I said under my breath, starting to laugh as I flipped the rusted penny into the fountain.

That night as I sketched naked bodies in my room, there was a light knock on my door.

I quickly shoved my sketches beneath the bed and slowly made my way to the door. "Who's there?" I asked.

"Me," he said.

Instantly, I recognized the voice and my pulse started to race. I glanced at the clock on the desk: 9:25 P.M. I could get into big trouble for opening this door and letting him in, both of which I did.

"What are you doing here?" I asked in a hushed voice.

"I wanted to see you again."

"You're going to get me in trouble."

"Relax," he said gently. "I know the owner."

And with that we both started laughing.

"I don't remember your name," I said.

"Dayglo," he said.

"That's right," I said. "Center of the universe."

"So, this is what they look like?" he asked, roaming about my room.

"What?"

"The girls' rooms."

"You've never been in any girl's room before?" I said. "I find that very hard to believe."

"Why?"

"Look at you . . . you're beautiful."

"I am nineteen," he said. "I have only done so much living at nineteen."

"I'm almost fifteen and trust me, I've done a LOT of living for a fifteen-year-old."

"Really?" he said, turning all of his attention toward me. "Tell me about your living. I want to know about you."

Whoa, I thought, feeling a breeze blow into the room, aware of his heightened fascination with me. It caught me off guard, making me feel uncomfortable.

Was he too familiar, too soon? Was this just too much? If Mayan catches us, there will be hell to pay. Could someone actually be this fascinated with me and my life?

"Sit with me," he suggested, patting the bed.

Cautiously, I approached and sat down beside him.

"Tell me about living," he implored.

"I don't know where to start."

"Start where every good story starts."

"And where is that?"

"The beginning," he said. And with that I recounted the story of my life, beginning with the death of my mother all the way through my father's tragic end. I hit the highlights with Reva Joe, paused at Anthem, and made a fat, round circle of conclusion at the Wintergreen Boarding School for Girls.

By the time I finished speaking, I was dry-mouthed and brain-rotted. He looked fascinated, love-struck, and filled with great lust.

We sat in silence for a long time, he and I, caught up in one another's gaze. I didn't know what he was thinking and he didn't know what I was thinking, but it appears we were thinking the same thing, as we leaned into one another and kissed.

Wow!

Sparks flew.

Thunderbolts fell out of the sky.

My skin caught on fire and burned a hole in the center of my chest. I pulled back, awestruck that I could kiss another man besides Anthem and actually *like* it. "You should go," I said, getting off the bed.

"Why?"

"Because it's after ten o'clock," I said hastily.

"Is that the only reason?" he asked, cornering me against the wall.

I didn't answer.

"Is that the only reason?" he said again, cupping my face into his hands.

"Yes," I said, quickly responding, eyes fixed on the floor.

"I don't believe you," he said, looking so beautiful and exotic. I started to fidget as he looked deeper and harder into my eyes. "I don't believe you," he said again. "You left out a big part of your story, no?"

"What do you mean?"

"A woman only pauses," he said, "when another man enters her field of vision."

"You don't know what you're talking about," I said, trying to brush it off.

"You have done a lot of living," he said. "But I have done a lot of *life*."

I looked down, and lowered my head. "Good night, Snow White," he said, kissing me gently on the forehead, then exiting.

I sat on the bed in a daze for a few minutes after he left, replaying the scene. A few minutes later, there was another knock on my door.

He had returned.

My heart started to beat fast and my pulse raced all over again.

What did he want this time?

Couldn't he leave well enough alone?

I quickly opened the door, saying, "We're going to get . . ." I started, then stopped midsentence as Mayan stood, larger than life, at my door, her hands on her hips. I didn't have the heart to make eye contact, which really didn't matter because Mayan bolted inside, slamming the door. She stood like a giant over me, disapproving.

"We are *not* studying anatomy this semester," she said with a stern accent. "You are breaking the rules."

"I don't understand," I said weakly.

"I think you do," she insisted. "You're very bright. You know the rules. You know them very well."

"I didn't do anything!"

"You've done plenty," she said with one raised brow. "Enough to get you into big trouble in this school."

"I've done nothing wrong," I insisted, turning away from her. Mayan was watching me from a distance. I could feel her heavy stare scan me up and down. "You've done enough to get thrown out of here," she said.

And again, I lowered my head.

"And then, where would you go?" she asked. "You could go back to live with your grandmother, perhaps?"

"I can't go back there," I said in a whisper.

"And you're not yet fifteen . . . ," she said. "You can't drive or work or do anything for money. Unless, of course, you want to lie on your back like a whore."

I gasped at the thought.

"You see," said Mayan, "you are playing big-girl games. Men are not wind-up toys. My son is a man, not a boy."

"You're making me uncomfortable, Mayan," I said, looking intensely into her eyes.

"You can't just turn them off when you feel the game is over, because the game is not over for them until they get this gigantic release . . ."

"Oh, God," I said, sitting down on my bed, feeling queasy.

"Stop with Dayglo now," she insisted, "before it is too late. He is beautiful, so I understand your attraction to him, ehhh . . . but stop it now! He is here for two weeks only for a visit and then he's back in Argentina with his father. Do you understand? There's nowhere to go with him. You're a child. My son is a man."

"I didn't do anything," I insisted.

"You are doing a lot," she said. "Do you think you are the first that I have had this discussion with about my son? Do your eyes see just how truly beautiful Dayglo is? Your eyes and everybody else's eyes.

"You think you are that special, Adrian? *That* pretty?" asked Mayan with a laugh. "Do not fool yourself . . . look around you. There are beautiful girls here . . . my son sees their beauty and they see his, so I am bored with this speech that I give you girls every year when my son comes into town. You are playing a very dangerous game . . . and I suggest you stop because there is nowhere to go with it."

I slowly nodded.

"Very well," said Mayan as she walked toward the door, stopped, and turned to me with those big black eyes. "Are you a virgin?"

"Yes!" I said emphatically.

"Good," she said. "At this time in your life," she said, "a virgin is the best thing to be."

Chapter 18

As I descended past the eighteenth floor, I remembered the night I lost my virginity.

The next morning when I woke up, Dayglo was standing over me in my bedroom. At first, it seemed like a sweet dream, and then I came further out of my deep sleep and sat straight up in my bed with the sides of my hair plastered against my head, and then it suddenly seemed like a nightmare.

"Oh, my God," I exclaimed, bunching the covers securely around my chest to hide my little pink nightgown. "What are you doing here?"

"I had to see you this morning," he said.

"No," I said in hurried desperation. "No, no, no."

"Do you not wish to see me?" he asked, with the blink of his gorgeous, chocolate-brown eyes.

"Yes," I said. "I mean no . . . yes . . . no . . . I don't know. I'm confused."

"There is no such thing as confusion. Only a rejection of the truth."

"And what is that truth, Dayglo? What is it?"

"You are as drawn to me as I to you . . ." he whispered into my ear. "That is truth, yes?"

"Yes," I said after a long pause, head lowered. "But we have nowhere to go . . ."

"What do you mean?"

"So, I like you," I replied defensively. "But what good is it?"

He pulled back, staring deeply into my eyes. "I do not understand Americans . . ."

"Why do you say that?"

"You feel, you live, you breathe, and then you stop and ask yourself what good is it to feel, to live, to breathe. So, it's like you never *really* live at all because you spend your whole life asking, *What is life?*"

"It's not so easy, Dayglo . . ."

"Why?" he insisted.

"Because . . ."

"Come again? Why?"

"Because it just is . . ."

"Why?" he asked, pressing further.

"I don't know . . ."

Dayglo stood up from the bed, and in looking at him, I could not believe how utterly beautiful he was—so beautiful, in fact, that I began to question his fascination with me.

I wondered about his interest in me; I wanted to question it to death, validate this experience, but I interrupted this mental absurdity.

"When you figure it out, Snow White," he said, gently kissing my forehead, "find me . . . I will not be far away."

And just like that, he was gone again. But I would feel his presence very strongly at the breakfast table that morning, sitting across from the girls, feeling the weight of their disapproval coupled with their cross-eyed stares and cackling laughter.

This was a typical breakfast in this house. It was also a typical lunch and dinner, too. Sprinkles of English surrounded by dialogue in Spanish.

"Pass the salt," Lolita would say.

"And the pepper," would add Benita.

"Water, please," said Pepper and sometimes Patricia, but beyond that they shut me out. *Salt, pepper,* and *water* were pretty much the extent of their conversation with me. Sometimes there was *hello*, but more often only *good-bye*. And yet again, Mayan did nothing to intervene on my behalf and command them to be civil. But in the end, it didn't matter. It all came to a crashing halt one morning as I sat at the table just before my fifteenth birthday, dangling somewhere between PMS and psychosis. I could feel the heat swell inside my body, leading me to a catastrophic display of anger.

"Speak English!" I demanded, slamming my hand down on the dinner table. Instantly, the room grew still.

"Every single morning you come down these stairs . . ." I said boldly, looking into the eyes of each girl, "rolling your r's and twirling your hair. Well, I've just about had enough of you rude, arrogant wenches!"

The girls gasped, holding their hands to their mouths, rattling Spanish to one another beneath their breath.

"Yes, I have just about had enough!" I spat, rising to my feet, feeling the giant within come alive. And suddenly, the girls seemed to shrink behind the shallow veil of their rude behavior.

Small.

Small.

And smaller they became.

"Do you *really* think you're better than me?" I asked each of them, looking into their eyes, expecting an answer.

"We think you are paranoid," said Pepper with a snap.

"And I think *you* are rude," I said emphatically. "All of you."

As I turned to walk away, Lolita spoke out of the silence. "We are not trying to be rude to you." I stopped, turned around, and looked at her. "Nor are we trying to exclude you," she continued.

"We are sorry for your feelings," added Benita.

"Yes," said Patricia humbly, "we are."

All eyes in the room turned to Pepper. She crossed her arms and said, "There is nothing that I should say . . . I am sorry for nothing as I have done nothing to be sorry for."

There's always one in every bunch.

I turned back around and walked slowly out of the dining room, the echo of my heels leaving their own statement.

It was silent for a long time and no one spoke a word, not in English or in Spanish, and for the rest of their time at the table, the room echoed a quiet that could be heard throughout the rest of the house.

That was the day I met the giant in me, rising up to a place where I could actually look over the top of their heads and see just how truly small they were.

The next morning, I woke up to a bed filled with rose petals. Obviously, Dayglo had snuck into my room while I slept. I thought about freaking out at first, but then realized I was enjoying the attention. And maybe I enjoyed it more because I was getting his attention and the other girls weren't.

Who was I kidding?

Maybe they had already gotten his attention and he was done with them and they with him. It didn't matter all that much. At least I was getting his attention *now*.

Suddenly, there was a strong knock on my door, and I hurried to fold back my bedsheets because I didn't want anyone to see the rose petals.

I opened the door and there stood Mayan with a giant bouquet of flowers. "Every beautiful girl should have flowers on her birthday," she said gaily, blowing in like a gigantic gust of wind. She set the flowers on the dresser, then arranged them.

"A young woman's fifteenth birthday is very special. This is a day to be remembered and cherished," she said gently, embracing me, holding my hands in hers. "This is a day to hold on to," she said, kissing each of my cheeks. Out of the corner of her eyes she saw a couple of rose petals on the floor beneath the bed. They had fallen there and were blowing in the soft breeze. In an instant, Mayan's expression changed from delight to disapproval. I shrieked at the blatant evidence blowing about in the wind, giving all of my secrets away though I didn't really have any. I had done nothing wrong.

Mayan walked to the bed and ripped the comforter and sheets

off, and it seemed as though the whole room filled with rose petals. They swirled in slow motion and vivid color. It was beautiful, indeed, and could have been a scene out of a love story, but this was nothing short of a nightmare.

Mayan lost it, right there in the middle of my room, on a beautiful morning in Tucson, Arizona, on daybreak's edge of my birthday.

"Why do you insist on breaking the rules, Adrian?" she screamed, almost frantic, almost desperate.

"I didn't do anything," I pleaded.

"The petals on the floor!" she said, dropping to her knees and gathering them. "What does this mean?"

"Nothing," I quickly responded.

"A man leaves red petals ONLY when his intention is to take your virginity."

Upon hearing the words, I blushed. These accusations were excruciatingly embarrassing.

"Are you still in possession of your virginity?"

I was silent.

Embarrassed.

"Well, are you?"

"Of course I am," I snapped. "Why wouldn't I be?"

"I know my son," said Mayan.

"And I know *myself*," I said confidently. "And I'll never do anything against myself . . . I have no plans to lose my virginity till I get married. The first time I sleep with a man, it will be with my husband."

"If that is your *true* wish," said Mayan, "then why do you flirt so intently against it?"

"I need to get ready for the day, Mayan . . . it's getting late," I said, looking hard and cold into her eyes. She looked back at me and for several uncomfortable beats, we stared, almost as if we were challenging one another.

"Very well," she said.

She left, slamming the door hard behind her. I stood in the center of the room, looking around, head held low.

"Happy Birthday to me," I whispered.

And that was my birthday morning.

The rest of the afternoon was uneventful in a grand way. I missed Juno so much. This was my very first birthday without him and it seemed empty indeed.

There were no calls from Reva Joe. I doubted she was even aware of my birth date. She had never called before, so why would this year be any different? I received a few birthday wishes from the snobby girls, and a mock birthday celebration after school was let out.

I stood in the center of the dining hall where the snobby girls and Mayan gathered, everyone holding a plastic expression, sustaining long, dull notes, butchering "Happy Birthday" to death.

"For you," said Mayan, handing me a large, wrapped package with a big, red bow.

"For me?" I asked, surprised.

"Yes," she replied and smiled humbly.

I eagerly accepted my gift, opening it quickly, tearing off the brown paper in great eagerness. "Oh my God," I whispered as the final wrapping peeled.

It was *grandiose* indeed! A charcoal drawing of a beautiful, young woman partially clothed and standing in the middle of a garden with her hand extended, reaching out to something not yet in the frame. It was just like the story pictures I'd admired on Mayan's walls.

"This is the beginning of your own story," she said. "The beautiful young woman growing into herself . . ."

"Wow," I said, amazed.

"Someday," said Mayan, "you will add to the story of your life . . . and you will give it a name as I have named my own."

I could feel tears well in my eyes as I stared at the picture. It was as if this beautiful piece of art gave me permission to claim my own story.

I did have a story.

The story of my life.

My own.

The evening would unfold in a way that I could not have imagined in a thousand years, or even a thousand and one. The rest of the day was uneventful. That night at the wishing fountain I stood by for a long time, holding onto a nickel I had come by the hard way, searching and searching for it.

I stood there a long time, squeezing the nickel tight, fondling and caressing it. I closed my eyes tight and made a wish.

"The wishing girl," said Dayglo behind me. "Here she is . . ." he whispered, inching his way behind me. I smiled at the thought of him being there, but I did not turn around to face him. He tried to slip his hands around my waist and draw me to him, but I backed away, and turned to face him.

"Naughty boy," I said.

"Why do you call me such things?"

"You got me in trouble this morning," I scolded.

"Trouble?" he asked, one brow raised.

"Rose petals," I said with an equally penetrating look.

"Oh, yes," he said, smiling. "Were they not romantic?"

"I don't think your mother saw it that way."

"Oh," he said, nodding. "Curious. How did my mother see it?"

"How do you *think* she saw it?"

"Not clearly," he said in jest. "Through clouds of judgment, I would imagine."

I looked at him, and in looking at him I couldn't be mad because he was so darned sexy, and so sincere in his expression of love for me.

"You're crazy, Dayglo," I said with a sigh. "Crazy."

"Only about you," he said, smiling. "Now what about that wish?"

"Oh, yeah," I remembered, clutching the nickel. I took a deep breath, closed my eyes tight, made a wish, and released the coin. It skipped across the water, stopped, and sank to the bottom.

"How will you spend the rest of your night?" Dayglo asked.

"I don't know," I said.

"Will you spend it with me?"

"We're not supposed to . . ."

"I don't care about the rules, Adrian. I am requesting the presence of your company on the evening of your birthday . . ."

I paused, staring at him, "Why do you want to?"

"Why wouldn't I want to?"

"Under one condition," I said with great insistence.

"What?" he asked, smiling.

"Behave," I said firmly.

"On my honor," he said.

Five minutes later we were back in my room, groping and fondling each other on top of my bed. We were doing anything but behaving; in fact, we were well on our way to misbehaving.

Dayglo slipped his hand beneath my shirt and gently rubbed my breasts before dropping his head to my chest, and consuming my breast in his mouth, licking the nipple. I allowed him to do it because it felt so good, and he repeated it again and again. But like so many things, it eventually lost its momentum, and it was time to move on; when that time came, he knew it. Now, I don't know why I expected him to move away from his exploration of my body. Perhaps this was a tragic error in judgment, and it would change my life forever.

We should have stopped right then and there.

I should have insisted, demanded, but I didn't. So, when he made his way to my jeans and began unzipping them, I should have honored my reservations and surrendered to the panic which had set in. But it was a low-grade panic so I did not honor it.

Sometimes, it's that low-grade panic, that uneasy, unsettled feeling that delivers a truth we should abide by and respect.

I should have listened.

Should have listened.

Listened.

But I didn't.

Dayglo kept going, gliding his hands over my genitals, rubbing and manipulating with every turn and twist of his fingers. And though it did feel good, it felt like too much. It felt like it went too far, and it was time to bring it back.

"No," I whispered between breaths as his heavy body consumed me, conveniently pinning itself against me. "No."

He didn't listen.

"No," I said again, trying to wiggle myself away from his

grip, but his lips pressed harder and his grip tightened, stronger. And this is where the low-grade panic rose up the scale.

"No," I tried to say, and this time, he took one of his hands and he muffled my mouth, then pinned me in a lock that immobilized me.

What was he doing?

What was happening?

This was my birthday night and I was spending it with a beautiful, gentle man, who, in the blink of an eye, was turning into the Not-So-Jolly-Mean-Giant. Forceful and abrasive, his gentle, erotic touch was now filled with heat, anger, rage.

What was happening?

He was changing like the Incredible Hulk, going from the Beauty to the Beast.

What was happening?

It wasn't gentle.

It wasn't kind.

It wasn't romantic and heartfelt.

It was edgy, and his embrace began to feel like strangulation, suffocation. His forceful kisses began to feel like tiny molestations. His voice went from soft whispers to the sounds of slashing razor blades in his throat.

What was happening?

A transformation.

Bizarre mutation.

A metamorphosis of man into sex-crazed monster, without a conscience or regard for consent.

With the strength of his upper body, he pressed me against the mattress, squashing me, without freedom of movement for air or breath, and with his hand he parted my legs and shoved his fingers inside, probing, molesting.

What was happening?

Something had gone terribly, violently wrong, and within seconds he had ripped me out of my jeans. What kind of persistence does it take to rip denim?

I knew I was in trouble.

Big trouble. It was a trouble bigger than I could climb out of, or see beyond.

What was happening?

Within seconds the denim was gone and my underwear was halfway down and he mounted my writhing body like he was trying to tame a wild stallion, break its spirit, crack its back.

I wanted to scream for help, or let the others know what was going on, but somehow he had managed to put a pillow over my head and I could barely breathe, much less speak, much less scream. I thought for sure he would suffocate me, and by accident, I would be dead.

Sheer and utter horror took me over. I was afraid for my own life and for my own death, both at the same time.

What was happening?

Something had gone terribly, terribly wrong.

Within seconds, I felt his rock-hard erection on the edge of my vagina, fighting for space inside. I arched my hips back, trying to wiggle my way onto my side, and throw him off somehow, but my strength was no match against his. His had immobilized my body. His aggression paralyzed me with fear. He was stronger—his body felt like liquid lead, crystallized in flesh.

I was fifteen years old.

Soft.

Delicate.

Fragile.

Feminine.

Fluid.

Violated.

And though my will was intense, his was undeniably stronger.

I could not fight him off.

Nor could I free myself.

What was happening?

Rape was happening.

Rape was happening.

Everything moved so fast.

So furious.

The next sequence of events are dulled in my memory because of their intensity and severity. He forced his way inside, moving, moaning, penetrating.

I couldn't make out anything, nor could I differentiate between his body and mine. His body had *become* mine, and I hated it. I hated his smell. I hated his breath. I hated the feel of his skin against my own. It felt like sandpaper.

I remember the drops of sweat that leaked from his forehead onto my chest as he buried his head between my breasts. After that, I checked out, mentally.

Shut down.

And there was no more recording of events.

When Dayglo was finished, he leaned into my ear and whispered, "I am the secret who makes himself known in a BIG way. All small things eventually must surrender to the thing that is much greater than themselves . . . it is the way of nature."

I looked into his eyes and spat in his face. In turn, he head-butted me.

I cried out.

He got up, pulled up his pants, and exited the room.

I was able to lift myself off the bed, dizzy and disoriented, but then I fell onto the floor. Rose petals blew around the room as I fell into them, sending them sweeping across the floor.

The beautiful, soft, gentle, red petals swirled about my broken, bruised body. It could have been a movie if it weren't so bloody real. It could have been a dream if it weren't such a gut-wrenching nightmare. I could have visited heaven if I were not so far down in the pit of hell. I could have retained my virginity if it weren't taken with such violence and vengeance on the night of my fifteenth birthday.

Chapter 17

As I descended past the seventeeth floor, I remembered the day the only wish I ever made came true . . .

After the rape, I found my way to the bathroom, which was down the hall from my bedroom. It was only a few feet but it felt like a trip from one end of the world to the other. I opened the door in a frantic rush and quickly locked it behind me before making my way to the commode where I spent the next several minutes throwing up.

Eventually, I undressed and eased out of my torn clothing, then examined the parts of my pale skin that had already started to bruise. My chest was beet-red and the upper part of my shoulder had Dayglo's paw print on it.

I slipped out of my torn panties and examined the spots of blood in the crotch, tangible evidence of all that had been taken from me. I turned on the shower as hot as I could stand it, stood under it, and allowed myself to be taken over by the steam.

I played and replayed the evening's events in my mind as the water impaled me. All I could hear were Mayan's words repeating themselves in my head:

You are playing big-girl games.
Men are not wind-up toys.

You can't just turn them off when you feel the game is over, because the game is not over for them until they get this gigantic release.

At this time in your life a virgin is the very best thing to be.

The words were loud, and filled with an eerie foreshadowing of my fate.

You can't just turn them off . . .

Not wind-up toys . . .

Gigantic release.

Between her warnings, I could see a gentle spirit who turned into a madman in moments.

Where in God's name did he come from?

And more importantly, what would I do now?

I must have been in the shower for a long time because somewhere in the second hour, there was a knock on the door. Actually, a series of knocks in succession.

I panicked when I heard it.

Was it Dayglo returning again?

What would I do if he returned to haunt me? And rape me again?

Surely, I would cry out as loud as I could, have my voice be heard in mega-decibels. I would cry out in many languages— English, Bulgarian, and French. I would be heard. He would *not* rape me again. I turned the water off and got out of the shower, then stood in the center of the floor, shaking, not certain what to do.

"Who's there?" I finally asked.

"Lolita," she said in a faint whisper. "I need to use the rest room."

"Okay," I said, trying to gather myself. "Give me a minute."

I collected my soiled clothing and tried to fix the towel around me so as to cover my body and bruises. Eventually, I opened the door and Lolita's brow raised when she looked at me.

I must have looked like a train wreck.

"Sorry," I said, inching my way around her.

She nodded, staring at me with a peculiar eye. "Are you okay?"

"Yes," I responded, surprised by her concern.

I quickly returned to my room where I propped a chair against the door to protect me from the bad man down the hall. I pulled the sheets off the bed and threw them on the floor. I sat on the bed, quivering and frightened, not sure what to do, but just knowing that I should do something.

I could call the police and turn him in, but when they came to take the report, how would I explain the rose petals in my room?

But it wasn't my fault.

And what of the previous late-night visits?

But it wasn't my fault.

How would I explain our very public flirtations at the wishing fountain?

But it still wasn't my fault.

How could I justify ignoring the warnings of his own mother?

But it wasn't my fault.

Did I stack myself up like a perfect row of dominoes, and then cry out when they fell in order?

This isn't my fault!

I had flirted with danger, invited him to my room, made out with him, pushed his desires to the edge, then dropped him there and tried to do the backstroke back to land, to safety, back to my virginity, but by then, it was too late.

Over.

Done.

Gone.

Forever.

Say good night to fourteen and good morning to fifteen.

Hell of a thing to be, fifteen.

I fell asleep holding a pillow very close to my chest for comfort and security. By morning, I had overslept and awoke to someone banging on my door.

It scared me.

I woke up, frightened and reactive. Disoriented, I stumbled out of bed and opened the door where Lolita stood, staring at me with haunting, penetrating eyes.

"You missed breakfast," she said.

"Okay," I said, trying to stir myself back to life. "Let me just . . . just find something to . . ." I moved away from the door and Lolita entered, closing the door behind her.

"Are you okay?" she asked with great concern.

"Yeah . . . yeah," I said, stumbling around the room, bumping into furniture.

"Here," she said, going through my closet, handing me a shirt and a pair of jeans. I turned to her, catching the tail end of her stare, surprised by her assistance.

Why was she being so attentive when prior to this she had never even noticed I was alive?

I accepted the clothing and looked at it, but all that I could do was sit down on the bed and stare at the dying rose petals. Lolita paid particular attention to the petals on the floor before returning her attention to me.

"Are you sure?" she asked, her words long and drawn out.

"About what?" I asked, eyes fixed toward the floor.

"That you're okay?"

"I'm not sure about anything," I uttered.

She rested her hand on my back, and I jumped. She pulled back. "I'm sorry," she mumbled. "Can I do anything to help you?"

I shook my head.

"What happened?"

I was silent.

"Adrian?"

And still, there was silence.

"I don't know," I said, half out of it.

"Dayglo?" she asked.

I became fully alert, and my face reflected fear at the mention of his name.

"I'm going to be late," I said, getting off the bed. "You'll have to excuse me."

Lolita stood, paused, then spoke. "Silence is *not* the answer to your problem."

"I don't have any problems," I said robotically.

"I look at the dead flowers on the floor," said Lolita, "and they tell another story."

"*Somebody forgot to water me*," I said sarcastically. "That's what they're saying. It's a crummy birthday gift," I said.

"But then I look at the bruises on your shoulder," she continued, "and they, too, speak their own truth."

Immediately, I attempted to cover my bruised shoulder with a towel. "It's nothing," I responded quickly.

"To Dayglo," she said, "it was nothing. To you, it was *every-thing*." And with those final words, she left me alone in the middle of my bedroom to deal with it. But it was just too much, so I got back in bed, pulled the comforter over my head, and went back to sleep.

I was awakened an hour later by Mayan, who was sitting on my bed taking my temperature, examining the devastation in my room with a critical eye.

Soiled sheets.

Dead roses.

A teetering chair against a wall.

Off-center mattress.

It was all an indication of chaos, but nothing was more telling than my own stance, tattered and unresponsive, hunched in the fetal position.

"What is the matter with you today?" she asked suspiciously, as though *I* had done something wrong.

Your son raped me last night, was my immediate thought. Yes, that would accurately summarize what happened, but I knew I couldn't utter those words aloud.

"You're not well today?" she asked with a critical eye.

"No," I said flatly.

"What are your symptoms?" she asked.

"I don't feel good, Mayan."

"What hurts?"

"What *doesn't* hurt?"

"Did you have a late night?" she asked, looking around the room.

I didn't answer.

"My son was here last night, wasn't he?" she said, circling my room like a vulture. "Wasn't he?" she snapped, growing agitated. "I smell him everywhere!"

I could not answer.

What would I say?

I could not tell her the truth about her son. I knew enough about Mayan to know that her son was everything to her—she praised him far more than he deserved. She believed him to be something better than he was, attributing a graciousness that did not belong to him.

Yes, your son was in this room last night. He was in this room pillaging and raping, violating and degrading. Yes, your son was in this room last night.

Suddenly, there was a knock on my door.

"What?" snapped Mayan, opening the door in anger. It was Dayglo. They had a brief, hurried exchange in Spanish, and though I did not look directly into his eyes, I could feel the weight of his stare.

"Hi, Adrian," he said, lighthearted and easy.

I did not respond.

"Adrian is not well today," Mayan said to Dayglo.

"Oh," he said. "I hope she recovers soon."

There was another brief exchange between Mayan and Dayglo, and then he was gone. She shut the door behind him and looked at me. "I will expect you for dinner." And with that, she left.

Dinner came sooner than I wanted it to, much like the rest of my life. Everything had come sooner than I wanted it to: the death of my parents, the development of breasts, the onset of menses, my first broken heart, and the unexpected loss of my virginity.

It had *all* come too soon.

All of it had left me feeling powerless and vulnerable to life and all of its untimely circumstances.

Dinner was quieter than usual. No one really spoke—it was

almost as if everyone knew. The air was so thick, you'd need a hacksaw to cut it.

I quickly ate, then excused myself and went to the fountain, where I stood with no coins to toss, no pennies to spare, no wishes to make.

I watched the bubbling water drip down the sides of the marble and thought about my life in painful detail. *What had happened to all of my wishes and why didn't any of them come true?*

A coin passed straight over my head and plopped into the fountain. Dayglo, who was standing directly behind me, had tossed the coin. When I saw that it was he, I immediately turned to leave the courtyard. He rushed behind me, grabbing my hand, but I yanked with a fierceness, pulling it back to me.

"Don't you touch me!" I said in a low but vicious tone. "Don't you *ever* touch me again!"

"I made a wish for you in the wishing fountain," he said, with a façade of sincerity. I could not believe this guy. He was actually standing in front of me as though it never happened. Standing there, boldly pretending to be gentle and humble, but I knew the bloody truth. And in knowing the truth, I knew his "kindness" was nothing more than a disguise.

"I made a wish for you," he said again, unaffected by my disgust.

"I made one for you as well," I said.

"You did?" he asked, surprised.

"Yes," I said with hatred in my voice. "I wished that you were dead." And with that I turned and stomped out of the courtyard.

Dayglo and I never exchanged another word.

The next morning, he returned to Argentina, cutting his visit short by almost a week.

Six days after his return to Argentina, Dayglo was killed in a bar brawl. According to witnesses, he lost a bet and welched on the payment. He traded his life for six American dollars, which was probably five dollars more than it was worth.

The "bad men" caught up to Dayglo in an alley outside the bar and pummeled him to death with the jagged edge of a broken beer bottle. They mangled his beautiful face beyond recognition. His own father was unable to identify him at the morgue. Alas, his exterior now matched his interior. The men were never captured, and Mayan was totally devastated. She flew to Argentina, where she buried him in a gold-plated casket.

I didn't feel anything when Dayglo died. There was no regret, sorrow, or sadness. He died as he lived, violently and deceitful, and all that I can truly say is that his death was the first wish I ever made that had ever come true.

Chapter 16

As I descended past the sixteenth floor, I remembered the day the Swan mangled the Rapist.

The Wintergreen Boarding School for Girls changed a lot after Dayglo died. Emotionally, Mayan shut down. She kept the curtains drawn in the house most of the time and stopped joining us for breakfast and dinner. She ceased participating in conversations, stopped giving advice, and closed herself off.

I think she stopped living and settled for mere existence, hiring a couple of part-time teachers who took over most of her curriculum. She also let it be known to all of us that there would be no more boarders, no new students to replace the ones who were leaving, and eventually, when the last student graduated *(and that would be me)*, she would close her doors forever and return to Argentina.

There was a sadness that blanketed the house, and most days I felt as though we existed beneath a cloud, and no matter how blazing hot the summers were or the intensity of the brightness of the sky, Mother Nature could never penetrate the fortress of pain erected by Mayan Santiago.

It was so depressing that at one point I contemplated returning to Milwaukee, but I quickly changed my mind, realizing it might be sad and depressing here, but back at Reva Joe's it was sad, depressing, poor, ignorant, *and* crazy.

The girls changed a lot, too. Their once festive, arrogant, jubilant Spanish chatter quieted to hushed whispers and cautious warnings not to disturb Mayan.

Mayan dormir.

Mayan dormir.

Sleeping.

Sleeping.

No one wanted to disturb Mayan, ever.

If the girls were too loud and woke Mayan from her nap, there would be hell to pay. And at least once or twice a week, there *was* hell to pay.

Mayan exchanged teaching, laughing, loving, and living for napping. She stayed close to her medication, pills for this, pills for that. Uppers, downers, and in-between. No one knew for sure what Mayan took, but knew that for certain she took a *lot* of it, whatever it was.

On average, she slept seventeen hours a day, and when she was not completely catatonic, which was most of the time, we could hear the sobs ricocheting off the walls of her bedroom.

Days turned to weeks, then months, then a year and nothing seemed to change; the only thing I could see that was moving was the date. Mayan's grief never seemed to ease. She was in as much pain on my sixteenth birthday as she was the day Dayglo died. The spirit of Dayglo seemed to haunt the house, haunting us all. None of us could get away from him, or so it seemed. He often crept into my dreams, taunting me with piercing eyes, asking me if I wanted to "come out and play." Telling me that he was "big" and I was "small," demonstrating his dominance over me, again and again. I woke up many nights in a panic, especially on the night of my sixteenth birthday, when, in a cold sweat, I saw the shadow sitting on the edge of my bed. I screamed, jumped up and away, but the shadow didn't speak, just sat.

I was breathing heavily, scared, trying to figure out what it was.

"What happened that night?" she asked.

"Mayan?" I asked, trying to confirm that it was her voice.

"What happened that night with you and my son?" she asked. "On the night of your birthday?"

I was silent.

"I want to know."

"I have nothing to say, Mayan," I said gently.

"You hated him after that night," she said. "I saw it in your eyes every time I looked at you."

I got back into my bed and wrapped myself up in the covers. "I don't want to talk about it," I said quietly.

"Talk!" She screamed so loud that it startled me when I saw the sudden, animated expression on her somber face. "Talk, dammit! Talk!"

"I don't know what to say," was all I could say.

"When you learned of his death," she whispered, returning to an unreliable sense of calm, "I saw light in your eyes. It was relief and joy that I saw."

"No," I said, shaking my head.

"Yes," she insisted.

"No," I countered again.

"What happened between you and my son?"

"Nothing!" I screamed.

"You lie!"

"Nothing!" I screamed again.

"Why won't you tell me?" she said, collapsing onto my bed, crying. "Tell me what hides behind the look in your eyes when you think of him . . ."

"Mayan," I said, pleading.

"Rage and anger?"

"There is nothing," I whispered.

"I read hearts," she said. "And your heart betrays your face."

I looked away, trying to spare her the pain I knew she could *not* take. It was the only humane thing left to do. Telling Mayan the bitter truth would only increase her internal agony, and drive a stake through the center of a heart already bruised and bleeding.

Mayan got up slowly off the bed and eased her way to the

door. She turned and gave me a look I will never forget. It was such an honest, penetrating moment—she looked into my soul and I am certain she saw the truth. The truth of what and who her son was, and if she were to grieve anything at all, it was to be the loss of her own deluded vision of Dayglo.

I did not say a word, but I did keep my composure and what I thought of as my dignity. And I did tell her the truth with my eyes, through the deepness and the stillness that lay behind them. The silence in between every breath I've taken since the brutal loss of my innocence. In that moment I told her *all*.

The most honest exchange between two human beings comes from the moments when they say *nothing* to one another, and yet *everything* is known. And in their silence, they speak their truths so loud, the sound is utterly deafening.

Mayan's eyes filled, as did mine. She blinked once and one tear streamed down the side of her face. "*Lo siento,*" she whispered before exiting.

Lo siento.

Lo siento.

It was a word I had picked up along the way, and one of the very few words in Spanish that I could translate.

Lo siento.

I'm sorry.

Lo siento.

I'm sorry.

Lo siento.

I'm sorry.

She left my room that day, deflated.

We would never speak of Dayglo again.

The next morning Lolita, the strange, beautiful girl, packed her bags and headed back to Argentina. She had completed the Wintergreen Boarding School for Girls and was headed off to a university in Buenos Aires to continue her lifelong dream of becoming a nuclear physicist.

On her way down to the car, she stopped by my room for a brief visit. She knocked on the door and I let her in. There was the typical odd, peculiar beats of silence between us that were always there. She circled my room, appraising. It was always so strange to me, her style. Then she quietly took a seat on the bed, motioning for me to sit beside her.

"Are you ready for college?" I asked.

She nodded.

"Must be exciting," I said. "I hope I get the chance to go to college."

"Why do you *hope*? Why don't you just go?"

"Money," I said flatly, staring down at the floor.

She nodded.

"There are scholarships, you know," she said.

"I don't really know," I said, "but I'll learn."

"Listen, Adrian," she began. "This is not easy for me . . ." Then she stopped and seemed to struggle with the words.

Stumbling.

Mumbling.

"What?" I asked.

"I can still see the rose petals on your bed *and* your floor," she said. Her words brought me back to a horrible place where I didn't want to be. The dying red of dried petals wilted on the floor have long since been swept up and blown away, but still I see them. And I look away, aghast at the memories. "You see them, too, no?" she inquired of me.

"Yes," I whispered.

"The vision haunts you at night, doesn't it?"

I looked at her, but offered no reply. What could I say?

"My first year at the Wintergreen Boarding School for Girls, Dayglo was taken with me," she began reminiscing. "And I with him . . ."

I smiled at her. She was *such* a delicate beauty.

"I was fourteen years old," she said. "And one night, Dayglo placed rose petals on my bed and onto my floor . . . and then in the blink of an eye he changed."

My eyes widened as I listened intently.

"He turned into something that I could not recognize . . . into something that seemed so opposite of him."

"Yes," I said spontaneously. "Yes . . ."

"He became a different person," she continued. "A violent, angry animal, forcing himself on me in a way that frightened me and made me scared to know him."

"I understand," I said slowly.

"He took *something* from me that night that did not belong to him," she said quietly. "It was something I did not give him, but I felt so . . . so . . ."

"Guilty," I said, staring at the floor, but reading her mind.

"'All small things eventually must surrender to the thing that is much greater than themselves . . . it is the way of nature,'" Lolita said, reciting Dayglo's mantra.

My eyes swelled with tears upon hearing it.

"How did you know?" I turned to her and asked.

"I saw it in your eyes that night when you came out of the bathroom. I saw the feeling that I had after he finished with me."

I nodded and we both sat in silence for a while.

"I scrubbed my skin till it bled," she said. "I covered my bruises. I swallowed my dignity . . ."

"Why didn't you tell?"

"The same reason you didn't."

"I don't know why I didn't," I said. "Mayan had warned me so to speak but I just kept walking the line . . . the edge . . . being too close."

"Being close shouldn't hurt," said Lolita.

"No," I said. "But being raped does."

"I want to tell you something," said Lolita, "and I only tell you this because I could not live with myself if I do not."

"What?" I asked, almost afraid of what she was about to say.

"I had convinced myself that Dayglo and I were a special circumstance . . . you see . . . unusual. You know?"

"I don't understand," I said.

"After he raped you, I lived the whole thing over again in my mind," she said. "I saw the roses on the floor, the look in your eyes, the bruises on your skin."

"Yes," I said.

"I am the youngest of seven, the only girl. Some of *mi her-*

manos walk on the other side of the law, you see. They are not so honest in their dealings."

I looked at her with a blank stare.

"In this country, you would call them criminals."

"Oh," I said.

"Understand?" she asked.

"Not really."

"I had him killed, Adrian," she blurted. "*Mi hermanos.* I called them and told them of the events here . . . and when he returned to Argentina . . . they took care of it on my behalf."

"Oh my God," I whispered beneath my breath. "Why didn't they just turn him in to the police?"

"Our system of justice is very different from yours," she said. "We make our own justice. My brothers did not do the deed with their own hands," she assured me. "But they found people who could do it for them and make it look like a brawl at a bar. It was a setup . . . the whole thing was a setup."

I stared at the floor, not knowing what to say. What do you say when someone drops news like this into your lap? And do you feel partially responsible for the violent, premature death of a young man?

"This is pretty heavy," I mumbled.

"Never a word to Mayan," pressed Lolita. "She has suffered enough."

"Do you feel guilty when you see her cry?" I asked Lolita.

"Not any more guilty than she feels when she sees *me* cry," she said, and without warning, she leaned over and kissed me gently on the cheek. "There is a whole world awaiting you, Adrian. Let nothing keep you from your journey. Expect a great adventure."

I smiled as she made her exit. And as she did, I stood at my window and watched this elegant swan of a woman glide into the backseat of a Lincoln Continental. She was as beautiful as a sunny day, as unpredictable as a sudden storm. She could probably be as charming as any woman could be, and certainly more deadly than any female should be.

Rape her and you'll find yourself dead.

Deader than dead.

Dead and unrecognizable, with a face so mangled your father won't be able to identify you in the morgue. So dead your mother will cry over you for a year and pay homage to you as though you were some kind of national hero. She'll carry on as though you died valiantly, defending old people and children.

Rape Lolita and you'll find yourself dead.

Dead and unrecognizable.

And that's a pretty tall order for a swan to fill.

I watched Lolita disappear behind the tinted windows and followed the car with hypnotized eyes till it vanished into thin air.

Rape Lolita and you'll find yourself dead.

Dead and *unrecognizable.*

Chapter 15

As I descended beyond the fifteenth floor, I remembered the day I discovered that I WAS art . . .

Summer ended.

Fall returned.

And I served out my last year with Mayan like a good prisoner, waiting for a reprieve.

Throughout the course of the year, the remaining girls dwindled in number down to nothing. Patricia and Benita returned to Argentina; each of them was accepted into trade schools. Patricia said they would study something like data processing or computer science.

"Nothing major," Benita said. "We don't want to *be* anything major. We prefer the simple life."

Pepper, the sassy one, returned to Argentina two weeks after Benita and Patricia. She went to do the tango for a professional dance theater.

Mayan did not encourage any of the girls to stay on another year. In fact, she eagerly anticipated their departure as she also hoped for mine.

My studies were accelerated so that I would be finished in

January instead of June. By the time I had completed my last course, Mayan already had the house on the market.

It sold two days later.

I knew it was over the day I stepped into the hall and the art display featuring Dayglo had been removed. The walls were empty and bare, just like the home's internal atmosphere.

I stood in the hallway, staring at the walls, making my own assumptions.

"You are ready to leave the nest," said Mayan, watching me from a distance.

"I guess," I responded, sounding uncertain.

"You'll be just fine," she said, approaching me from the side, resting her hand on my shoulder.

"I hope so," I said with little confidence, as I continued to stare at the wall. "Not looking forward to going back to Milwaukee."

"It's only for the summer," she said. "Then you are a free bird, off to art school."

"I'm not going to art school, Mayan," I said, head lowered. "I don't have the money. I'll try to get a job in Milwaukee and save up enough cash to get away from there once and for all. I feel like a hamster on a wheel, going round and round."

"Well," she said with about as much of a smile anyone under the weight of that kind of depression could muster, "your wheel has just come full circle."

She handed me an envelope and I opened it to see something that ignited my faith in God *and* in miracles.

It was a check for $50,000.

My eyes widened to the size of dinner plates.

"You *are* going to art school—in Evanston, Illinois," Mayan said. "It is a lovely place. Your transcripts have already been forwarded to admissions and I have arranged a dorm room for you there . . ."

I was speechless.

Flabbergasted.

"Don't worry," said Mayan, winking, "I have connections. They'll take very good care of you there."

My eyes filled.

"Why?" I asked, breathless. "How . . . ?"

Mayan looked at me, all her pain, heartache, and tears evident in her expression. She looked like a woman who appeared, for all intents and purposes as if she would spend the rest of her life trying to come to terms with Dayglo's life—and death. She looked at me with apology, sincerity, and regret. She looked at me, then she looked through me, past me.

"The money," she said, "is from Dayglo's life insurance policy. I figured he owes you that much, at least . . ." And with that, she exited and went into her bedroom.

She never came out again, not even to say good-bye. The next morning, when the same Lincoln that had taken Lolita, Patricia, Benita, and Pepper off to the airport came for me, I knocked at Mayan's door for a long time and stood and waited.

Waited for her to say something.

Anything.

Or nothing at all.

"Mayan?" I called. "Mayan, I'm leaving."

There were no sounds.

No signs of life.

"Mayan?" I called again.

In that moment the housekeeper approached me and tapped on my shoulder, "Miss Adrian," she said in her beautiful Argentinean accent, "she's sleeping."

"I want to tell her good-bye," I said, almost pleading. "Mayan . . . Mayan . . ."

The gentle housekeeper placed her hand more heavily against my shoulder, "Miss Adrian . . . please."

"I have to say good-bye," I said, tears welling in my eyes.

"I will make sure she gets the message," said the housekeeper.

"Thank you," I said.

"Claro que si," she said, nodding her head.

"Okay," I said, releasing myself enough to walk away. I walked out of the house for the last time and eased into the Lincoln's backseat. The driver promptly got out of the car and loaded my suitcases. As we drove off, I looked at Mayan's bedroom window and saw the curtains open briefly, then gently close. And that was the last time I laid eyes on Mayan.

Beautiful.

And divine.

Tormented, tortured.

But never forgotten by me.

Ever.

Within two hours I was boarding a plane heading back to Milwaukee, Wisconsin.

Back to Reva Joe.

Back to hell.

But it would be a minimal stay. In other words, I knew I could do the time, a short-term departure from humanity and descent into the abyss. August would come soon enough and I would be on my way to Evanston, Illinois. Granted, Evanston was only 81.1 miles from Milwaukee, but 81.1 miles was 81.1 minutes of driving and put a lifetime of distance between me and Reva Joe.

I would study art.

Learn about it.

Delight in it.

At long last, it would be a formal completion of my informal studies, but it wouldn't be easy. I'd have to make that skate through hell first to get to the Promised Land, 81.1 miles away, 81.1 minutes by car, 8 minutes by plane. A lifetime and no less. Eight months of hard time at the Institution for the Mentally and Criminally Insane. The Great Wall of Ignorance, the House of Reva Joe. If I could just keep my mind right and tread water while there, I'd be okay.

I hadn't been to Milwaukee in three years.

Never had a reason to go there.

Never had a reason to be there.

Juno was gone.

Anthem never returned a single letter.

Reva Joe was stark, raving mad. In fact, we had only spoken once or maybe twice in my entire three-year absence. She paid the tuition promptly, though, which only reinforced the sincerity of her efforts to keep me away. And trust me, I was only too happy to stay away. But I had to break down and let her know that I was returning to Milwaukee—well, just "passing through for a couple months" is the way I put it.

"How long you plan on staying?" she asked me over the phone with the same nastiness she always had.

Some things never change.

"Few months," I said.

"You said a couple," she said flatly. "A couple is two, a few is more than a couple."

"Few months," I repeated.

"How long is a few?"

"Four, five, eight," I mumbled.

"Eight months!" she squawked.

"Just till school starts up again in August, Reva Joe," I spat.

"Eight months," she said, sounding out of breath. "A lot can happen in eight months. We'll change presidents by then, seasons will change a couple times over. Country could go to war. Hell, Jesus could come back for an encore in eight months. Eight months is a long time," she huffed on the other end of the line. "You gonna have to get you a job this go 'round," she spat.

I know.

"And pay rent first of the month," she said.

I know.

"And help around the house with the weeds and all," she said.

I know.

"And no niggers . . ." her final word.

"Jesus, Reva Joe," I said out of impulse.

"No niggers. House rules," she insisted.

God, she made my stomach turn, and the simple recollection of our conversation on the plane ride home alone was enough to land me in the airlines bathroom, puking in the little gray sink.

It was January in Milwaukee, and, of course, I arrived in the middle of a freaking blizzard and went from a 71-degree day in paradise to a 13-below-zero descent into hell. It was inverted, the whole thing, my life *and* the weather. Find your way to hell in the middle of January and you will freeze to death.

Guaranteed.

I caught a cab to the other side of town where the slow, stupid people lived. And I continued to feel sick to my stomach staring at the houses, the people, and their lost dreams blowing in the Milwaukee wind, covered in dirty snow and slippery ice.

My God.

What happened?

Poverty.

Rusted cars, condemned houses, and lost hope.

My God.

What happened?

Poverty.

The cab pulled up in front of Reva Joe's house and when I laid eyes on the run-down dwelling, my heart sank. The structure looked like it had taken quite a beating over the years, if that was at all possible.

Dead of winter.

Everything was dead.

The house even looked like it had gotten smaller, or maybe I had just gotten taller.

"Sweet Jesus," I mumbled to myself, looking down at the cabbie's lint-filled floor.

My God.

What happened?

Poverty.

"Twenty-three bucks!" shouted the cabbie, bringing me out of the somber trance I had drifted into.

I gave him a twenty and a five and slowly eased out of the car. As I approached the front door, it felt like the slow walk of death. One foot in front of the other.

As I stood on the doorstep trying to muster the strength to knock, I could smell an array of odors seeping beneath the door and in between the cracks. It smelled like sickness.

Smelled like death.

My God.

What happened?
Poverty.

"Oh, boy," I said to myself as I knocked.

There was no answer so I knocked again. Still no answer, and I knocked once more. After about three minutes, I was beginning to worry that she wasn't home, or worse, that she had changed her mind about me staying there.

I was beginning to feel the extreme chill that 13 below zero brings, as the wind ripped through me. If crazy Reva Joe decided not to open this door, where would I go? What would I do? Would I freeze to death on her doorstep waiting for her? Could I actually stay here? As the many possibilities ran wild through my head, there was a click behind the door as it unlocked.

I never thought I'd be so happy for the old wench to let me in. That's just how desperate I was in that moment. When Reva Joe opened the door, I was taken aback.

She was using a walker, barely able to maneuver. She moved excruciatingly slowly and looked as ragged and run-down as the house did.

She looked like decay.

"Well!" she snapped. "Don't just stand there letting out my heat!"

Upon entry into the house, the heat was such a drastic change from the outside temperature that it felt like suffocation.

Goodness gracious, I thought. It had to be about 100 degrees in that house. The air was stifling.

My God.
What happened?
Poverty.

The wood paneling was falling off and the old carpets were stained with food and filth. The place smelled of urine and Ben-Gay.

Dear God.

Dishes were piled in the sink, crumbs and other unidentifiable items sprawled on the floor. The moment I stepped inside the living room, my skin started to crawl.

"Are you okay?" I asked Reva Joe as she wobbled back toward the dining room table, where it looked like she had six months of newspapers stacked in the center.

"Does it look like I'm okay?" she snapped.

"Not really," I said in a low voice. "What happened?"

She backed into the seat, balancing herself with the walker, the table, and the chair. It was a great juggling act—I couldn't help but wonder if she was going to make it into the chair or fall on the floor.

"Took a tumble off the front porch a couple of years ago. Broke a hip," she said.

"I'm sorry," I mumbled.

"Had a stroke six months ago," she added. "Not a big one, but big enough to land me on this damn thing," she said, hitting the walker.

"Wow," I said, looking around the house. "Why haven't you gotten someone to help you?"

"Do I look like one of those rich bitches to you?" she huffed. "How am I going to pay for it?"

"I'm sorry," I mumbled again, looking away.

"Ain't much," she said. "But I do the best I can . . . best I can."

"I know," I said reassuringly.

"You look *real* nice," she said, pausing a beat to look at me.

"Wow, thanks," I said, shocked to hear a compliment from her.

"You kinda grew up out there in Arizona," she said. "Sprouted up like one of those cactuses."

"Yeah," I said. "Kinda did . . ."

"How tall are you now?"

"Five-nine."

"Jiminy Crickets!" she squealed. "You're a cross between a cactus and a giraffe!" Actually, for the first time *ever*, I think Reva Joe said something I thought was funny. And so I laughed, hard and heartily.

And so did she.

It seemed like there was a moment where we were able to

meet in the middle, and I dropped my stuff against her and she let go of her stuff against me. And just for the heck of it, we were able to be "cool."

"Glad you're back, kid," she said, reaching for my hand across the table. "I've been needing somebody to pull them damn weeds."

"Thanks," I replied sarcastically. Her hand remained extended and I looked at it, uncertain what to do. She *was* extending herself to me, so perhaps I should take it, or shake it, or something.

I slowly brought my hand to the table and allowed it to rest inside of hers.

Wow, I thought. Life and people never cease to amaze me. Compassion stretches a long, long way. Sometimes it takes years to get to where it's supposed to be.

Over the course of the next couple days, I readjusted to Milwaukee. I had gotten my driver's permit, and that was good enough for Reva Joe to let me take her old, raggedy station wagon to the grocery store and run simple errands for her.

Since the rape, I had not allowed my mind to drift to the topic of boys, but I had recently begun to think about Anthem a lot.

I had always wondered what had happened to him and why he just dropped off the face of the Earth. I sent him letters every week the first six months of my stay in Tucson, but after none of them was answered, I gave up, surrendering to the fact that he was disinterested or had moved on. Or maybe he was just angry with me for leaving so abruptly. Or maybe he was unable to forgive Reva Joe's public humiliation of him that day at the lake when she caught us showing affection for one another. A thousand scenarios played out in my head and none of them brought me any closer to an answer.

On the way back from a local errand for Reva Joe, I found my way to the address I had sent so many of my letters to.

I pulled up in front of a simple house on a simple street in a simple little neighborhood. Actually, most of Milwaukee could be described that way: simple, simple, simple.

The house that he lived in looked as dead as the rest of the street. It looked like the people who lived inside had worked the same jobs for thirty years. They drove the same way home day after day. They ate the same thing for dinner. They listened to the same songs over and over again on the radio. They did the same dances and wore the same five outfits in rotation.

Nothing was extraordinary.

Everything was ordinary.

Below average.

Boring.

Poor.

Dull.

Depressing.

I glanced up at the sky, and even it appeared to open and close the same way. Day and night came about the same way every day. It was all one huge, tremendously overexaggerated production of boring.

I sat out in front of the house for a long time before getting out of the car. I sat and stared at the street, the houses, the dead trees and barren yards.

I sat and waited for courage to come and help me make the journey from the front seat to the front door. Eventually, I opened the car door and got out.

The cold air hit with such intensity that it brought me back to sobriety.

I did a slow, lazy walk to the front door and knocked. I knocked so lightly, perhaps I was hoping that no one would answer. But eventually the door opened and on the other side stood a scrawny, haggard-looking woman, ghastly white, with long, stringy blond hair, smoking a cigarette. She seemed rather unconcerned about life, though her physical appearance dictated she had been beaten to death by it.

"Yeah?" she asked in a deep, raspy voice.

"Does . . . does Anthem live here?" I asked, stumbling over my words.

"No," she spat.

"Oh, okay," I said, turning to walk away, assuming I had the wrong house. "Sorry to bother you."

"What are you doing looking for that loser, anyway?" she asked, stopping me dead in my tracks.

I turned back around to face her.

"Do you know him?"

"I ought to," she snapped. "Gave birth to him."

I anxiously returned to the top of the steps.

"What do you want?" she asked, staring at me suspiciously.

"I'm an old friend."

"Bullshit," she spat.

"Excuse me?" I asked.

"I said bullshit," she said.

"I don't understand."

"He doesn't have any friends," she said.

"We were friends back when I lived here a few years ago. He was really nice to me. I moved here to live with my grandmother after my parents died."

"Sounds like a sob story if I ever heard one," she said rudely.

"Not really," I said, angered by her callousness. "If you can just tell me where I can find him."

She started to laugh wildly, throwing her scraggly, damaged hair backwards.

"I don't know . . . you tell me," she said, staring at me with impenetrable eyes.

"I haven't seen or heard from Anthem in three years," I said.

"Then that ought to tell you something, girl," she said, taking another hit off the cigarette, examining me top to bottom. "What's a skinny, pretty white thing like you doing looking for my tall, fine black son? Don't you want nothing out of life?"

I didn't answer, just looked at her with increasing discomfort.

"In the wrong neighborhood, wouldn't you say?" she asked, smiling. But it wasn't a sincere smile. It was a wicked smile, one that hid bad intentions.

"I don't understand what you're saying," I said.

"Oh, come now, doll face," she scoffed. "You're not so naïve, are you? You look sophisticated enough to get it . . ."

"I don't understand . . ."

"C'mon, kid . . . PULL your head out of your ass! Look around you . . . look at this shit hole! You're dead in the center of it, floating around like a lost turd."

I was horrified.

"Listen to me, doll, and listen up *real* good. I don't know what your deal is with my son. I can't imagine why in God's name you've decided to track him down after all these years, but I will tell you this . . . you're in the middle of a sinking shit hole, but you got one thing going for you . . . you got one real, real good thing going for you."

"What?" I asked curiously.

"Your pretty white skin," she said. "It's like porcelain."

She started to laugh on the edge of her last words and I began to feel even more uncomfortable, if that was possible.

"I used to be pretty like you," she said, obsessive with her cigarette, puff, puff, puffing. "My good looks should have carried me outta this dump of a life . . . fucking should have. I was damn fine. Prettiest girl in the neighborhood . . . then I fell in love with a no-good-for-nothing, minimum-wage-earning store clerk."

She swung her door open wide. "C'mon in here," she said. "Heat's getting out . . ."

"No . . . really," I said, hesitating. "I should be going."

"This story is gonna save your lily-white ass," she said with a serious tone. "So I suggest you get in here and listen to the rest of it."

Reluctantly, I stepped inside her warm living room. It was a very average, run-of-the-mill, no-frills kind of room. Looked like the rest of Milwaukee, boring and uninspired. She had clutter everywhere, knickknacks, oddly colored furniture. Everything in the room looked old and dusty. It was all covered with a layer of smoke, ash, and soot.

Gross.

The house stunk to high heaven, reflecting years and years of cigarette smoke. At the far end of the wall there were two pictures. One was her daughter, a fair Caucasian girl with a pretty smile and straight hair, and Anthem, a gorgeous mixture of white and black.

"Sit down," she said, suggesting I sit on the filthy, torn couch in the corner.

Oh God, I thought to myself.

Horrific.

I sat.

Barely.

Butt cheeks hanging off the end.

The dust moved and blew around me, disturbed by my presence. It appeared as though she had not had company in quite some time.

"Smoke?" she asked, offering me a cigarette.

"No, thank you," I said, trying to be polite.

"Sure?"

"Yes."

"Good," she confirmed. "Don't ever take up these fucking things. Quickest way to frown lines, crow's feet, and an early grave, but not necessarily in that order."

"I'll keep that in mind," was my response.

"So," she said, sucking smoke down into her lungs. "I got a couple things I wanna teach you, mainly cause I'm feeling generous today."

There was a sudden loud squawk in the background that scared the living daylights out of me. I jumped about two feet off the couch, disturbing the dirt, smoke, and debris.

"Shut the fuck up, Winston!" screamed Anthem's mom. "Don't mind him . . . he's just a grumpy parrot going through nicotine withdrawal."

"The parrot smokes?" I asked, eyes wide, jaw dropped low.

"Not really," she confirmed. "I used to blow the smoke in his beak and I think he got off on it . . . but I stopped doing it 'cause he started getting smoker's beak."

I literally did not know what to say as I sat in the middle of her old, dusty living room, jaw lingering close to the floor.

She began laughing so hard she started to cough. She

seemed about eight days away from contracting lung cancer. At the end of her choking, she was spitting up phlegm and other unrecognizable body fluids.

Major gross.

"So," she said, finally catching her breath. "I'm feeling fucking generous, which means I'm gonna teach you a few things. That cool with you?" she asked, putting out one cigarette in exchange for lighting another.

My God.

This woman was a walking tar pit.

"Use what you got," she said, giving me a solid, strong look in the eye. "Don't be a goddamned fool . . . use what you got. Now, what you need to do is take inventory."

"Take inventory?" I asked naively, though I was intrigued. "What does that mean?"

"Your goods . . ." she said, exiting the couch, going to grab a sheet of paper, then bringing it back to me. "What are your fucking goods? Write that shit down!"

"Well, I don't know."

"What do you mean, you don't know?" she screamed, slapping my knee as hard as she could, which actually scared the daylights out of me again.

"Your goods. Assets. What are you working with? That's your inventory! That's what you ride on! You gotta have something to ride on! Are you a scientist?"

"No," I said.

"Are you a genius, bookworm, brainiac . . . like an Einstein?"

"I'm kinda smart."

"Fuck that. How smart?"

"Kinda . . ."

"*Kinda* doesn't count. We can't put that down," she said, obsessed with the list.

"Are you career-oriented? Goal-oriented?"

"I never really thought . . ."

"Forget about it," she said. "Can't put that one down."

"Do you come from money?"

"Well," I said, "Reva Joe's probably got a life insurance policy."

"Forget about it," she hollered. "You can't list an insurance policy as an asset."

"Why not?"

"Are you rich?" she snapped, cutting me off. "Is your family made of money? Do green dollar bills grow on trees in your backyard? And I'm serious about that shit . . . unless you can pluck Benjamin Franklin off your fucking sycamore tree, we can't put it on the list."

"No money," I said, looking down.

Anthem's mother shook her head, sighed aloud, then sat down on the couch. She grabbed the paper out of my hand and ripped it in two, and threw the pen in the trash.

"Just like I thought . . ." she said, shaking her head.

"What?" I asked concerned.

"You ain't got no money," she said, shaking her head. "You ain't got smarts. You ain't really got much family. You ain't got but one thing."

"What?"

"You got looks. You not only got looks but you got THE LOOK. Okay???" she insisted, rising off the couch with a second wind and soaring enthusiasm. "You're a tall, skinny, long-legged, blond-haired, blue-eyed, pale-skinned, purebred Aryan. You are the heartbeat of American culture. You're everything from California dreaming to upstate New York royalty. You coulda been a Kennedy . . . and maybe, if you're lucky, you can change your last name. You are the "it" girl. You are the cover of every high-fashion magazine in the world. You are the envy of every nation, you dumb motherfucker. You are the centerfold that every red-blooded American male masturbates to while taking his morning shower. *That* is your inventory list!"

I was speechless.

I was all of that?

For real?

I didn't know how to take it or how to respond. I don't know if I should have been grateful because maybe, just maybe, she had given me the greatest compliment a girl could ever get. Or that I had ever gotten. Or maybe, just maybe, she was calling me stupid and telling me the only thing I had going for me was a pretty face and a set of long legs, neither of which seemed to matter at that moment.

"What you got to say for yourself, girl?" she asked, hovering over me like a devastated coach who had lost her dynasty, heritage, and legacy—all in the flip of a bad coin or bad bet.

"I like art," I whispered.

"You dumb motherfucker!" she screamed at the top of her lungs. "You *are* art!"

I shrieked and backed away from her.

She was damn crazy.

It was no small wander Anthem didn't live here anymore.

"You ARE a retard!" screamed Anthem's mother. "You *are* art! USE what you got! Girl with your looks should never spend a day standing over a sink washing a dish. A girl with your kind of looks should never speak the words, 'May I take your order!' Girl with your looks should be pushing one of them nice SUVs around town, a Mercedes or something. A girl with your looks should never want for nothing. Girl with your kind of looks lives in a gated castle on top of a hill overlooking the poor, ugly fucks who didn't have what it took to get a prince!"

I looked down.

"I . . . I . . ." she said, poking herself in the chest with a finger. "*I* was one of those kind of girls," she said. "And then I fell in love with a poor bastard from the neighborhood. Pretty black man who loved the feel of porcelain white skin against his fine black ass."

She stopped speaking and looked at her reflection in a dirty mirror on the wall.

"Yeah," she said, continuing, rubbing what could have once upon a time been a beautiful face with her hands, stroking and caressing. "Fell in love and cheated myself out of the good life. He never made more than minimum wage . . . spent most of his life a no, sir/yes, sir man till he said, *fuck it*, and left home one morning, and never looked back. Left me with a two-year-old and a string of bad gigs asking the general public, *May I take your order?*" She starts to laugh, "Then I married me a stupid-ass white man, had another baby a year later, and he was a drunk so we didn't get that far . . . backed over him one day with my station wagon . . . and he was kinda pissed so he moved out after that . . . yeah . . . we didn't get that far."

"I'm sorry," I said, mumbling the words.

"Kid, you ain't brilliant. You ain't rich. You ain't talented, far as I can see . . ."

Tears began to form in my eyes.

"I got art," I said in my defense.

"You *are* art, stupid," were her final words. "You are art."

Use what you got.

Chapter 14

As I descended beyond the fourteenth floor, I remembered the day I decided to "use what I got."

I left that day with her words heavy on my heart. I never did get Anthem's address or whereabouts. By the time I bolted from his mother's house, I was so undone I didn't even want his information anymore.

I got in Reva's old car and drove away down the dirty, filthy street. And as I looked around the neighborhood, I began to feel suffocated. I could feel the dirt and air cling to my skin, grounding me, condemning me to Milwaukee. And even though I had a fabulous scholarship to an art school, I began to doubt my ability to believe in myself anymore. How far would art take me? I had been so halfhearted about it. I could put together a sketch or two, but I was no great shakes. And if I was no great shakes, I would probably end up back in Milwaukee when school was over.

Washing dishes.

Mopping floors.

Welcome to Sloppy Jack's.

May I take your order?

The thought of that kind of future was staggering. It was as close to death as I could imagine. My skin began to crawl and itch. I started scratching like I had cooties, scabies, or something.

I scratched.

And itched.

The words from Anthem's mother began to play and replay in my mind, against my better judgment, possessing me.

You're a tall, skinny, long-legged, blond-haired, blue-eyed, pale-skinned, purebred Aryan girl. You are the heartbeat of American culture. You're everything from California dreaming to upstate New York royalty. You coulda been a Kennedy, and maybe, if you're lucky, you can change your last name. You are the "it" girl. You are the cover of every high-fashion magazine in the world. You are the envy of every nation.

Use what you got.

Use what you got.

As I continued down the street, I paid special attention to the old cars and the people who drove them.

Dead of winter.

Pale, white skin.

Blue-collar heaven or hell.

Ordinary living.

Ordinary life.

It all seemed so bland, black and white, void of color. All I could hear was this crazy, dried-up woman's words echoing around in my head.

Use what you got.

Use what you got.

By the time I made it back to Reva Joe's house, I was so disconnected I had forgotten the real reason I had left—to get Reva Joe some epsom salts so she could soak in the tub.

When I opened the front door and stepped into the living room, I remembered.

"Oh, damn," I said, slapping myself in the forehead.

The house was quiet, more than usual. Reva Joe usually had something on, television, radio, something. But it was so quiet, the silence was deafening. It was so sticky and hot in her house, miserable.

"Reva Joe!" I called out. "I gotta go back to the store . . . forgot your epsom salts."

No reply.

"Reva Joe!" I called again, and still there was silence.

Unusual.

I eased my way to Reva Joe's bedroom, skirting past the bathroom off to the side where she lay on the floor.

"Help . . ." I heard her whisper. "Help."

I quickly ran into the bathroom and there she lay, sprawled on the floor, just to the left of the commode. It appeared that she tried to sit on the toilet, missing the seat altogether. I was hit with a stench that almost knocked me out. It smelled like poop.

"Reva Joe!" I screamed, running to her side. "Are you all right?"

"You got shit for brains!" she yelled. "Do I look okay to you?"

I stooped down to lift her up and as I did, the stench was so violent it knocked me backwards. When I toppled toward the door, I saw that Reva Joe had what appeared to be some form of diarrhea and had pooped all over herself. Squishy and brown, it lined her bottom and the back of her legs.

Oh God.

Oh dear God up in heaven, I thought.

And who in God's name is going to clean this up?

"What took you so goddamned long?" she screamed. "Get me up off this floor!"

Okay.

Well, here is where we have a parting of the ways.

I was about 117 pounds soaking wet and Reva Joe was about 197 pounds bone dry. How could I possibly lift her up off the floor without a forklift?

"Don't just stand there, shit for brains . . . get me up off this floor!"

Okay.

I bent down, slowly, trying to hold my breath because the

odor was so atrocious. Tried to work my way around her dimpled flesh.

She grabbed hold of my neck and pulled me as I tried to lift her off the floor.

"Sit me on the commode!" she screamed. "Sit me on the commode!"

Oh, sweet Jesus!
Dear Lord!
Father up in Heaven!
This is going to be the end of me!

She pulled so hard the vertebrae in my neck began to protest and for a moment, I literally thought I would snap in half. Slowly, she rose off the ground like a freaking mountain being supported by a long, skinny crane.

Oh, sweet Jesus!
Dear Lord!
Father up in Heaven!
This is going to be the end of me!

When I had just about gotten her to the pot, she tilted backwards and took a tumble, pulling me down into a pool of liquid chocolate syrup.

She screamed.

I cried, and then she screamed some more.

I think she called me a list of readily accessible insults and names. I tuned Reva Joe completely out, to the point that all I was aware of was the god-awful smell of her loose bowels.

Diarrhea.

I had fallen into a pool of poop, and upon that lovely note I began to cough, gurgle, and regurgitate my breakfast.

She was screaming.

I was crying.

Screaming.

Crying.

Eventually, I got up and was able to get the two tons up off the floor and onto the pot where she finished pooping.

I gave her a washcloth and she cleaned her butt somewhat,

but she did a "poopy" job of it (no pun intended), because I could smell her behind the rest of the day. And after the storm passed, it was my glorious afternoon duty to scrub the bathroom floor and wipe down the commode with bleach. By this time, it had hardened and I had to scrub extra hard to get it off. The combination of bleach fumes and poop fumes sent me into a frenzy, and I started to cry. It was too much to take, the stench and the humiliation of being screamed at and blamed. It wasn't my fault she missed the target. I wasn't the one to blame for her fall. I couldn't be responsible for her diarrhea.

It was on rewind, her rudeness.

You got shit for brains!

Shit for brains!

Those words rode the wings of these words:

Girl with your looks you should never spend a day standing over a sink washing a dish. A girl with your kind of looks should never speak the words, "May I take your order!" Girl with your looks should be pushing one of them nice SUVs around town, a Mercedes or something. Girl with your looks should never want for nothing.

"Girl like me," I whispered to myself, "should never be on her knees scrubbing shit off linoleum."

I stood up.

Walked out of Reva Joe's bathroom.

Went into the makeshift, filthy excuse for a room and packed my bags.

"Girl like me shouldn't be in a place like this," I said.

"Shit for brains!" I could hear Reva Joe screaming from her bedroom.

Shit for brains!

Shit for brains!

I collected the entire sum I had saved during my three-year stay in Tucson, all $197, and hit the road. In that moment, I walked out, and never even said good-bye.

I never said a word. Instead, I ran out of her house like it was on fire, running down the street, running for my life.

I caught the next bus smoking out of Milwaukee, Wisconsin,

and headed straight for Evanston, Illinois, which was exactly
81.1 miles from Milwaukee, and that was the first day of the rest
of my life.

I got a hotel room, pay by the week.

A dive, for $79.

One week's worth of lodging.

One single lifetime's worth.

I would work it out somehow.

Managed to get a job in the dive as a clerk, but just through
the remainder of winter and into the summer. At the end of
summer, I left the hotel and went to school full-time at the art
school and lived on my scholarship.

The day I arrived at the school, my life changed forever. In
that one courageous, hopeful moment, I finally felt good enough
about myself to call myself *SOMEBODY*. Not just anybody, but
a tall, skinny, long-legged, blond-haired, blue-eyed, pale-skinned,
purebred Aryan girl. The heartbeat of American culture. Everything from California dreaming to upstate New York royalty. I
could be a Kennedy, and maybe, if I'm lucky, I'll change my last
name. I am the "it" girl, on the cover of every high-fashion
magazine in the world. Envy of every nation . . . and now . . .
now . . . now . . . I'm gonna use what I got.

Forever.

Use what I got.

Chapter 13

As I descended past the thirteenth floor, I remembered the night I learned the art of counterfeiting . . .

I lived in a tiny dorm room with a roommate. Her name was Damian, odd name for a girl. A Seattle native, she was as beautiful as her name was unusual. With pale white skin, long coal-black hair and deep blue eyes, she never wanted for attention. Everyone noticed her. They also noticed me, and when we ventured out together, it was a show-stopping event.

The day I met her I wondered if she, too, would use what she had. From the sway of her hips and the toilet paper she stuffed inside her bra, it certainly appeared that she was trying to get the most mileage out of what the outside delivered.

Now, the interior—that was a different story. In truth, Damian was an unfocused airhead. She grew up a spoiled princess, daughter of a multimillionaire. She was slightly interested in sculpture, which is how she found her way here, but she was more interested in blazing a trail in the opposite direction of parental authority.

She was rather stupid, but lots of fun, so we ended up becoming great friends.

Our friendship was dualistic in nature. It was good *and* bad.

Good because I had never really had any female friends to bond with, but bad because Damian was so flighty and unfocused in her studies and her life. Nothing mattered to her, probably because her daddy would always be available to bail her out. But me, on the other hand, this really was life or death. This could have been my last chance to get an education and make something of myself.

I couldn't piss it away.

There were no millionaires waiting to rescue me.

I had no backup plan.

No mother.

Father.

Nothing.

My focus right now was general education with an emphasis on portraiture. I had no idea where that would lead, but it was a hell of a lot better than a job as a desk clerk in a run-down motel.

"Let's go out," whined Damian one night, while she lay on her bed, bored to tears.

"I can't," I said, face buried in a book.

"You'll be eighteen tomorrow . . . let's go celebrate your birthday."

"We can celebrate tomorrow . . . I have a test in the morning."

"No tests," she insisted. "Party."

"Damian," I said, "we've been out every night this week. I really need to get into these books."

"What you need to get into . . ." she said, closing my book and sitting on my bed, "is a boy."

"No . . . I don't," I said, snatching my book out of her hand.

"Yes . . . you do," she said, closing the book again. "What's up with you and boys?"

"What do you mean?"

"Are you gay?"

"No!" I quickly replied.

"Be honest," she pleaded.

"I am being honest," I said angrily. "I'm not gay!"

"Well, you never pay attention to boys," she said. "And they *always* pay attention to you. It's not normal."

"That's because I have my mind on other things."

"Doesn't your mind ever wander?" she asked, playfully tickling me.

"Stop tickling me," I said, laughing.

"Doesn't it?"

"No!" I shouted, laughing.

"You never think about being with a boy?" she repeated, her face becoming serious. "Really?"

"Yeah . . ." I said, almost irritated. "Really . . . why are you so surprised?"

"It's not normal," she said.

"Okay," I said, snatching my book from her hand and turning away, "you're being so weird right now."

"Oh, my God . . . it's worse than I thought," she said dramatically.

"What?" I snapped.

"You need therapy!"

"You need Jesus!" I insisted.

"So you're a religious freak, or something?"

"No, Damian," I said. "Stop it!"

"Why don't you ever pay attention to boys, Adrian? Your hormones are screaming for attention, but you never give boys the time of day . . . never talk to them . . . never give your number out . . . you never even try."

"I don't have to," I said. "You try hard enough for both of us."

"And what is *that* supposed to mean?" she asked, pissed off.

"Look," I said, "it doesn't mean anything . . . it's just not my style, okay?"

"Well," she said, lightening up, "get some style and throw on your jeans . . . we're going out tonight."

"You're brutal," I screamed.

"I'm right," she said, jumping off the bed and disappearing into the bathroom to shower. She opened the door one more time to scream, "And I'm in style."

Outside of one hour, we were cruising up and down Chicago's world-famous Rush Street in Damian's BMW, looking for bars and guys.

I wasn't really looking. I was riding, and thinking about my art history exam that I was about to fail tomorrow. It was a Monday night and Rush Street wasn't as crazy as it could get. Actually, it was pretty mellow.

"What are you thinking about?" Damian asked me, shouting over the top of the blaring music.

"What do you mean?"

"You're a million miles away," she said. "What are you thinking about?"

"Art history."

"Lose it," she said.

"Lose what?" I asked, growing more and more aggravated.

"Lose the whole worried schoolgirl act. It's so unattractive," she said, cracking out a cigarette from her purse.

"When did you start smoking?"

"What do you mean, when did I start smoking?"

"You weren't smoking last week when we went out."

"I know," she said, lighting the cigarette, taking a puff, coughing. "I started smoking yesterday. Take a hit."

"No, thanks."

"No, really," she said. "It's cool. Take a hit."

"No, really," I said forcefully. "I don't want one."

"Why not?"

"Quickest way to frown lines, crow's feet, and an early grave, but not necessarily in that order," I said with a grin.

"Yeah, right," she said. "Except you forget something."

"What?"

"You gotta LIVE before you die, girl . . . LIVE before you die."

Damian pulled up in front of the valet at a plush-looking lounge. "Let's do this one."

"Okay," I said reluctantly, uninspired.

"Gee," she said, grabbing her purse, "TRY to pretend tonight that you're not a corpse, okay? Jesus."

Her comment hurt my feelings, but I sucked it up and got out of the car, threw on a smile, and walked inside. It was a beautiful lounge, and the music was easy. It was exactly the kind of place that Damian would stay for five minutes before insisting on leaving to soothe a sudden onset of boredom. We walked up to the bar and ordered a couple of Long Island Iced Teas, courtesy of our on-campus fake I.D.s that Damian, the party girl, hooked us up with.

"This place is dead," said Hyper Girl. "I'm looking for some action tonight."

"It's nice," I said. "Mellow."

"Whatever," said Damian. "If I want mellow, I'll go to a funeral home."

"Okay," I said, "but drop me off at home first so I can study for my art history exam tomorrow."

"Look, I don't know about you, virgin girl, but I'm looking to get laid real soon, so work with me," she said, rolling her eyes. "I'm going to the powder room . . . maybe I'll get off on the pretty wallpaper hanging in the stall."

When she walked away, I was relieved. Lately, Damian was just way too much to deal with. It was painfully obvious that we were on opposite ends of the spectrum, traveling in two different directions. Dealing with Damian was becoming my own personal nightmare.

"It's beautiful in here, isn't it?" said a strong voice behind me.

"Yes, it is," I said, turning around, and when I did, I saw a *boy*! He was a beautiful All American Boy.

Broad shoulders.

Chiseled features.

All American Jock.

Tall.

Blond hair.

Blue eyes.

He was the heartbeat of American culture. He was everything from California dreaming to upstate New York royalty. He coulda been a Kennedy, and if I was lucky, maybe I could change my last name to his, whatever it was. He was the "it" boy, on the cover of every high-fashion magazine in the world. He was the envy of every nation.

"Hi," he said, flashing that pretty, All American smile, extending a hand. "I'm Michael Keifer Cage."

"Hi," I said, taken back a bit.

"You have a name?"

"Yeah," I said, almost mesmerized.

"That you're willing to share?" he asked, penetrating me with his baby-blue eyes.

"Sorry," I said, tapping myself against the forehead. "It's Adrian . . . Adrian Moses."

"You're beautiful," he said, towering over me like a giant.

"Thank you," I said, looking down and away.

"Live around here?"

"Evanston," I said. "And you?"

"I'm in a loft downtown," he said, squeezing next to me at the bar. Actually, there was no reason to squeeze. The bar was virtually empty, so I took it that he just wanted to be close.

"What do you do, Adrian Moses?" he asked seductively.

"Student," I said, feeling like I was running out of breath.

"What do you study?"

"Art."

"So you're an artist?" he asked, impressed.

"Not quite yet . . ." I said. "Working on it. And you?"

"Criminal attorney," he said.

"Wow . . ." I said, sounding like an overly impressed geek.

Beautiful.

Employed.

And NOT a loser.

This was three sevens on a Vegas slot machine if I ever saw it. Not that I ever did.

"It's not as impressive as it sounds," he said lightly. "A lot of long hours. A lot of lonely nights."

"I can't imagine," I said.

"You can't imagine lonely nights?" he asked, smiling.

"Can't imagine long hours."

"I am so over this place!" squealed Damian, the ultimate mood-slayer, as she returned to the bar from her potty break. "This place is a dud," she said, before dropping the words mid-sentence upon seeing Michael Keifer. "Hello," she said. "It just got a whole lot better. And what's your name?"

"Michael," he said, trying to be polite, extending a hand. After their handshake, it suddenly got very quiet and Damian got the hint that we were in the middle of a *personal* conversation. "Oh," she said. "So I'll let you two lovebugs chat . . ." she said sarcastically. "Listen, Adrian, not to rush you or anything, but I'm gonna be in the corner waiting to roll outta here. So if you can make it snappy, sister, I'd appreciate it." And with that she spun off to the other edge of the room. It could have been the other edge of the world, as far as I was concerned.

"Wow," he said, taking a sip of the beer he was working on. "She's a piece of work."

"Yeah," I said. "Brutal."

"Can I see you again, Adrian Moses?"

"Yes," I said, looking down. He rubbed his hand gently against my face and for a second it frightened me, so I pulled away. I wasn't used to anyone touching me, and the last time a boy got close it was a catastrophe. I ended up raped and he ended up dead, not a good combination.

"I'm sorry," he said, pulling away, taking note of my apprehension.

"No," I said. "I just . . ."

"Time's a-ticking, sister!" screamed Damian in the background, tapping on the face of her watch.

"Dinner, tomorrow night?" he asked.

"Yes."

"Write your number on my hand," he said, handing me a pen.

"Serious?" I asked, laughing as I wrote my number up his arm. "Now, don't wash it off before you write it down."

"Good night, pretty girl," he said with a beautiful smile.

"Good night."

As we drove off, Damian attempted conversation but I found myself lingering somewhere between being over her and caught up by him.

"This night was such a waste," she pouted. "Sucked wind."

I didn't respond.

"Let's hit the other end of Rush Street," she insisted.

"No, Damian," I said strongly. "I need to go home and study."

"You're such a dud," she pouted.

"And you're rude."

She gasped.

"News flash," I said. "You are *not* the center of the universe, Damian!"

For the most part, *that* comment ended our series of late-night rendezvous around the city. Damian ventured out on her own, or from time to time she hung out with her other dizzy girlfriends. We remained the best of roommates but less than the best of friends. And honest to God, it was better that way. None of it was of grand concern to me because I had begun to learn a whole new language.

It was the language of a magical courtship between an eighteen-year-old art student and a twenty-eight-year-old criminal attorney, Michael Keifer Cage.

We soon became the All American couple, that striking beautiful duo, seemingly incomplete without the other. Everyone noticed us, and even more, they wanted to *be* us. I took it in stride most of the time, and allowed myself to be enchanted by it all. For the first time in my life, I didn't seem like a low-class girl from Saxon. I wasn't the daughter of a sexually confused, eccentric theater actor who had killed himself. And I certainly wasn't the dirt-poor grandchild of an old bigoted, bitter woman. For the first time in my life, I felt a little *normal*. Dare I say I even felt like royalty?

There was little in the way of intimacy between Michael Keifer and me. He was very charming and elegant, and always played the part of the prince very well. He kept us busy with a flurry of activities at a private club, of which he was a member.

I think that somewhere along the way, we both got caught up playing the part. I had finally learned to master the art of "using what you got."

I lived in the public eye, hiding behind the prestige of my white skin, sky-blue eyes, and my "serious" studies at an outstanding art institute.

Michael Keifer lived the prestige of being third-generation stock, born and raised in Hoffman Estates, Illinois, where his grandfather and father had built an empire, anchoring it in one of the country's most prestigious law firms. Yes, the beautiful Michael Keifer came along just in the nick of time to stand on their shoulders. He was a golden boy, savvy and charming, brilliant and breathtaking in every way.

The man came from good stock, definitely good breeding. The way I saw it, it was a win–win situation, and with each passing day I felt more like a movie star and less like the common woman I was deathly terrified of being. No one knew that I was barely skating by on scholarship money that was due to run out at any moment, and when it did, I could very well be that girl behind the counter wearing an apron and saying, "Welcome to the end of the world—may I take your order?" But until that day came, I would play this part to the hilt, borrowing much of Damian's designer-label clothing to make my many entrances and exits.

The more events I attended, the bigger I smiled. The bigger the smile, the greater the compliments. The greater the compliments, the more pleased Michael Keifer was, and the more satisfied he was to have me as the "it" girl by his side.

We were America's sweetheart couple, but beneath it all, it didn't feel like a *real* relationship, it felt more like an alliance. I made him look good, and in return, he wined and dined me, chauffeured me around the city in luxury. He exposed me to everything wonderful. This was a world away from Saxon, and at least two worlds away from Milwaukee.

On one such occasion, at another elegant dinner party for overpriced attorneys, Michael Keifer escorted me to the garden patio, where we slow-danced alone.

"Your beauty is staggering in that dress," he said, rubbing his hand along the width of my back.

"Why, thank you, sir," I responded with giddy laughter. He kissed me gently, and I kissed him back. Within minutes, he had pulled me aside to a corner and was vigorously rubbing my backside in Damian's long, tight dress. He was fondling me in the dress and moving his tongue around wildly inside my mouth. I could feel the perspiration forming on the top of his forehead.

"What do you say?" he whispered into my ear. "Spend the night with me tonight?"

Michael Keifer and I had been dating for three months and I had always managed to skate around it. We were always so busy entertaining the masses, and I always had my fallback excuse of studies or "creating great art."

It was legit.

Respected.

And *never* questioned.

But the native was getting restless, as it had been a long three months and counting. The bulge inside his pants was growing stronger, harder, commanding more and more of his attention. In the past week, he had started to press.

Pressure.

Push.

Prod.

For sex.

This was the third night this week he had asked me to spend the night with him. "What do you say, baby?" he asked again.

My eyes widened over his shoulder and my face was struck with panic. The thought of being sexual was terrifying. I still had plenty of nightmares about Dayglo—in fact, more than I cared to admit.

"I can't," I quickly replied.

He pulled back, sighing deeply.

Pressure.

Push.

Prod.

"Why? It's Saturday tomorrow. There are no exhibits . . . no classes . . ."

"I know," I said shyly.

"Then no issues," he said. "Right?"

"Um," I said, stalling for time. Knowing that no matter how

fancy the footwork, I couldn't stall for three more months, probably couldn't even get three more days.

"It only goes so far," he said. "Then it stops."

"Michael," I responded, trying to comfort him.

"You take me to the edge," he said, "then drop me."

"It's not my intention."

"But it's what's happening," he said, pulling away, pouting. "I've been patient, but I've got needs."

"I know. I know . . . I just need time."

"Time for what?" he asked, perturbed.

"To take it all in."

I looked into his eyes and saw how hungry he was, not just for sex but also for validation.

"What do you need?"

"Time," I said.

"Are you afraid?"

"I think so."

"What are you afraid of? That I'll leave?"

"I don't know," I said, exasperated. But of course I did know. I was terrified of being raped and overpowered, humiliated and degraded. He looked into my eyes, and then, with great frustration, he turned away, released me, and walked to the other end of the courtyard and began a conversation with a group of attorneys.

He left me standing there, alone in the corner, watching him, feeling awkward and out of place. He laughed with friends, told jokes, and shared stories. He nodded his head back and forth, exchanging stories with strangers, while I stood alone, isolated, and disconnected.

My gorgeous, backless sequined gown did not seem to deliver me from my own feelings of inadequacy. And no matter how pretty or elegant I looked from a distance, I still felt alone and insignificant.

I didn't shine without him. We looked great together but merely good apart. I must have stood alone for nearly an hour, minus a few empty conversations with strangers and passersby.

A waiter approached, asking if I wanted a glass of wine or something to snack on.

No, thank you.

As I stood against the wall, staring at the beautiful image of a man, Michael Keifer, I began to feel his distance and separation from me, as though he were punishing me by leaving me to fend for myself in a room filled with wealthy people with whom I had nothing in common. I saw Michael getting smaller and smaller, pushing himself farther and farther away from me.

Oh God, I said to myself. *What has happened to me?*

Without him, I didn't feel tall.

Nor did I feel complete.

Without him I felt poor, and the sequins on this dress didn't sparkle bright enough.

As I watched Michael Keifer from across the room, I paid close attention to how many single women jiggled their behinds in his direction. Obviously, he could be swept away by a young, beautiful girl with a trust fund and a secure future. Without him I felt as though I were destined to be regurgitated into the hard, brittle winter of a Milwaukee morning, reborn into poverty and anguish.

There were no crystal stairs in the houses that took up too many square miles between Saxon and Milwaukee. I knew it, and I could barely catch my breath because of it.

"Are you ready?" he asked, finally returning to where I stood.

"Yes," I said, pissed that he had left me all night.

By the time we reached the car, I was incensed. Our ride was silent for the first few blocks.

"Did you have fun tonight?" he asked, pretending there was no great wedge between us.

"About as much fun as a girl could have *alone* at a party," I said sharply.

"You weren't alone," he remarked.

"I wasn't with *you*," I insisted. "That's for sure."

"What do you want from me, Adrian?"

"I don't want anything from you," I said before flipping it back to him. "What do you want from me?"

"I want to make love to you," he said. "Am I wrong for wanting you in that way?"

"No," I whispered, quiet and defeated.

He pulled the car off to the side of the road, turned off the ignition, and put his head down on the steering wheel.

There was silence between us.

Tension was thick.

I knew it was time to give in or give up. I wasn't ready. I wasn't secure. I didn't feel safe. Honestly, I don't even think I was connected to him deeply. But what I did know was that I didn't want to be the girl I was before I knew him. The *nobody* who walked around afraid she'd never meet anybody.

I didn't want to be her anymore.

Little Bo Peep.

The blue-eyed girl who lost her sheep, parents, and future all at once. I began to run my hands through his hair, then kiss the back of his neck gently. Within minutes, he rose to the occasion.

My first instinct was panic. Then he reassured me by whispering, "relax," as he turned his attention toward me, moving his body against mine.

He laid my seat back, almost reclining it to the floor.

Relax.

Relax.

Relax.

I repeated the words inside my head.

Relax.

Relax.

He lifted my dress up, kissing me passionately. But maybe it wasn't passionate, maybe it was just hard and forceful. The shame of it all was I didn't even know the difference. All I knew was that I felt sexually incompetent. I should have been enjoying his touch and attention.

"I like you so much," I could hear him whispering in my ear. "You're so, so beautiful.

"So, so beautiful," he repeated.

Relax, I told myself.

"So, so beautiful," as his hand slipped beneath my dress.

Relax, I told myself.

"So beautiful," he whispered, unzipping his pants, assisting my hands in the direction of his erection.

Relax, I told myself.

"I want to make love to you," he said, climbing on top, parting my legs, and inserting himself inside. It was no easy task. It was as if he were trying to park an oversized RV into a tiny little garage.

It was virgin territory, minus one rape.

A very tight fit.

It was an uncomfortable exchange of give and take, him thrusting, withdrawing, and thrusting again.

"Yes," he said, riding me like a zoo animal at a state fair.

Relax, I told myself.

Relax.

"You love it, don't you?"

Yes, I moaned.

Yes.

Yes, I moaned.

Yes.

It didn't last long. He could not contain himself, so in essence, he cut himself short of that thing he had longed for. He let out a squeal or a yell or a scream, a howl or a gurgle, or something like that, and then, without further ado, it was over.

"How do you feel?" he asked upon catching his breath.

"Relaxed," I said with a forced smile.

He thought I loved it, and he thought I was there. But it was only an act.

A script and a lovely cast of characters. I was the character. The moans and contortions of my hips were my dialogue. The elegant dress that belonged to someone else was my costume, and the fabricated stories of two dead parents who allegedly died in a car accident and left me with a hefty trust fund was my back story.

Michael Keifer Cage and all of his intellectual friends were my audience.

I was the woman that everyone saw and the stranger no one knew. And it is for this reason that in that moment I coined myself counterfeit. Almost good enough to be the real thing, but only if you don't look too close, examine too deeply, think too much, or expect something overly grand.

Welcome to the rest of my life.

Chapter 12

As I descended beyond the twelfth floor, I remembered the day I got to keep the last name.

Six months into my relationship with Michael Keifer, he decided it was time that I met his parents, the illustrious and prestigious Cage family. It was a Sunday afternoon and I was silent during most of the beautiful country drive through Hoffman Estates.

Spring was upon us and everything was in full bloom—the flowers, trees, even the air seemed crisp with the spirit of rejuvenation. It was beautiful as we drove, classical music flowing through the car.

"You okay?" he asked, squeezing my hand tight. "Don't be nervous. They're just people."

"I'm fine," I said, playing the part. After all, being "fine" on the day you meet the parents had already been written into the script.

The invitation to meet his parents had come on the edge of my own financial crisis. I had almost depleted my allotted scholarship fund for the year and it would not be too long before I would have to find a job. I had abused a lot of the funds, spending in excess of what I should have on "costumes." But the jig was almost up. Trust-fund girls don't work side gigs to supplement their lifestyle, or, God forbid, get a job as a waitress or a cashier.

How could I continue to hide my desperate financial situation?

Use what you got.

Use what you got.

"How much farther?" I asked, feeling as though we had been driving forever.

"Not much," he said.

My armpits were starting to sweat. I could feel the air filling up my lungs and it seemed as though I had to take bigger breaths to sustain myself.

"You okay?" he asked. "You look a little pale."

"I'm fine, honey," I said, losing my grip on the part I was supposed to be playing.

He pulled up to the Cage's gated estate and from the outside it was awe-inspiring. From the inside, it looked like Jurassic Park.

"Wow," I said, my jaw dropping. There were fountains, trees, and wide-open spaces that went on for miles. In the center of everything was a house that looked Greek, with giant columns and marble steps leading up to the entryway.

The house was colossal.

Pristine.

Perfection.

Elegant.

Timeless.

I began to fidget as he took me by the hand, almost dragging me out of the front seat.

"You're beautiful," he said, kissing me on the forehead. "Just be yourself. They're going to love you as much as I do."

"Okay," I said, forcing a smile as he turned around in a whirlwind and we started trotting up to the front door like a pair of wild stallions.

Hey buddy, I wanted to say. *What's the mad rush?*

By the time we arrived at the front door, it was already open and a lavishly maintained woman in her late fifties stepped onto the giant front steps wearing a cream-colored pantsuit and glorious diamond-and-pearl earrings.

"Darling!" she yelled, arms extended in the direction of her son. "I'm *so* glad you could make it!"

"Mom!" said Michael, eyes beaming, flashing a bright, warm smile. They embraced for what seemed like an eternity, which left me standing at the bottom of the steps, slowly making my way to the top, humbly waiting for an introduction. And just as it was about to happen, an elegant, charming man, who also appeared to be in his late fifties, joined the mother and son on the front steps, where they all embraced some more.

Wow, I thought, watching them. They're beautiful, wealthy, and they actually like each other.

"Mom, Dad," he said, extending an arm in my direction, "I would like you to meet Adrian."

Slowly, I began to walk toward them. They paused, and I felt myself being watched, studied, examined, dissected, and appraised. But as I crossed the front steps, I felt flawless. The old man's eyes were popping out of his head and the lady of the house observed me quietly but intently.

"Hello," I said, flashing one of those beauty-pageant smiles. "It's so nice to meet you."

"Pleasure," said the father, almost trampling the mother to get to my hand so he could gently kiss it. "Call me Alfred, and this is my wife, Jean."

"We've heard a lot about you, Adrian," said Jean, offering a professional smile and a solid handshake. But when I touched her skin, I felt the heat of her thorough yet subtle interrogation. It was the kind that was done *without* words. It was the kind of inspection that was almost impossible to pass. It was the scanning of the eyes and the making of mental notes—attire, shoes, jewelry, and purse.

"Let's go inside," suggested Alfred, and we all followed him. *Dear God.*

When we stepped inside, I felt as though I had entered a museum. It was immaculate, with marble everywhere, two winding staircases, and a skylight that took up what appeared to be the whole roof.

"Your place is beautiful," I said.

"Thank you," said Jean proudly as she led us onto their terrace, a garden-like paradise where a glorious brunch had been laid out for us.

We each took our respective seats.

I was so nervous I didn't know what to say, as Michael's parents sat opposite me, and Michael sat beside me. It was anything but relaxed. This was dead center of the stage and the spotlight was on me.

It was now or never.

Do or die.

Time to belly up.

Perform.

"So you're a student?" Jean said.

"She's an artist," said Michael.

"Oh, yeah," said Alfred.

"Yes," I replied.

"What kind of art?" asked Jean.

"Portraiture."

"I would love to see some of your work," said Jean.

"Yes, of course."

"Are you exhibiting anywhere?" Alfred asked.

"Not yet."

"Oh," she said, tone dropped. "I see."

"But she will be soon," injected Michael just as quickly as he could.

"Yes," I said.

"Of course," said Jean.

"Tell me about your family," said Jean.

"My parents were killed in an auto accident when I was a child," I said.

"We're terribly sorry," said Alfred.

"Thank you," I said.

"So, where did you grow up?" asked Jean, hell-bent on continuing the interrogation. Don't let a silly little thing like the untimely passing of both parents stop you.

"Tucson," I said.

"Oh, Tucson," said Alfred, raising his brows. "That's such a lovely place."

"It's hot, Alfred," said Jean, scolding.

"But it's lovely," he insisted, confronting her with his eyes.

"Who raised you after you lost your parents?" asked Jean.

"Mother," said Michael, "let Adrian have a rest . . ."

"That's right, Jean," said Alfred. "She didn't come here to be put on the stand."

"Well," she said with an insincere laugh, "I certainly wouldn't want to make our guest feel uncomfortable. I'm just looking out for my son."

"Mom," warned Michael.

"There are so many, Alfred," she said to Michael's father.

"Mother," said Michael.

My heart dropped.

So many? I thought. *What does she mean by that?*

"Jean," warned Alfred. "Let's enjoy lunch."

"Of course," she said in a way that was rather unconvincing. I clenched my teeth, locking my jaws together. By this time, perspiration had dripped down my underarms, spilling over onto the sides of my dress. My body ached from the tension of holding everything together so tightly. We ate in excruciating silence, minus a light word from Michael's father here and there.

After lunch I was ready to leave, but instead of an early departure, I was delivered to the lion's den with a steak sitting on top of my head.

All of this was done at Michael's suggestion. "Baby," he said, "why don't you let my mother show you her lovely rose garden?"

I looked at him as though I would die, and his mother shot a look at me as though she were planning to eat me alive.

"Come," she said. "They're quite lovely."

Cautiously, I joined her as we went out into the backyard.

"How long have you been dating my son?" she asked.

"Six months," I said.

She looked at me, rolled her eyes, and made some sort of impolite grunt beneath her breath.

"Sorry?" I asked, calling her out on her rudeness. "Is something wrong?"

"You," she said flatly.

"Pardon me?"

"You," she repeated without qualms.

"Excuse me?" I replied. "But I . . ."

"Save the act for Broadway, honey," she said, scanning me up and down with critical eyes. "I don't believe you are who you say you are."

"What do you mean?" I asked. "Do you need to see my driver's license?"

"Cheap perfume," she said with her nose turned up.

"Excuse me?" I asked, flabbergasted.

"You're dressed to the hilt, head to toe, playing the part, but you missed a critical detail in your presentation . . . you're wearing cheap perfume."

"I don't know what you're talking about!"

"Oh," she said, putting her fingers on my lips to silence me. "I think you *do* know."

"It's absurd, what you're saying," I replied defensively.

"The issue lies not in the absurdity, but in the truth," she stated. "If I asked you to produce a financial statement of your assets today, could you?"

"Could you?" I asked, calling her bluff.

"I wouldn't need to."

"And I do?"

"You're a fraud," she declared flatly.

By this time we had made our way down to the rose garden while Michael and his father looked on, smiling. His manipulative mother smiled back, as though we were engaged in great conversation, but it wasn't great. It was awful and humiliating. And I could not believe that I had ended up a part of such insanity, especially from rather normal-looking people.

"All you'll ever be is a pretty toy," she said. "Nothing more, nothing less . . . until your face falls flat and wrinkles come, and your body gives in to gravity." She paused a beat for laughter; "That's a real fun time, by the way . . . gravity."

"Why are you saying these awful things to me?"

"Because they're true," she said flippantly. "And I only deal with reality. You and my son have nothing in common."

"We have lots in common," I said defensively.

"Don't flatter yourself," she said. "I know him like the New York stock market, and I can see through you like a magician who leaves his trick book open on the table while he performs for the people. You have *nothing* in common, and you're only getting by because you've mastered the horizontal position. But don't stay down there too long and let your *real* life pass you by while you're busy playing make-believe with my son."

I looked up only to see Michael and his father smile at me from the garden patio.

"Don't fool yourself, Adrian. You haven't a chance in hell with my son," said his wretched mother that day as she turned her back on me and began her ascent to the back of the house. "A toy is a seasonal item. You toss out the old one when a new one comes along. New toys come along every day . . . so don't get too attached to the name."

Three months later, at the end of my first year of school, Michael and I eloped to Vegas.

His father was disappointed because he felt he had been cheated out of a "good, old, traditional, American wedding."

Upon learning the news, his mother suffered a mild "heart attack," but I think it was nothing more than a whole lot of drama. And in the end, I got to keep the last name.

Chapter 11

As I descended beyond the eleventh floor, I remembered the impecca-
ble day aboard a first-class flight going from Las Vegas to Chicago. It
was the first day I learned to do the math . . .

Marriage is not for the fainthearted, nor is it intended for
anyone who plans on being happy for any length of time.

The day we married was bliss.

The day *after* the day we married was the introduction to the
rest of my life. Dress rehearsal was over and the real show had
begun, and it appeared we both had been playing deceptive
roles.

I was flat broke, pretending to be a movie star, and he was an
all-out ass pretending to be charming.

Michael Keifer, in what I calculated as a twenty-four-hour
period of time, went from being a charming, elegant, caring
man to a controlling, condescending, self-righteous, judgmental, indignant freak.

The moment I said, "I do," the whole thing went straight to
hell.

I was actually waiting for his head to do a 360-degree spin
and green stuff to spew from his mouth.

The descent into hell began at 6:00 A.M. the next morning. I woke up to him tugging, pulling, and fondling me roughly. He didn't caress or kiss me. He was behind me like an impatient truck, honking the horn, trying to get inside.

I was asleep.

He didn't care.

When I woke up, he had already worked his way partially inside.

"Michael?" I asked, groggy and incoherent. "What's . . . ?"

"Shh," he said harshly, doing the deed. "Just be still."

"You're hurting me," I said.

"Be still!" he insisted. "Don't move!"

He pinned me against the bed, holding me still against his wild thrusts, till he finally got off. Then he rolled over and got up without so much as a *Good morning.* I lay with my face pressed into the pillow and tears in my eyes, fighting against the ghost of Dayglo, reliving our brief encounter for the one-hundredth time.

"Let's get a move on," he said coldly. "Checkout time is noon."

I glanced at the clock.

It was 6:07 A.M.

"It's six o'clock in the morning," I said. "I'm tired."

"Well," he said, emotionless, "then you'll be flying home alone, because I'm on the next plane outta here."

I sat up in the bed and looked hard into his eyes, flabbergasted. "What's wrong with you?" I asked. "Where is this coming from?"

He continued about the room, busying himself, packing clothes into a suitcase.

"Michael," I called out to him again. "I thought we were going to be here all weekend. It hasn't even been a full day yet."

"I have a meeting!" he snapped.

"What?"

"I have a very important meeting in the city and I can't miss it."

"Wait . . . wait . . . wait . . ." I said, getting out of bed in a whirlwind of panic. "This is our honeymoon! What do you mean, you have a meeting?"

"Listen, Adrian," he said harshly. "I don't have time to go through this with you. We're taking the next plane out of Vegas and that's final!"

"But . . ."

"It's *final*," he insisted before going into the bathroom and slamming the door.

I stood in the center of the floor blindsided, as if something big and heavy had fallen out of the sky, hitting me on top of the head.

Brick and mortar.

Brick and mortar.

I had been hit by brick and mortar.

I listened to the sounds of running water as I sat up on the bed, stunned into disbelief at the sudden shift.

What had happened?

He was charming yesterday.

We took vows at midnight.

Made love at 2:00 A.M.

I fell asleep in his arms at 3:00 A.M., and woke up to a complete stranger at 6:00.

What the hell?

I went through the motions of getting ready, stunned, wondering if I had done the right thing. I didn't want to jump to any conclusions, but *something* had changed.

The four-hour plane ride was pretty quiet. We sat in first class while Michael dissected the *New York Times* and I scanned through the most recent issue of *Vogue*.

"What are you reading about?" he asked, looking at me with a critical eye.

"Makeovers," I said under my breath.

He took the magazine from me and put it in under the seat, replacing it with a page from the *Times*.

"I don't want to read about missiles being produced in Russia . . . I want to read something light," I said, sighing.

"You'll read something educational," he insisted.

I looked at him hard.

"What is wrong with you today?"

He didn't respond.

"I went to sleep with a charming man and woke up with a dictator . . ." I said. "What the hell is that?"

He squeezed my arm tight, leaned over, and whispered into my ear, "We all have jobs to do here, and yours is to make me look good."

"I didn't marry you to make you look good," I said, emphatically drawing my arm back. "I have no intention of being your trophy. I'm your *wife*, for God's sake."

"You married me so you could live well," he said with a tone of finality. "And I married you so I could look good. You clean up nice for parties and impress the hell out of potential clients."

"What?" I asked, gasping.

"Adrian, simply put . . . you bridge the gap between people I could meet and the people I *will* meet. A pretty face and a nice set of tits go a long way."

"I *cannot* believe you," I scowled. "You're using me?"

"Not any more than you're using me. We both have jobs to do," he said. "You will live very, very well as my *wife*."

"What about love?" I asked, staring into his eyes. He didn't respond. "What about the love, Michael?"

"You got the wrong guy," he said. "This isn't about *love*."

"Then what's it about?"

"It's about looking good and living well," he said. "Look at my parents."

"What about them?"

"You think they love each other?" he asked, laughing. "They can't stand the sight of each other."

"Then why are they together?"

"Why does any great merger happen?" he asked. "It's good business. Oh, don't tell me . . . you're one of the last people on Earth who actually believe in happily-ever-after . . . love for the sake of love? Pull your head out of your ass, Adrian. Shakespeare wrote those love stories hundreds of years ago. The world doesn't spin that way anymore. And if you really don't know that, then you definitely need to put down whatever nonsense you're reading and pick up a copy of the *Times*."

"I think I'm going to be sick," I said, staring at the floor.

"I think you're going to be rich," he said, turning his attention back to the *New York Times*.

"I can't go through with this . . ." I said. "I just can't."

"Oh, yeah?" he said. "What are you going to do? Climb back into that Milwaukee shit hole you climbed out of . . . ?"

At that moment, my skin lost all of its color.

"You gonna crawl back to your impoverished, crippled grandmother and tell her that you walked away from a dynasty because you got tripped up on a little four-letter word called *l-o-v-e*?"

He started to laugh, thoroughly amused—the sounds of his merriment echoed throughout first class. His laughter was appalling, and in that single moment I began to hate him.

"What are you going to do?" he asked. "Get another job as the night clerk at a cheap motel? Now, that sounds like a promising career. They could promote you to the cleaning crew and you could spend your life changing cum-filled sheets and scrubbing people's shit out of toilets. Now there's something to aspire to . . ."

My eyes began to fill with tears.

"Or," he continued, "you could pursue a career in the arts and write a one-man show and perform it in a run-down dive, pro bono, and kill yourself at the end of the run because you realize you're never gonna be anything *ever* . . . but poor and desperate."

The tears began to fall down my cheeks.

"You have two pennies in your account," he whispered. "Last time I checked I had two million, and I'm just getting started, baby . . . so, you do the math."

"What did you do, Michael? Run a background check on me?"

"For God's sake, Adrian . . . I'm a criminal attorney. What did you expect me to do?"

"You could have asked."

"I did," he said, "and you lied."

I began to shrink back into my seat.

"I won't stay with you forever."

"Bite your tongue, young lady," he said with a condescending ring to his voice. "Marriage is a lifelong commitment."

"You son of a bitch," I said.

"You'll play the part for as long as I want you to," he said. "And when you get too old to make me look good anymore, I'll retire you to greener pastures and replace you with a younger version of yourself . . . you really are one of the most beautiful women I have ever laid eyes upon."

He rambled on, but I paid little attention. I had already faded into the background, thinking and plotting my next series of moves.

At the age of eighteen, I had two pennies to my name. At the age of twenty-eight, he had somewhere in the neighborhood of two million.

I could get off this plane in Chicago and get a job at Mc-Donald's flipping burgers. Or I could catch the bus to Milwaukee and go take care of Reva Joe and wish every day that I were dead. Or I could "suck it up" and stay with him, accompany him to functions, force a fake smile, and live like a queen. I could numb the ache for *real* love with a series of hefty purchases.

Oh, God.

Would it ever be enough?

Probably not.

But I could fake it until I couldn't take it anymore. At the very least, I would be comfortable on the outside, and maybe, just maybe, someday I could get used to my skin crawling. And even if I couldn't get used to it, I could grow accustomed to the feeling of cashmere and mink rubbing against my crawling skin.

I wanted to turn around, walk away, and never look back. But then I contemplated just how much dignity I would have cleaning shit out of toilets, and in that moment, dignity seemed slightly overrated.

Live poor.

Die rich.

You do the math and see which side you come out on.
Live poor.
Die rich.
You do the math.
Live poor.
Die rich.
You do the math.

Chapter 10

As I descended beyond the tenth floor, I remembered the day I accidentally blinked and lost thirteen years of my life.

We landed in Chicago from Las Vegas on a hazy Sunday afternoon. Numb, I stared out the window at the runway as the pilot announced weather conditions, temperature, local time, and date.

June 1995.

No, I mumbled to myself.

Repeat the date one more time.

Repeat it one more time.

Can't be.

I'm not.

This isn't.

Can't be.

Repeat the date one more time.

1995.

1995.

Thirteen years had gone by.

I glanced over at Michael Keifer, who was seated beside me in first class, and I nearly leapt out of my skin. His hair was salt-and-pepper, and his face, though still very handsome, was finely lined around the sides of his eyes and mouth. Distinguished and elegant, he was a man who had known a great measure of success at forty-two years of age.

A chauffeur awaited our arrival at the airport. We weren't returning to the lovely, sophisticated downtown loft Michael Keifer owned when we married. No, that had been given up ten years ago in exchange for the 8,000-square-foot home we built in Hoffman Estates. It was gorgeous but geographically undesirable, as the lot and the house were only one block away from Michael's parents.

And that was just way too close for comfort, privacy, or anything else.

The house was beautiful.

The grounds immaculate.

The neighborhood was one big photo opportunity.

The schools were progressive, the citizens impeccable.

As we rode in the backseat of the chauffeured limousine, I caught tiny glimpses of my own reflection in the mirror.

I scanned the surface of my thirty-two-year-old face. It had matured while I wasn't looking, and with my attention focused elsewhere, there was a subtle sign now hanging on my forehead which read, "Aging in Progress."

Aging in Progress.

I was still rather beautiful.

Michael Keifer made sure of that.

There were Botox and collagen injections to smooth me out injected beneath the skin to smooth me over. There were weekly facials and peels, and a plethora of moisturizers and miracle creams to make me look younger, better, stronger, and more vibrant, ever tapping into that fountain of youth out of fear that Michael would send me to greener pastures, keeping his word to exchange me for a "younger version of myself."

I would probably be an eighty-year-old woman with the face of a seventeen-year-old and the heavy heart of a thousand-year-old. But for now, I remained attractive, elegant, and refined.

Michael Keifer Cage had kept the promise he made thirteen

years ago while sitting in a first-class flight from Las Vegas to Chicago when he uttered, *You're going to be very rich.*

And I was.

We lived very well and I wanted for nothing, except love.

I had sold my soul to the highest bidder.

Good job, Adrian.

Good job.

Our ride home was silent, which, by the way, defined most of my life. I lived in and out of emotional desperation. I sold my soul at the age of eighteen for a price not translatable in our language. By the age of thirty-two, it was nowhere to be found.

When we arrived home, I stepped into our lovely palace unimpressed, though it was one of the most beautiful homes in all of Hoffman Estates.

Michael Keifer saw to that.

It was professionally crafted to a standard of excellence that most people will *never* experience. And yet, I remained untouched by its beauty. All I could really see was the muddied underside of all that was not visible.

I quickly ascended the winding marble staircase to the east wing of the house and disappeared into our bedroom.

I stood at the French doors, which gave way to a sprawling veranda overlooking the thirteen acres upon which our home was built, with a running stream, fountains, and an English-style garden. I waited there for a long time, on the edge, taking in as much air as I could.

I ran a bubble bath and immersed myself, closing my eyes to it all, sinking into my own version of oblivion.

Then he came.

Michael Keifer, entering my private sanctuary, standing in the center of the floor, staring at me, as he often did, admiring my beauty.

Not a man of many words or emotions, he lived life robotically. He removed his clothing and got in the tub with me.

It was time.

Time for him to be gratified.

It was not rehearsed, but yet it was very staged. There was no spontaneity to our lovemaking, if you could even call it that. I called it the great gratification session. It was about me pleasuring him sexually and giving unto him his due. It was the manner in which I repaid him for all the luxuries.

It was gratification.

Nothing more.

Nothing less.

He would present himself before me and I automatically knew what to do. We never talked about it. There were no tender caresses or gentle embraces. We did not kiss and God knows we never cuddled. He presented himself to me and I fulfilled my obligatory wifely duties.

Once he immersed himself in the bathwater, I rose from my relaxation to greet him as he knelt in the oversized tub. His penis was already erect, assuming the natural position for me to insert it into my mouth, which I did. From there, I would grab each side of his buttocks, inserting him into my mouth, and then pulling him out.

In.

Out.

In.

He moaned.

In.

Out.

In.

He came.

Stood up.

Exited the tub.

I spit out the leftovers.

And resumed my bath.

End of discussion.

It was perfunctory and served its purpose, releasing him of excess pressure.

"Check on Mayo," he said before leaving the bathroom.

"Of course," I replied.

I should probably have gone to the other side of the house

before drawing a bath, but I wasn't prepared to deal with *him* yet.

I got out of the tub and stood in the center of my sprawling bathroom, sighing deeply.

I dressed and began the descent to the other side. I called it a descent because once I got to the other side, I would be reminded of the true hell in which I existed.

I knocked on the door, whispering gently, "Mayo . . . Mayo."

"What?" he asked with a bitter edge.

"It's Mother," I replied, and even I couldn't believe it myself.

I was the mother of a ten-year-old "demon." In fact, I really did call him that when no one was listening.

"Open the door," I insisted. "It's Mother."

He didn't open it.

I tried to open it but he had something wedged against it.

"Mayo!" I called. "Mayo!"

No response.

"Nanny Brown!" I called, going back down the hall, seeking his caregiver. "Nanny Brown."

Nanny Brown, a staunch Midwesterner, entered my field of vision. She was a heavyset lady with an equally heavy voice, and was probably the only person who had any control over Mayo. For whatever reason, he seemed to respond to her, or at the very least, respect her.

"Come quickly," I said in haste. "He's got something blocking the door."

"Right away, madam," she said, following me.

Back at the door, I put all of my weight against it, trying to force it open, but by then Mayo had removed the object that was originally blocking it, so that when I pushed it, I fell onto the floor. When I looked up, there he sat on the bed in all his glory.

Rosemary's Baby.

But his name was Mayo instead.

He was a striking young boy with beautiful sandy-blond hair and deep blue eyes. He was so absolutely perfect that it was hard to believe he was *crazy*.

But he was crazy—violent *and* also masochistic. When he was seven, his father bought him a rabbit and I dare not say what cruel things he did to the little animal. (He crucified him, driving nails through his paws one day while his father and I slept.)

He had been to therapy, church, treatment centers, and special schools. I had gone everywhere to try and make him sane. But he only seemed to get crazier with every passing day, a little more over-the-top, a bit more extreme, to the point where I didn't know what bothered me more, him hating me or me hating him.

Perhaps I could deal with him if I had loved him just a little bit, and maybe that would have made it all seem worth it. But as it stood now, Mayo was one of the biggest reasons, even more so than his father, that I wanted to pack my bags, walk out that door, and never look back. And if that made me a god-awful person, then a god-awful person I would be.

It was my truth.

"Why was this door jammed?" I asked him as he sat on the bed, laughing at me as I picked myself up off the ground.

"Mayo," scolded Nanny Brown. "Be nice."

"The door wasn't jammed," he said, evil intent behind his eyes. "I think *you're* jammed," he spat with a twisted grin.

"Don't speak to me that way," I said to him, exasperated. "I came in here to check on you because I wanted to know what you've been doing while Daddy and I were away."

"Eating crickets," he said.

I looked at Nanny Brown, who looked back at me with a blank expression.

"Eating crickets?" I asked him.

"Biting their heads off and enjoying them as a snack," he said, with this crazy, far-out look in his eyes.

I looked at him and thought to myself with such intense emotion, *I wish to God I could send you back.*

Back to where you came from.

Parents enjoyed their children.

Children enjoyed their parents.

But Mayo was the biggest mistake I had ever made, and I knew it. And the tragic horror of it all was *so did he*, and we were both condemned because of it.

The guilt was immeasurable in the *knowing* of it all.

I walked out of his bedroom, past Nanny Brown, and slammed the door.

I could hear his laughter echoing throughout the hallways.

I hated my son.

Despised him.

I was indifferent toward my husband, and apathetic to my lifestyle. The past thirteen years of my life had been lived in a golden prison.

"Mrs. Cage," called Nanny Brown from one of the side bedrooms.

I paused a beat before entering the darkened room.

"Mrs. Brown?"

"He's not getting any better," she said, concerned.

"I know," I said, nodding.

"Yesterday, I caught him in the garden setting ladybugs on fire. This morning he was on the veranda pulling the wings off the butterflies."

I put my head down and started to cry. Nanny Brown rested a strong, comfortable arm upon my shoulder.

"I just don't know what to do with him anymore," I said, exasperated. "Not that I ever did. He wasn't a normal baby. He was just so angry."

"What does Mr. Cage say?" she asked delicately.

"Mr. Cage doesn't say . . ."

"What do you think he *thinks*?" she asked with an inquisitive eye.

"I think he *thinks* he's beautiful but insane," I said. "Tries to keep him away from everything . . . you know. Tries to stay away, works seventeen hours a day so he doesn't have to look at one of his greatest failures."

"Do you see Mayo as a failure?" she asked gently.

"I see him as a disaster, a nuclear holocaust," I said without pause.

"That must be devastating," she said quietly.

"I feel lost and desperate . . . trapped," I said. "I am the world's biggest irony, Mrs. Brown."

"I don't understand," she said.

"I can buy anything I see—I snap my fingers and it's mine. But the one thing I really want is to be *free*, and I can't have that for all the money in the world."

Nanny Brown looked at me with eyes of sympathy.

"I want to be free, Mrs. Brown," I said with tears streaming down my face. "I want to know love. I want to dance in the rain!" I shouted. "I want someone to set me on fire and consume me. I want my flesh to burn to the bone. I want to know I am alive and if someone has to kill me to prove it to me . . . then so be it, but I want to know that the last thirteen years of my life is not a preview of what's to come . . ."

I collapsed onto the floor and started to sob hysterically.

Nanny Brown knelt down to my eye level and shoved a paper inside my hand.

"What is this?"

"Call that number," she suggested.

"What is it?"

"Help . . . for Mayo," she insisted. "That number belongs to a man who lives in downtown Chicago. He works with local kids, using song to bring them back from their demons."

"What?" I asked, staring at the number on the card, trying to digest it all.

"He teaches music to disturbed children. I got his number from a friend of mine . . . he had worked with her daughter and I must tell you, I saw quite a change in the little bugger. Go see him, Mrs. Cage," she said earnestly. "He could be the miracle you're looking for."

I looked at the paper, intrigued. There was only a number, no name.

"What's his name?"

"I don't remember," she said. "Something unusual. I have to run along now, but do call, okay?"

"Of course," I said, trying to pull myself together. "Mrs. Brown?"

"Yes?"

"Do you have any idea what it's like to be me?"

"Can't say that I do, ma'am."

I looked deep into her eyes, and then I went a little deeper. And just as I tried to show her, she turned away, and there was an uncomfortable silence between us. So I filled it with happenstance conversation. "I'll call the number tomorrow . . . Thank you, Mrs. Brown."

"Thank you, ma'am," she said, exiting without further eye contact.

Chapter 9

As I descended beyond the ninth floor, I remembered the day the demons took a vacation from Mayo.

Early the next morning, I dialed the number Nanny Brown left for me. The phone rang nine times before it was answered, and I counted every ring, waiting for a human voice or an answering machine. Just as I was about to end the call, there was an abrupt, "Hello."

"Hello," I responded, surprised.

Then silence.

"Hi," I said, searching for the right words. "I umm . . . wanted to make an appointment."

"What are you looking for?"

"Looking for someone to work with my son."

"What's his story?" he asked abruptly.

There was a long pause.

My forehead started to sweat.

"What's his story?" he repeated.

"He's crazy," I whispered.

"Be here tomorrow at three—816 Michigan Avenue, Loft 3."

"Okay," I said, scrambling to write down the address.

"If you're late," he said, "I don't see you."

"Okay."

"If you're early," he said, "I don't see you."

"Okay."

"Three o'clock," he repeated sternly. "Sessions are one hour and they're private. While I'm working with your son, I don't see you. You get lost for the hour."

"I've been lost a lot longer than an hour," I said in jest.

"You tell your son nothing," he said. "I'll do the talking when he gets here."

"Okay," I said.

"Three o'clock," he said again.

"What's your name?" I asked, but before I could get an answer he hung up.

Gee whiz, I thought. *This guy's intense.*

The next day I picked Mayo up from school at 2:15 P.M. promptly, to ensure our timely arrival, but not to be too prompt or he "wouldn't see us."

"Where are we going?" asked Mayo, kicking the dash of my brand-new Mercedes SUV with the heels of his shoes.

"We have an appointment," I said.

"I don't want to go to an appointment!" he screamed at the top of his lungs.

"No screaming!" I screamed back at him, feeling my blood pressure rise.

"I don't want to go to an appointment!" he shouted again.

"No screaming!"

"No appointment!"

"No screaming!"

"No appointment!"

"Stop screaming! Jesus Christ, you're driving me crazy!"

"Stop the car and let me out!" he insisted.

We were driving down the expressway and I was doing 79 miles per hour. At one point, I wanted to open the door and push him out.

"Mayo, shut up and sit in that seat!" I demanded.

He removed his seat belt.

"Put your goddamned seat belt back on!"

"I'm not going anywhere with you!" he shouted.

"Mayo!" I warned, growing more concerned. "What are you doing, son? Put your seat belt back on!"

He opened the door and the wind ripped through the passenger's side and into the driver's seat. I immediately slammed on the brakes, and the car swerved off the road and onto the shoulder. Once the car came to a complete stop, Mayo opened the door and jumped out, screaming, "You bitch!" as he raced down the side of the expressway.

"Mayo!" I screamed. "Shit!"

I threw the car into reverse and backed down the shoulder till I cut him off and he ran right into the Mercedes and almost knocked himself out.

"Oh my God!" I screamed. "Shit!"

I jumped out of the car and raced around to the side where he lay sprawled on the ground with a bloody nose.

"Mayo!" I screamed, running to assist him. I bent down and tried to help him up.

"Get off me! Off me!" he shouted.

I opened the trunk, reached inside, and pulled out a custom-made leash designed especially for Mayo. It was a chain that attached to the side of his pants and could also fit around my waist to tie us together.

"No leash! No leash!" he screamed, his nose dripping blood.

"Get in the car!" I screamed, as traffic whizzed by while we stood on the side of the road, attracting stares. "Get in the God-blessed car and don't you dare move!"

He got in the passenger's side and when I was certain he had calmed down, I removed the leash and put the childproof safety lock on all the doors so he couldn't get out on his own. *Why didn't I think to do that before?* I asked myself as I walked back to the driver's side.

We rode the rest of the way in silence. Actually, silence and despair. He was silent, I was in despair. When we arrived at the building, what a sight it was. As we entered, careful to follow precise instructions, we wound our way around a corridor to Loft 3.

I looked a tattered mess.

Mayo's nose had dried blood on it and his left eye was starting to swell. He looked a mess, too.

"I don't want to be here," he said under his breath.

"We're here, so deal with it," I mumbled.

"I'm going to kill myself on the way home."

"You won't have to," I suggested. "If you embarrass me, I'll do it for you."

When the door opened, I came so close to passing out there were no words.

I recognized him upon sight.

I knew that face.

It was *him.*

I could not believe my eyes.

Astounded, I could have been knocked over with a feather.

What a beautiful, beautiful man.

He was a big boy now, all grown up.

I could not believe what a gorgeous man he had become.

Broad shoulders.

Six-foot-four.

Wide-eyed.

Alive.

Passionately connected to the instrument that hung from his shoulder strap. *Oh yes*, I remembered. He and his guitar had always been soulmates.

"Anthem," I whispered, so low it was barely audible. "It's you."

His eyes held such depth as he looked at me; then his stare penetrated me completely.

I felt it.

I could see his struggle, trying to recall my name, but it was lost to him.

"The dove," he said. "The dove from Milwaukee."

"Adrian," I had to remind him.

"Oh, yeah," he said as it all came back to him. "Adrian from the lake."

I smiled, embarrassed.

Is that all he remembered?

The girl from the lake?

I was so disappointed. I certainly remembered a lot more than that. The girl from the lake was easy to forget, but the girl who actually loved him, once upon a time, wouldn't be.

Oh God, maybe I was being dramatic. Maybe it wasn't that deep for him. It had just been so long since I remembered anything remotely close to love, and in remembering, I found myself wanting to grab hold of it, even if it was nothing more than a memory.

We embraced, and I just wanted to hold onto him. He smelled so good and his skin was soft and I didn't want him to let go. I also felt as though it was obvious, so I pulled away quickly before my desperation became apparent to everyone else in the room, including my son.

"This is my son, Mayo," I said, clearing my throat. Actually, I was trying to catch my breath.

"Hey," said Anthem with a smile, extending a hand.

Mayo did not accept it, just glared at him with evil eyes.

This was surely Satan's child.

"Mayo," I cautioned.

"It's cool," said Anthem. "Come on in."

We entered his loft and stood there like strangers. His place was simple and very bachelor-looking, definitely a guy's house.

There was nothing quaint or homey about it.

It was big, brick, and empty. He had several pictures of Jimi Hendrix scattered about the room, some hanging from walls and others on the floor.

"I like your place . . . it's rather *lofty*," I said with a laugh.

"It'll do for now," he said, walking to the other side of the room.

Mayo and I stood out like two sore thumbs.

"Dude," he said to Mayo. "We're gonna do some cool music in my studio back there."

Mayo stood like an ice sculpture, unmoved.

"Go check it out," he suggested to Mayo.

Reluctantly, Mayo slowly obliged.

I was relieved when his feet began to shuffle in that direction because I didn't know if he was going to flip out and cause a scene.

Once Mayo left, I stood in the center of the room staring at Anthem, slightly uncomfortable in my skin because I was so drawn to him. And he was looking at me, too.

"You look good," he said.

"Thank you," I replied with a huge grin that I couldn't suppress. "You, too."

"Real good," he confirmed.

"Thank you," I said again.

I smiled.

He smiled.

Silence.

And another smile followed by even more awkwardness.

"I can come back in an hour," I said. *Or I could stay forever,* I thought as I looked at him.

He didn't respond, just looked at me with those beautiful eyes. He had grown into his manhood so well and was truly, truly fine.

I was thinking all of the things that people think when they're strongly attracted to someone.

If you could read my mind, I thought.

If you could only read my mind.

"An hour's good," he said.

"Okay," I said, feeling uncomfortable as I made my way to the front door.

"Is he going to be okay?" I asked, referring to Mayo. "He's not the easiest kid."

"He'll be fine," said Anthem. "Don't worry—if he gets out of hand I have a Taser."

My face lost its color.

"Adrian," said Anthem, laughing. "I'm just kidding."

"Oh," I said, bursting into a forced laugh. "Okay."

"Are you okay?"

"Yes," I said, trying to quiet my own memory of a Taser. I had purchased one for self-defense once upon a time, and about six months ago, Mayo had such a violent fit, I actually used it on him.

The memory was not a pleasant one.

That night his father threatened to send me to jail.

I surrendered the Taser that evening and Mayo has never looked at me the same way. Before the incident, he had a grotesque dislike of me, but after being stunned by the gun, his hate was so brutal it was palpable.

"I'll be back in an hour," I said hesitantly.

"Okay," replied Anthem lightly. "See you then."

I went down to the car and sat in the front seat, stunned and a little bit confused.

I didn't know what to make of it all.

Anthem.

Mayo.

Music lessons.

Taser guns.

In-laws.

Hoffman Estates.

The exceedingly wealthy.

The morally bankrupt.

High society.

Downtown poverty.

Socialites.

Homeless people.

Parenthood.

I sat in the front seat and for the whole hour stared blankly at the steering wheel.

I just didn't know what to make of it all.

By the time the hour had passed, I found myself racing back to Anthem's door. I was anxious as I knocked, hoping that Mayo had not set the apartment on fire or tortured the old lady upstairs. To my surprise, Anthem opened the door with a smile.

Good, I thought. *He's still breathing.*

Okay.

So he must have won the war and my son is dead.

I shuddered at the thought of it, because, sadly, the contemplation of Mayo's demise brought me pleasure.

Surely, this could not be a normal parental experience.

"How did it go?" I asked as I entered, prepared to see my son hanging from the top of the roof by a string with his tongue hanging out.

"Great!" said Anthem with a smile.

I paused, glanced at him, then looked around for signs that Mayo was actually still alive. In that moment, he emerged from the bedroom holding a guitar. It was the first time he appeared as a normal child, a little boy of ten years old.

He did not seem like a giant.

Bigger than I.

Bolder than I.

Stronger than I.

Someone I needed to overpower.

Someone I had to body-slam onto the ground and Taser.

He was ten years old.

A little boy.

A beautiful boy.

Blond hair.

Blue eyes.

Perfect face.

Tortured soul.

He was just a little boy.

Not a beast.

Or a monster.

Or someone to be feared.

"Did you drug him?" I whispered, amazed by his calmness.

"I didn't," said Anthem. "The music did."

I nodded, cautiously watching him, and for the first time in this little boy's life, he seemed at peace.

"One week, buddy," said Anthem, rubbing the top of Mayo's head.

"Cool," he said with a smile.

"You stay cool," said Anthem.

"Okay," he agreed, wild-eyed.

I don't think I've ever seen Mayo *authentically* smile, not even as a baby.

He was born violent.

I never knew where it came from.

Mayo headed out the door, and I followed.

"So, next week?" he called after me.

"Yes," I said, amazed, shocked, and so surprised I could barely speak. "One week."

The drive home was pleasant.

It was pleasant because Mayo didn't try to jump out on the expressway and kill himself, or perhaps it was pleasant because he wasn't trying to kill me.

The conversation between us was minimal, as always, but at least it wasn't antagonistic, which was usual.

"So you like him?" I asked.

"Yeah," he said, nodding.

"What did you do?"

"You know what we did," he said defensively.

"No . . . I mean," I started stumbling over the words. "I know what you did but I'm not sure exactly what you did."

"We did music, man," he said. "We did *music*."

"Did you like it?"

"No, I didn't like it . . ." he said, shaking his head. "I *loved* it."

And he smiled again.

Second time in his life.

I could have cried all the way home.

I felt like this was the first time I was meeting my son, Mayo.

Later that night, around midnight when Michael Keifer came home, his usual arrival time, I related the story to him as he slipped into bed.

"That's lovely," he said, distracted, reading his paperwork.

"Michael," I said. "He actually smiled!"

For the first time I was excited about something that he and I could actually share.

"He smiled!" I repeated enthusiastically. "He smiled!"

"Adrian," he scolded. "You're disrupting my paperwork!"

"Do you know what I'm saying to you?" I asked him, irritated that he wasn't acknowledging it.

"I know that you're destroying my work!"

"Your son is coming to life, Michael," I said, exasperated. "Doesn't that mean anything to you?"

He looked at me and sighed, putting his papers down and removing his reading glasses. "Yes," he said.

But his *yes* didn't sound sincere.

It sounded obligatory.

"Michael," I said dramatically, "he said he loved the music. He used the word *love* . . ."

Michael Keifer stared blankly at me as though he had no soul. I looked into his eyes and saw no evidence at all that he was human.

"Love," he said dryly, "as I have told you so many times, is overrated."

I looked at him in disgust.

"Do you care about anything?" I asked him. "Anything at all? Give me one freaking thing you care about. This house? Your car? Your god-awful parents? The people who work for you? Your dynasty? Do you care about the money you've made? Do you care about *me*, Michael? After thirteen years of marriage, can you drum up some emotion for *me*?"

And still his expression was blank.

"Do you care about your son, Michael? Do you give a shit about your son?"

"Do you know what I care about?" he replied in a not-so-kind manner. "I care about being *right*."

My eyes widened and the hair on the back of my neck stood up.

"And right now the only thing that's going to help me be right is this goddamned paperwork, so let me get back to it. Do you mind? Can we put the evening's theatrics behind us now?"

I gave him the dirtiest look I could summon, then turned over and went to sleep.

Bastard.

The week had gone by rather quickly and before I knew it, it was Tuesday again and Mayo and I were returning to Anthem's world so he could do whatever magic he had done last week.

I must confess that the past week had been one of the most joyful I had experienced in a long time. I felt like a dead tree in winter slowly coming back to life in spring.

I went shopping and bought a new pair of jeans and a sexy little blouse. I actually took great care with my makeup and put some real work into my hair.

I always looked elegant and well put-together, but today I knew I looked my best.

"Mom," said Mayo as we drove down the expressway. "You look kind of cute today."

I almost wrecked the car.

"What?" I asked him, jaw dropped to the floor. "You think I'm *cute?*"

"Not usually," he said, "but today you're all right."

I couldn't believe my ears or eyes—my son had stopped his violent anger and was not only civil, but *kind.* It was behavior that had carried over from last week's session. The past week he had been much more gentle, but there were still moments here and there bordering on the impossible.

"You really think I'm cute?" I asked again, because I just couldn't believe it.

"Oh God, Mom," he said, rolling his eyes. "You're such a girl."

It started raining pretty hard on the way to Anthem's. It hit rather suddenly, and we weren't prepared, so by the time we got to Anthem's, we were soaked through and through.

"Come in," said Anthem, opening the door.

"Whoa," I said, taken aback. His house smelled of weed.

"Sorry, dude," he said to Mayo. "Sometimes musicians need to take a hit of something to stimulate creativity." And when I saw that smile I began to reminisce about moments we'd shared down by the lake in Milwaukee, back when living was easy, or at least appeared to be.

"An hour, right?" I asked him.

"Yeah," he said, looking at me with red-streaked eyes.

"Mayo," said Anthem, "head on back to the studio and I'll be there in a bit."

"Cool!" shouted Mayo, scurrying out of sight.

"What have you done with my son?" I asked with a smile. "I don't even recognize that little boy . . . he's actually happy to be here."

Anthem laughed.

"I mean . . . we still had some moments last week, but for the most part he seems a little more settled, after just one session."

"That's cool," said Anthem, smiling. "You don't have to leave."

"What?"

"You can hang out in here," he said. "But the studio is off limits. I'm doing the whole trust thing with Mayo right now."

"Interesting," I said, nodding my head.

"What?"

"He's never trusted anyone." I said quietly. "Does he trust you?"

"No," said Anthem, "but he trusts the music. We can build on that."

"I forgot my checkbook today," I said. "I know I owe you for the session."

"Don't worry about it," he said, eyeing me. "Looks like you're good for it."

I laughed, somewhat embarrassed.

Anthem turned to walk away, and instinctively, I grabbed his hand. He stopped, and his eyes shifted to my hand as I held onto him, and he contracted his fist around my grip.

"Thank you," I whispered, and with his free hand, he gently caressed the side of my cheek. My eyes dropped to the floor as I stood mesmerized, taking it all in, soaking it up.

I had not been touched like *this* in years. So much so that even when he pulled his hand away and walked back into the studio and shut the door, I could still feel the heat of his touch against my cheek.

I reached up to touch it back.

My cheek.

His heat.

At last.

Chapter 8

*As I descended beyond the eighth floor, I remembered the night I be-
came a thirty-two-year-old cheating virgin.*

That evening, I called Nanny Brown to come sit with Mayo
so I could return to Anthem's loft and bring him a check for the
sessions. It was about 7:00 P.M., and I knew Michael Keifer
wouldn't be home till past midnight, and I wanted to see Anthem again. I also had an urge to see him alone so I could have
a *real* conversation with him.

He answered the door looking sexy, wearing a nice blue-
collared shirt and a pair of jeans. He looked like a bad-ass music
man—a naughty boy, perhaps.

"I'm sorry," I said. "I didn't mean to intrude . . . I was just in
the neighborhood and wanted to come by and bring you a
check."

He looked surprised to see me. I hadn't let him know that I
would stop by again so soon.

I couldn't tell if the look on his face was surprise or disappointment. It could have been either.

"I ain't the man to turn down a check," he said, accepting the
money with a smile.

"Good," I said, relieved. "I really didn't mean to intrude."

"Don't be silly," he said strongly. "Money is never an intrusion."

His place seemed cozier at night. He had jazz pumping in the background and candles lit, so I thought that perhaps I was interrupting a possible romance.

He turned around and looked at me, and somehow all my defenses fell. Internally, I got the green light to speak honestly. "Why didn't you ever write me back?"

He looked at me but did not respond.

Okay.

Maybe that light wasn't so green after all . . . maybe it was yellow or red instead.

"Didn't you get my letters?"

"Yeah," he said, but offered no reply, just turned away.

"I was really crazy about you, Anthem," I said, following behind him.

"Thank you," he said, emotionally disconnected and distant, which only really made me want him more.

"I didn't just disappear," I said, my face coming close against his.

"I know," he said. "I did."

"Where did you go?"

"Texas."

"What did you do there?"

"The check is blank," he said, staring at the check I'd just handed him.

"Oh," I said in a daze. "Sorry. How much?"

"Six weeks of sessions are a grand."

"Okay," I said without a second thought, and began writing the check.

"So what were you doing in Texas?" I repeated.

No answer.

"So money's not a big deal for you?" he asked, with a charge of emotion.

"No," I replied, embarrassed. "Texas?"

"Oh . . . school," he said.

I could feel his eyes scanning the full length of me, head to toe.

"You got a lot of money, don't you?"

"I do okay."

"Whole lot, huh?" he repeated.

"Don't judge me," I said, cutting it off.

"No judgments here," he said, holding up his hands.

"You don't know my story, Anthem."

"No," he said, looking at me. "I don't know the details but it sure looks like they're written in gold."

"Haven't you heard?" I asked, tears forming in my eyes. "All that glitters is not gold."

"Sorry," he responded.

"You married?" I asked, trying to take the attention off me.

"Does it look like I'm married?" he asked, pointing to the obvious bachelor nature of his house.

"No," I said, laughing.

"Girlfriend?"

"No," he replied.

"Kids?"

"No," he said, shaking his head.

"Divorced?"

"No," he said.

"Lonely?"

He didn't respond.

"You better get going," he said. "Looks like a big storm's coming."

No sooner had he uttered the words than thunder and lightning lit up the night sky. Water poured from above like a dam had been broken, and if I weren't absolutely certain that I was indoors, I would have confused the raindrops with my tears. The ones I had never allowed myself to shed.

"Oh, boy," I said, looking out his window. "Looks really bad."

"Looks like you're trapped," he said with a sly grin. "But I'm sure you've been trapped before."

I didn't know how to respond to that comment.

"Can I stay till the storm dies down? Just a little while, and I'll be on my way."

"Suit yourself," he said, disappearing back into his studio. "I'm gonna go get high."

Well, I thought. *This is odd.*

Sometimes things don't go as you planned, and even though I wasn't expecting anything romantic, I guess I was hoping for a warmer reception.

Well, I thought again. *This is really odd.*

"You get high a lot?" I asked, standing at the door of his studio while he lit a joint.

"Enough," he said. "Takes the edge off."

"The edge of what?"

"Being a fucking hustling musician."

"A hustling musician?" I asked, in need of clarification.

"Read between the lines, rich girl," he said. "Being poor."

"Oh," I said, embarrassed.

"Struggling," he said, grabbing his guitar. "You know what I'm saying?"

"I've struggled, too, Anthem."

He looked at me good and hard, then said, "But not in a long time."

He started to play the guitar, and the melodious sounds poured throughout the room. It was inviting, even primitive.

It called me to him.

One beat at a time.

What was he playing?

What was he doing?

What was he smoking?

How was he living?

And how was he dying?

I slowly took a seat at his feet. My heart was beating so hard, my palms were sweaty.

He was playing.

Luring.

Calling me without saying my name because that's what sexy, sultry musicians who wear collar shirts and ripped jeans do. The kind that have developed backsides with wide shoulders and big, strong hands, smooth skin, and *intentions*.

Heavy.

Heavy.

Intentions.

Unpredictable.

Calling me with every pick of his acoustic guitar.

Adrian.

Adrian.

Calling me to finish what we started long ago before we were interrupted by Reva Joe and her ignorance, because the town didn't want to see my white skin against his brown skin, and because back in the day, biracial love was *not* in style.

And so I am.

Here.

Waiting for an invitation. He was lost in the music *and* the guitar, and I couldn't tell the difference between the two. I didn't know where the note ended and he began—all I really knew was that I wanted to be part of the song, and before it was all said and done, I wanted to *be* the song, especially if he was going to play it.

Play me, too.

When he realized I was mesmerized, he stopped.

"Is it okay if I sit here?" I asked.

"Yes."

I will never forget the way that word rolled off his tongue— *yes*.

And we did the dance.

The mating ritual, though I had no intention of being unfaithful to Michael. It was not motivated by some deep love or reverence for my marriage, but simply because I felt that as long as we were married I had a contractual obligation to honor my word.

I belonged to him like high-priced real estate.

He paid.

I stayed.

And the rest was ancient history.

Thirteen years' worth, to be exact.

"You're still as beautiful as you were the last time I saw you," he said, strumming gently under his words.

"Thank you," I said, blushing. "You're not so bad yourself."

He put out the joint and lit a cigarette.

"Wow," I said. "It doesn't stop . . ."

"Never does," he said.

"Got any more bad habits?"

"I gamble," he said, taking a hit.

"How much?"

"Couple grand a month."

"Is that a problem?"

"Only when I'm losing," he said.

"Anything else?"

"I get high every day," he said.

"Anything else?"

"I'll cheat you right out of your tits," he said with a laugh.

"Anything else I should know?"

"I'm a slut, too," he stated emphatically.

"Your marketability is dropping."

"But you still want me," he said with confidence.

"How do you know?" I asked. Actually, he was right, even though everything he was saying was disgusting to me. I did still want him, which was a true indication of just how desperate I was.

"Because everybody does," he said.

"Everybody does what?"

"Want me."

"Cocky," I stated.

"Confident," he rebutted.

I nodded.

"It started on the road," he said. "Playing in these dives all around the country."

"What started on the road?"

"Every bad habit I got . . . cigarettes, pot, gambling, women . . ."

"How long have you lived in Chicago?"

"About a year," he said, taking a drag off the cigarette. "You?"

"Thirteen years," I said. "Came right after high school. Went to school for a year. Met a guy. Got married. Never went back to school. You know . . . classic Cinderella tale."

"Fairy tale?" he asked.

"Dreams that start out like fairy tales," I said, looking down, "usually end up like nightmares."

"From the looks of your life," he said casually, "that's the kind of nightmare I'd like to have."

"You don't know anything about me."

"I know you're rich as shit," he said.

"And how do you *know* that, Anthem?"

"Heard it through the grapevine," he said.

"What do you mean?" I asked defensively.

"Word travels fast in small towns."

"Chicago's not that small."

"It's smaller than you think it is," he assured me. "Are you ashamed of being married to one of the richest men in the state?"

"Oh," I said. "I see you've done your research."

"Maybe."

"It's funny," I said, shaking my head.

"What's funny?"

"You think how I *used* to think," I said.

"And how is that?"

"That money could solve all of my problems, and that if I could get enough pennies in my savings I'd be set free."

"Listen," said Anthem, "I ain't never said money can solve *all* of your problems, but it can sure clear up a whole lot of them."

"You're just like the rest," I said, disappointed, getting up to look out the window and stare at the pouring rain. "I'm just like you, Anthem. I hurt. I bleed. I'm human."

"Yeah," he said. "I guess there's only one difference between you and me . . ."

"What?"

"You're rich," he said with a snicker. "And I'm not. But hey, what's a billion dollars between friends?"

I stood at the window, staring outside as the rain poured down in buckets, and my eyes filled with tears.

I turned around and he was standing in front of me, in my personal space.

"I don't have a billion dollars," I said.

"Don't sweat it, Adrian . . . I won't hold it against you. The rich and the poor meet here for a little love and happiness."

I smiled.

He smiled.

And for a beat of time, there was an awkward silence. I looked at him, he looked at me, and for a moment we both seemed transparent. Somewhere in that transparency, the rain stopped falling.

"It stopped," I whispered.

"Yeah," he whispered back.

"Guess I should be going."

"Yeah," he said, towering over me.

We stared into each other's eyes and I could feel his energy envelop me. He reached out his hand, touched me, and I reached back. With our hands intertwined, we began to caress one another.

It was so intense.

My skin began to tingle.

He kissed me on the cheek, as I allowed my head to fall backwards.

"So beautiful," he said gently into my ear. "You're so beautiful."

He embraced me and I wrapped my arms around his tall, sculpted body. I could feel the rippling of the skin on his back.

He locked me inside his arms and I could feel the energy between us. I held on because I didn't want to let go. And for the first time in what seemed like ages, or maybe even a lifetime, I felt completely human.

His lips found their way from my cheek to my lips and once they did, he kissed me long and passionately. I could feel my knees quiver and weaken. Eventually, we locked tongues. He moved in closer as his hands began their ascent and descent, up

and down my spine. He rubbed aggressively, heating up my
back.

I moved in closer, so close that I could feel the muscles beneath his clothing. Within moments we were pressed against
one another with such ferocity that there was no room left to
breathe.

"Can't go any further than this," I said, breathless.

"Why?" he asked.

"I'm married."

"Okay," he said.

"In about ninety seconds, I'm going to go."

"Okay," he said.

"This is wrong, isn't it?"

"Feels right enough to me."

"I'm a wife."

"You're a woman," he countered.

"I'm human."

"You're divine."

Somewhere between one last kiss and intending to go home,
I began to tug at my shirt, trying to get it off. Next thing I knew,
I was standing in the middle of his studio with my bra, jeans,
and blouse on the floor. The rain had begun again, so I had no
choice but to talk myself into staying "a little longer." Soon, he
began to play with my nipples, circling them gently with his fingers. My body was responding of its own accord. It was a sensation I had never quite felt before.

Within minutes, we had removed all our clothing and were
fondling one another intensely.

He dropped to his knees, parted my legs, and pleasured me
in a way I'd never known before.

It felt so unbelievably good, and I was actually surprised that
I was allowing myself so much freedom.

I felt as though my knees might give way. He gently laid me
down and continued—within two minutes I experienced a sensation that I had never known in my life.

It was a *gigantic* release.

My first orgasm.

Michael Keifer had never concerned himself with my pleasure long enough to extend me the courtesy of an orgasm. It was an intense and violent contraction of muscles somewhere deep within me.

I arched my back.

I screamed.

He held me.

I cried.

We stopped.

He began to kiss me gently, my navel, stomach, and breasts. And with his tender affection, I came to life again.

I opened my legs to experience it more fully, and that is when he mounted and penetrated me.

I gasped.

And moaned, continuing to allow it to be. It felt good, the authentic joy of pure connection. Even if it was only a glimpse into my past, with a boy I used to know who had fallen by the wayside years ago, and who was now a man with a lot of dirty habits that up until five minutes ago I would have stood in judgment of, now I was a part of him, and felt just as naughty as I imagined he did.

Together we found a rhythm very quickly. We had done this before, if not in this life, then surely in another. I was certain of it.

Our bodies moved in sync, slow then quicker, till he worked his way up to a pleasurable frenzy, exploding inside of me. When it was all said and done, there was an *inevitable* moment of awkwardness as he rolled over and off me, and we lay side by side. He reached over and grabbed a cigarette, lit it, and began smoking.

Bad boys never change.

He made rings with the smoke, filling the air with them. I started to choke.

"Sorry," he said, putting out the cigarette.

"It's okay."

"What are you thinking about?"

"I don't know," I responded quietly.

"Regrets?"

"Never."

"You ever cheated before?"

"No."

"Has he ever cheated?"

"Probably," I said without great emotion. "But not with his heart."

"How do you know?"

"He doesn't have one," I stated emphatically. "*Everything* is business with Michael. If it doesn't serve him, it doesn't matter."

"Do you serve him?" he asked, looking into my eyes.

"Thirteen years of service," I said, heavy-hearted.

"So I take it you're not digging the gig?"

The look in my eyes told a thousand truths.

"Then why stay?"

"He takes good care of me," I said. "Have you ever been married?"

"Never," he said dramatically.

"Why?" I asked, curious to hear his response.

"House of pain," he said. "Who needs it?"

"That's a sad outlook on life," I said. "It doesn't have to be like that."

He started to laugh.

"Women who live in golden castles shouldn't venture down to the slums and tell the peasants how to live."

"I don't live in a golden castle," I said defensively. "And this is a far cry from a slum."

"You're defensive about having money," he said.

"You're defensive about *not*," was my response.

"Touché."

"I should be going," I said, standing up and putting my clothes back on.

"Yeah," he said. "It's about that time. The ivory tower awaits you."

"You got it wrong, Anthem," I said, under the weight of a great deal of emotion. "I'm miserable."

"Then get the hell out."

"It's not so easy," I said, frustrated. "Where would I go?"

"Anywhere you want. You're married to a man with a zillion dollars. Take the kid and run. Get paid."

"I can't."

"Why?" he asked.

"It's complicated."

"I don't know how hard it could be to pack a bag, load up the kid, put the car in reverse, and back the hell out of the driveway."

"This is my *life* you're talking about," I said.

"Exactly," he said. "All the more reason to take it seriously."

The words echoed back to me on the drive back home.

This is my life.

This is my life.

My life.

Exactly.

I felt odd.

Guilty, yet exhilarated.

Free.

Yet caged.

I felt disconnected and unlike myself. I had actually cheated on my husband but I didn't feel bad. I had cheated on my husband with a bad boy.

Actually, I didn't feel anything, which made me feel something, and that kind of made me feel bad.

I had no emotional connection to Michael Keifer, and sadly, I had very little, if any, emotional connection to my son. I felt like a stranger, a visitor to a foreign land, despite a lavish lifestyle.

So, I cheated. The only regret I had was that I did not do it sooner.

So what?

Had my first orgasm and lost my virginity tonight. What did that make me?

A thirty-two-year-old cheating virgin.

I arrived close to the ten o'clock hour and Michael Keifer was already home, which surprised me.

I entered the house where he was already in bed, wearing his silk robe, a pile of papers sprawled over the bedding.

When I entered, his eyes cut sharply to me.

"Where were you?" he asked with a tone.

"Got caught in the storm downtown and had to wait it out," I said, barely able to hold eye contact with him, trying like hell to pull it off. As I scurried across the room, I could feel the weight of his gaze upon me.

"What were you doing out in the storm?"

"It wasn't storming when I left," I said. "I went to pay for Mayo's lessons at the studio and . . ." my voice trailed off. I didn't feel like lying, so I replaced my words with silence.

"I sent Mrs. Brown home," he said. "Her corns were aching. She spent thirty minutes telling me about her corns and bunions. I didn't want to hear about corns and bunions. I don't care about corns and bunions."

"Okay," I replied, grabbing my nightgown. "I'm going to take a shower . . . I got hammered in the storm."

"I thought you waited it out *indoors*?"

"I did."

"Inconsistent."

"Why are you cross-examining me?" I asked. "I'm not on your witness stand."

"Inconsistencies," he stated flatly.

"What do you mean by that?" I asked, irritated.

"Your behavior is inconsistent this evening. It is the opposite of your typical behavior, which leads me to further examination."

"Well," I said sarcastically, "I'm living on the *edge* tonight!"

"I would mind my tone if I were you," he cautioned.

"Well . . . I'm not a pet or a child—therefore, I see no grand benefit in *monitoring my tone*," I replied mockingly.

"No," he said, "but you do exist in very fine fashion on the grace of my courtesy."

I looked at him and anger rose in my eyes.

"Why do you always feel the need to remind me?"

"Of what?"

"That *I* don't exist outside of this arrangement. That you are the force by which the sun shines on me, and the rain pours on me."

I walked over to his pants and pulled his driver's license from his wallet.

"What are you doing?" he asked.

"Just checking the name on your license."

"You already know my name! You're being ridiculous!"

I paused a beat in heavy contemplation. "No," I said. "For a second I thought it might have read, *God*."

I quickly withdrew into the bathroom and showered.

I tried to stay there as long as I could, hoping he would be asleep when I was done, but he wasn't, of course. He was sitting in the same stiff position.

I got in the bed in silence.

I turned over, closed my eyes, and was on the verge of sleep when I heard him speak.

"You smell like smoke," he said.

My eyes opened and I stared at the wall.

"Why do you think that is?" he asked.

"Because I was in a room where people were smoking," I said, greatly irritated.

"You should keep better company," he said. "Smoking can be hazardous to your health."

I kept my eyes steady on the wall without responding. He tapped me on the shoulder.

"I need a release," he said.

"Michael," I said, exhausted by it all. "I'm really tired."

"I need a release," he repeated.

"Tomorrow."

"Tonight," he insisted.

"I'm too tired."

"Have I ever said I was too tired to pay for all of the things you like to buy? Have I ever been too tired to fund the checks you write?" he asked. "Spa trips, jewelry, shopping sprees."

I sat up in the bed, exhausted and sad.

"Sometimes," I said, looking into his eyes, "I think I hate you."

"Well," he said, undoing his robe, "hate and love are both mute emotions, and neither of them means anything to me."

"They mean something to me!" I declared.

"You climbed out of a sewer and have spent the better part of thirteen years living like a queen. The only meaning you should be concerned with is how well you mean to please me tonight."

He stood up, then dropped to his knees on the bed, inserting his erect penis into my face.

Honestly, I wanted to bite his dick off, but it would be bad press for the family if I did that. So, I obliged him and gave him what he wanted, a release.

A gigantic.

Violent.

Release.

When it was over, he watched.

He always watched, and waited.

Waiting for me to do that thing which brought him so much pleasure.

Swallow.

And I did.

Swallowed.

And barely kept from gagging. Desensitized, I rolled over and went to sleep with his cum on top and Anthem's cum down below.

The two would never meet.

Or be friends.

Just distant strangers.

Chapter 7

As I descended beyond the seventh floor, I remembered the day I met Lucifer.

I drove Mayo to school the next morning, spacey and disoriented, obsessing over thoughts of Anthem, feeling him deep inside of me.

Penetrating.

Concentrating.

Emancipation.

"Early dismissal today, Mom," said Mayo as he sat in the passenger's seat.

"Huh?" I said, barely acknowledging him.

"Early dismissal," he said again.

"Okay," I whispered.

"I need lunch money, Mom" he said, holding out his hand.

"Huh?"

"I need LUNCH money!" he said loudly.

"Okay . . . okay," I said, zombie-like. "Get twenty dollars out of my purse."

"When is my next lesson with Anthem?"

I didn't respond.

"Hey!" he shouted, jarring me back to real life.

"Mayo," I scolded. There was that angry kid again.

"You're not LISTENING to me!" he shouted. "Where are you?"

"Mayo," I said, "lower your voice."

"Listen—DEAF!" he screamed.

"Don't you dare talk to me like that!" I shouted, gripping the steering wheel intensely.

"Then don't be DEAF!" he shouted.

I pulled up in front of the school and slammed on the brakes, sending him forward in his seat.

"Get out!" I shouted. "Out! Now!"

He opened the door, looked back at me, and cried, "Loser!"

"What did you just say?" I screamed.

He slammed the door.

"Shit!" I screamed.

Shit!

Shit!

I pulled off, skidding and fishtailing, jumped on the expressway, and headed straight for downtown Chicago.

I landed on Anthem's front doorstep, a million-dollar orphan.

I knocked, unannounced.

He answered, unprepared.

"What's up?" he asked, looking at me strangely. He looked like he was in the middle of something important and I was in the middle of interrupting it.

"Are you busy?"

"In the middle of something," he snapped.

And suddenly, I felt small and intrusive. I was not as welcome as I thought I would be. As welcome as a girl who had just had the best sex of her life with the sexiest man in Chicago.

"Sorry," I replied meekly, turning away. "It was a mistake."

"Hold up!" he said. "Where you going?"

"You're busy, right?" I asked, turning back to him.

"Yeah," he said.

"So I'll come back later."

"Come back *now*," he said with a hint of smooth and sexy.

I walked inside his place and as soon as he shut the door and our eyes locked, I began to take off my clothing.

Stripped.

He embraced me wildly, grabbing, caressing, fondling, exploring, and expecting.

I couldn't wait for him to be inside of me. I wanted to experience the fullness of him again.

"Put it inside!" I screamed.

Inside.

Inside.

But he was a tease and unwilling to accommodate me at the moment. And to my chagrin, I was growing rather impatient.

"Inside!"

"Inside!"

"Wait," he whispered. "Wait."

"No," I howled.

"I just want to look at your fine white ass," he said. "Yeah . . . I used to call you 'Dove.' Pretty white thing," he said, caressing my naked body with his hands. "So pretty you could fucking fly . . . fucking fly, man."

I was so taken by his comment that I stopped and just looked at him.

"Are you serious?" I asked with great surprise.

"Yeah," he said, staring at my naked body. "I don't just wanna fuck you, Adrian," he said. "I wanna connect with you," he said sincerely.

"Connect?" I asked. "What do you mean by that?"

"Feel your spirit . . ."

"I don't think I have one," I said, confused.

"Then you're in fucking trouble," he said. "Do you know what I call someone without a spirit?"

"What?"

"*Dead,*" he said. "You used to have passion behind those beautiful blue eyes. You were so full of life. What happened to you, Dove?"

Tears began to form.

"Grew up," I whispered. "Married a man I didn't really love.

Had a child I don't feel at all connected with . . . became part of a community I have no affection for."

"That doesn't sound like growing up to me," he said. "That sounds like selling out."

"I don't need *anything*," I said with so much conviction, I almost believed it myself.

"Yeah . . . only difference is, now you want for *everything*," he said. "Shame . . . you really coulda flown . . ."

And in that moment I knew it. It was not as if I had not known it before, but now it was just harder to run.

The morning passed us by, and the funny thing was, we never got around to sex. Instead, I exchanged it for something a little deeper—real conversation.

I hadn't felt connected to anything or anyone in so long.

Anthem wasn't the kind of guy I would ever meet in my circle. He wasn't wealthy, or important. And since he wasn't, I had always thought, *why waste the time?*

But oh, how wrong I was.

I'd almost forgotten how beautiful being human could be.

Naked, I lay on Anthem's floor, facedown. He rubbed my back and it felt so good, I fell asleep. He fell asleep beside me, arms wrapped around me, until I was shaken awake by the blare of his cell phone.

"What time is it?" I asked, groggy and disoriented.

"It's three," he said, slowly coming to life.

"Shit!" I screamed. "Mayo!"

"What?"

"He got out of school early today . . . and . . ." I said, leaping up and scrambling to put on my clothes. "Shit! Shit! Shit!"

"Adrian, calm down," said Anthem. "It's going to be okay."

"No! It's not going to be okay!" I screamed. "My son got out of school two hours ago!"

"Can't you call somebody?" he asked. "Don't you have a nanny?"

"Doesn't work like that . . . I pick him up! Me! It's my responsibility!"

I didn't register the balance of the conversation as I was already out the door and down the hallway before another word was said.

I bolted out the door and into my car where I saw seven missed messages on my cell.

"Shit!" I screamed.

I threw the car into drive and sped my way through downtown traffic, which was heavy in the congested area where Anthem lived.

I sped through stop signs and crosswalks, zigzagged through traffic jams, and even managed a couple of turns on two wheels in a mad rush to the expressway.

I tried calling the school on my cell phone, but got no answer.

I tried Nanny Brown and still no answer.

I did 110 on the expressway and made it to Mayo's school in exactly 22 minutes. As I pulled up, Mayo was getting into Michael Keifer's mother's car.

"Oh God," I thought. "There she goes—Jean Cage, the original Monster-in-Law."

I beeped the horn and pulled up alongside her Mercedes.

"Hi, Jean," I said, rolling down the window, trying to keep my composure. "I'm really, really sorry . . . got held up in a meeting."

Brutal eyes staring back at me.

Mayo looked at me with something resembling hate as Jean peered through eyes of intense disapproval.

"He was waiting two hours!" snapped Jean in her usual judgmental tone. "That's unacceptable, Adrian."

"I know . . . I know," I said apologetically. "I'm sorry, Mayo. Mommy got held up at a meeting and lost track of time. If you could find it in your heart to forgive me . . ."

"Grandma," Mayo said to Jean, "I want to go to your house."

"Okay, darling," Jean replied, cutting her eyes to me.

"Next time, honey," I said to Mayo, shouting over Jean. "We really need to go home and get dinner prepared!"

"I don't want to go with her!" he screamed.

"He'll have dinner at my house," said Jean.

"No," I said sternly. "He'll have dinner at home."

"He doesn't want to go with you," said Jean. "Let him come over and I'll have Michael pick him up later."

"No," I said, almost in a panic. I didn't want Michael to know what happened, though he probably already did. That being said, my immediate future consisted of a whole lot of doom and drama.

"Jean," I said more intently. "He needs to come home with me now. This is nonnegotiable. I am his mother."

"Sad but true," she said with a sigh. "Mayo . . ."

"No, Grandma!" he protested. "I don't want to go home with her! She's crazy!"

"Mayo!" I shouted, getting out of the car. "You're coming with me!"

"No!" he screamed.

Jean's eyes widened as I ran to the passenger's side, opened the door, and began to pull Mayo, kicking and screaming, out of the car.

"Oh my God!" screamed Jean, hands on her forehead. "What in God's name are you doing to him?"

"Get out of the car!" I shouted, pulling him harder

"Grandma!" he screamed, holding onto the sides of the door.

"Oh God!" screamed Jean. "Let him be!"

"You're coming home for dinner!" I screamed.

"I don't want to go anywhere with you! I hate you!" he screamed.

"Let him be!" screamed Jean. "Let him be!"

"I hate you!" he kept shouting.

Hate you.

Hate you.

"Mayo, stop it!" I screamed. "Stop it!"

I literally picked him up off the ground and carried him to my Mercedes, opened the door, strapped him inside, put the child safety locks on, and shut the door.

I walked around and got in the driver's seat, and once I shut the door, he began to fight me. And something happened in that moment: I lost it, snapped, came completely undone. And I began to punch him back.

Hard.

Hard.

And harder.

I hit him so hard he was sucked back into his seat by the velocity. And then he stopped moving, eyes wide with shock and disbelief. He was as surprised as I.

No one moved.

Or said a word.

I glanced up and allowed my eyes to meet with the horrified gaze of the outside world. It was the combined reaction of all the people who had never lived a single day of my life, united in condemnation.

I saw teachers at the school, and people driving by in their cars, staring. I saw them all taking notes, potentially to be used in a court of law, about the event that would eventually come into question: the "vicious beating" of my son. A single act, which the world would hold against me forever. They were all watching, mesmerized.

Jean's face was pale, drained of color, and she had tears in her eyes, horrified, as she stared at me.

I looked as though I had been in a train wreck. My hair, which had been in an elegant updo, was now half down and falling around my face.

My shirt had been ripped and part of it was hanging off my shoulder.

I was exhausted.

Tattered.

Wrecked.

The silence in the car and on the street was deafening.

I slowly turned and drove away, with the weight of the world on me, as I rounded the corner and disappeared from sight.

By the time I made it home, Michael Keifer had already arrived. Obviously, he had been well informed by his mother.

When I turned into the drive and saw his big black four-door

Mercedes parked crooked, I knew that the angled car was a reflection of just how angry he was.

"Shit," I said out loud.

Mayo was practically catatonic in the seat beside me.

As I pulled up beside Michael's Mercedes and put the car in park, this was the first time I wanted to run away from home.

I wanted to deposit Mayo at the front door, pull off, and drive into the sunset, never to be seen again. When Michael Keifer opened the door and bolted out onto the front steps, in that moment I honestly wanted to kill myself.

It wasn't worth it to go through what was about to happen to me. Mayo burst open the car door and ran into his father's arms. It could have been a Hallmark moment if this was not about to become the biggest nightmare of my life. Just as I got out of the car, Michael's parents, Jean and Alfred, pulled up behind me.

Michael walked Mayo to their car, where he bent down and proceeded to have a four-minute private conversation with his parents, which didn't seem so private at all. Obviously, they were discussing the most appropriate manner in which to punish me and make my life even more miserable.

I paused for a moment and looked at them. Michael Keifer bent over the driver's side, engaging Alfred and Jean in theatrical conversation.

Mayo, the great victim, was standing behind his father.

Michael Keifer, the hard-working, brilliant knight-in-shining-armor who rescued me, the Milwaukee peasant, eternally unworthy even to be in their presence.

Michael opened their door and Mayo got in the backseat, and in that moment they all paused and looked up at me. Our eyes met in intense hatred—me for them and them for me.

I had never felt like such an outsider.

I turned around in anger, went into the house, and shut the door.

I withdrew to the upstairs bath where I sat on the toilet, bawling uncontrollably. When Michael Keifer returned to the house, he slammed the front door so hard, I heard it all the way upstairs.

"Adrian!" he shouted, running up the stairs, going from room to room on a rampage, searching for me.

"Adrian!"

"Adrian!"

Slowly, I emerged from the other end of the house, only to meet his perspiration-drenched face, beet-red with anger.

"What the hell is wrong with you?" he screamed.

"Don't scream at me!" I shouted. "I've been through enough today!"

"Are you going to stand there and make this all about you?" he shouted. "You left your son standing on a street corner for two hours!"

"I didn't do it on purpose!"

"It's inexcusable! What the fuck is wrong with you?"

"I lost track of time!"

"You must have lost your mind!" he shouted. "And to make matters worse, you beat him in the car while the whole world watched!"

"He was hitting me, Michael . . . I was trying to get him under control!"

"He's ten years old, for God's sake!" he yelled. "If you can't control a ten-year-old, that's pretty goddamned pathetic!"

"Well, you try it!" I screamed. "You try taking care of a violent, angry kid who hates your guts!"

"You should have joined the theater like your crazy, impoverished father! All I ever get from you is dramatics!"

"You don't understand what my life is like!"

"It's rich!" he shouted. "You crazy bitch . . . you have the mentality of a poor nigger!"

"Oh my God!" I said, horrified by his bigoted comment. "I can't believe you, Michael Keifer Cage."

"What more do you want?" he asked. "You want for nothing! You have everything, Adrian Cage. Do you know what the official definition of everything is? *Everything!* You're a beautiful Caucasian female with sky-blue eyes living the American dream in the greatest country in the world! You live in the biggest house in Hoffman Estates, married to one of the top criminal attorneys in the country! People would kill to live like you for one day! How can you be so ungrateful?"

"And if they did live like me for one day, Michael," I said in a lowered voice, "they would see just how overrated the American dream is!"

"I gave you everything," he said.

"I don't have *everything!* So if you truly gave it to me, *where the fuck is it?*" I shouted so loud I almost broke the glass in the window. "I don't have LOVE, Michael! I'm talking real, honest-to-God, jaw-dropping, breathtaking, I-could-die-tonight-and-it-would-be-all-right kind of love! I want to be breathed back to life again. I want to wake up with a song in my heart and go to bed with a smile on my face."

He threw up his hands, cutting me off.

"I could choke to death listening to this idiocy," he said. "Thirteen years of luxury have made your mind painfully dull. I cannot believe what a goddamned idiot you are!" he shouted. "You were Milwaukee trash when I took you in off the street. I rescued you from a life of poverty . . . waitress jobs, and low-life losers with bad credit who would have set you up in a trailer park to live out your days on welfare. I delivered you from a hand-to-mouth existence, brought you to Hoffman Estates, gave you a name, and made you somebody."

"How much?" I asked with hatred in my eyes. "How much?"

"What?" he asked, surprised by my question.

"I want you to tell me how much I owe you because I am SICK to death of owing you! I have spent the last thirteen years of my life trying to pay off an *inexhaustible* debt! It's like I'm having a nightmare that everyone thinks is a fairy tale! Well, here's a news flash for you . . . not every pretty place is a fairy tale! And not every man with money should call himself wealthy. You're not rich, Michael—you just have money. And the saddest part is, you don't even know the difference."

I turned and began my retreat down the hall, but he grabbed my arm.

"If this happens again," he said menacingly, "I will pack your things in a trash bag and throw you out of here! I will excom-

municate you. You won't see a goddamned penny. Do you understand me? I will take Mayo and you'll never see him again!"

"Is that right?" I asked, challenging him with my eyes.

"I want you to know just how right it is," he said, in a deep,
threatening voice. "I will personally escort you to hell."

"Don't you dare threaten me," I said.

"No threat," he said, turning away. "This is as real as the
devil himself. Push me and you *will* meet Lucifer. I'll see to it."

Chapter 6

As I descended beyond the sixth floor, I remembered the day my life fell to the ground, shattered to pieces, and burned to ash.

The next morning Michael Keifer woke up very early. He usually woke at five, but this morning he got up at 4:00 A.M., showered, and left.

We did not exchange words.

Gestures.

Even looks.

I pretended to be asleep and as soon as he left the house, I got up, showered, and left, backing my Mercedes out of the driveway at dawn. Blazing out of the gates of Hoffman Estates, I headed straight for the expressway and downtown, where I must have sat in my car for two hours, waiting outside of Anthem's loft for a respectable hour so I could knock on his door.

At around 8:30 A.M., Anthem came outside looking as though he was on his way for a jog, but when he saw me, he stopped.

I slowly got out of my car and approached him, and from his point of view, I can just imagine how desperate and pathetic I must have looked.

My feet were heavy and so was my heart.

My life was unrecognizable to me.

My son was gone.

My husband and I were at war.

I was having an affair with a fantasy from childhood, a man who I really didn't know at all, except through the vague memory of a fourteen-year-old girl who liked pretty things.

My DNA was changing.

I couldn't be that little girl chained in the ivory tower anymore.

I could feel wings growing down the center of my back—they were starting to flutter, and I was preparing to fly. For the first time, I was about to leave the ground, but I also knew that these so-called *new* wings had been there all the time, waiting patiently to propel me into flight. And all I had to do was turn around and look. *They were always there.*

When I finally made it across the street and met Anthem face-to-face, there was silence. In a loving gesture, he ran one of his hands along the side of my face; the simple touch evoked tears. They fell down my cheeks one by one and Anthem wiped them all away.

I felt as though I were being brought closer to my own humanity, just feeling him touch me.

I had been missing this feeling, this moment, all of my life.

"The ivory tower cracked," I whispered.

"What does that mean?"

"I want to fly," I said, laying my head on his chest. He wrapped his arms around me and, for a moment, I felt complete and whole.

For the first time in my life, I *felt* rich.

"Let's take a walk," he suggested.

And we did, holding hands.

Talking.

Eventually he had me laughing about everything and nothing, all at the same time. And I was able to look at him and appreciate his simple ways.

He wasn't a man of great means. He didn't have an extensive vocabulary, and I doubt he had any education beyond high school. He was a brilliant musician, but I doubted he would ever live any better than he did now. There would be no material riches, no gated estates or exotic travel in Anthem's world.

There would be no claim to fame.

He smoked, gambled, partied, and didn't seem to be particularly connected to any one thing, except his music.

In essence, he seemed like a true loner. He was a lot like me, and there was something about *him* that actually understood *me*.

This beautiful black man understood me beneath the white of my skin, the blue of my eyes, and the richness of my lifestyle.

He understood.

We took safe harbor in a park, where we sat under a tree and I lay in his arms. He kissed me gently on the back of my neck, caressing and teasing the tender spots with his tongue.

"Run away from home," he suggested.

"Yeah, right," I said. "Where would I go?"

"What are you waiting for?"

"I don't know. Where are *you* going?"

"With you," he said in jest.

"Great," I said sarcastically. "Two lost people."

"Speak for yourself," he said. "Ain't shit wrong with me. I always know where I'm going."

"You always know where you're going?"

"Yeah," he said. "That's 'cause I always know where I'm *at*," he replied. "Figure that out and the rest is easy, baby."

"Who are you, Anthem?" I asked, turning around, looking into his eyes.

"Just a guy."

"Why didn't you marry?"

"That's a loaded question," he said with a smile.

"No," I said. "I really want to know. Why?"

"'Cause," he said, "I never loved anybody before."

"You've never been in love?"

"You sound so surprised."

"But you're so beautiful," I said, caressing his face with my hands. "I know . . . beauty and love aren't twins, are they?"

"Not even distant cousins," he replied.

"You've really never been in love?"

"I'm a musician," he said. "We don't fall in love."

"Do all musicians have a lot of sex?"

"Only the good ones," he said with a smile.

I playfully punched him in the chest.

"What's the deal with you and your mom?"

His eyes cut a piercing look to me. "Why you asking about her?"

"You don't talk, do you?"

"You a psychic or some shit?"

"No," I said. "Just got a feeling."

"We're in two different worlds," he said.

"You're 81 miles apart."

"We're a whole hell of a lot farther apart than that," he said. "Let's go grab some food," he suggested, changing the subject quickly. "You hungry?"

"Yeah," I said with a smile. "That actually sounds really good."

We ventured to a café and eventually went back to his loft, where we napped and made love the rest of the afternoon. I felt free from the relentless daily obligations of wife and mother.

There were no errands to run for Michael Keifer.

No household to organize.

No dealings with Mayo.

I was certain Michael Keifer's busybody mother was all too pleased to take care of him for a few days, and while she was at it, slander my name all over Hoffman Estates.

I fell asleep in Anthem's arms and by the time I woke up it was early evening. Time to leave the fantasy and return to the real world.

"I have to go," I said, rising sluggishly from the makeshift bed we had created on the floor.

"Stay," he said.

"I can't."

"Why?"

"Michael's going to be home soon," I said. "And I haven't been there all day."

"What if you *were* gone all day?"

"It just doesn't look good," I said, snapping on my bra and sliding into my jeans.

"Why do you live like that?"

"Please, Anthem," I said. "I can't go through this right now."

He looked away, obviously disturbed.

"Anthem," I said. "I'm married."

He got up and went into the bathroom, closed the door, and turned on the shower.

He didn't say good-bye.

And I didn't bother to knock on the door and say good-bye, either. I don't know what he wanted, but whatever it was, I couldn't give it to him.

I was married with a kid, and granted, though my world was slowly unraveling, I still felt obligated to do the dance.

I wasn't ready to be a divorced woman with a child, responsible for doing it all on my own. I didn't feel strong enough for that yet.

Michael Keifer had always taken very good care of me, and I had grown accustomed to being taken care of.

Right or wrong.

Good or bad.

The ivory tower may have been the loneliest place on Earth, but at least the view from that part of the world was spectacular. I wasn't ready to return to the land of the common people. I had been gone for so, so long.

The drive home was intense.

I was dreading the possibility of another confrontation with Michael. All was far from well in never-never land, and last time I checked, the prince and I weren't even speaking. I was reluctant to hear the horrific details of Mayo's return, and God knows I couldn't bear a parental lecture from the all-wise, all-knowing, omnipotent Jean Cage.

My heart was heavy as I entered Hoffman Estates. It was home to many sprawling gated homes, gorgeous architecture, bubbling fountains, fine automobiles, and maidservants.

It was the enchanted place where perfect families dwelled,

those whose real claim to fame was their unnerving ability to disguise dysfunction beneath stocks, bonds, cash, and collateral.

As I approached our estate, my stomach knotted and tightened. My underarms perspired profusely, and my forehead began to bead with sweat.

I pulled into the driveway and when the gate opened, I saw the front door of our home standing wide open.

"What's going on?" I asked out loud.

Michael Keifer's Mercedes was parked at a bizarre angle in the driveway again, which prevented me from pulling my car beside his.

Jean and Alfred Cage were standing on my doorstep, their Mercedes still running.

"Uh-oh," I said to myself. "Something's going on."

I had no idea that I was about to have an encounter that would change my life forever.

The first taste of my own death.

I put the car in park and slowly emerged, looking around cautiously for clues.

Michael Keifer came to the front door carrying three large, black, plastic trash bags. When I looked into his eyes, I saw the devil himself, the cast of his blue eyes having faded to black.

He dropped the bags at the bottom of the steps.

Alfred and Jean looked at me with great disgust.

"What's going on?" I asked him. "Where's Mayo?"

Alfred and Jean turned their backs on me, went inside, and shut the door.

Michael Keifer brought out one more black trash bag and set it on the doorstep.

"What's going on, Michael?" I asked him, surveying the trash bags. He handed me a brown envelope, which I opened, and when I did, I almost passed out.

The envelope contained several black-and-white photos of Anthem and me in the park from earlier that day, kissing, holding hands, and lying in one another's arms.

I turned pale.

I looked down.

Ashamed.

"Your things are in these bags," he said.

"Michael," I said desperately. "Please."

"Be on your way," he said. "It's done."

"Michael, please . . ." I begged.

"I want you off this property NOW before I call the police," he said.

"This is MY home, too!" I screamed. "Where's Mayo?"

"He doesn't want to see you, Adrian," said Michael. "Don't make a scene. Get your things and get the hell out of here!"

"Mayo!" I screamed, running toward the door.

I tried to turn the door and go inside, but it was locked. I could see Jean and Alfred watching through a window on the other side.

"Mayo!" I said, banging on the door. "What are you doing!" I screamed at Michael. "You can't do this!"

"I want you off this property!" he yelled.

I started banging violently on the front door, screaming, completely out of control.

Mayo!

Mayo!

Mayo!

Michael Keifer body-slammed me down to the ground, picked me up by the back of the neck, and escorted me down to my car.

"Get in your car and get out of here!" he yelled.

"You can't do this to me!" I screamed. "That is *my* son!"

I tried to fight him, kicking, swinging, but I was too weak and he was too filled with rage and vengeance.

I kicked him in the shin, bit his arm, and he fell to the ground. I jumped on top of him and we began to wrestle in the middle of the driveway. He head-butted me and the pain seared through my body.

It was outrageous, the sensation in my nose. It felt broken and started to bleed violently. Just at that moment, one of our neighbors, who just happened to be the president of a huge law firm, drove by with his lovely, charming wife in their fine Mercedes with their two adorable, robotlike, perfect children sitting in the backseat, witnessing it all.

The Mercedes slowed down as they all stared, aghast. *Could this really be Michael Keifer Cage, our elegant next-door neighbor and frequent golf partner, rolling around on the cement in a three-thousand-dollar suit, kicking the shit out of his poor, helpless wife?*

I will never forget the horrified look on their faces as they passed us by. The man wanted to help, but I think he was probably confused. Should he run to the aid of his prestigious attorney friend or forsake him for the wife who was being beaten, thrown out of her house, and humiliated in public?

I guess it didn't really matter because once he saw the photos, he would probably join in and beat me as well.

"You fucking whore!" Michael screamed at me. "You fucking, fucking whore!"

Bloody.

Exhausted.

Humiliated.

Devastated.

Horrified.

Terrified.

The scene was so outlandish and out of character for this perfect, beautiful place. The sun was just beginning to set and it was a gorgeous evening, so beautiful that in fact, it just didn't seem real.

Couldn't be.

I had to be dreaming this nightmare, and all I wanted to do was wake up and go back to the ivory tower. I knew it wasn't perfect there, but at least it was safe.

Miserable, perhaps, but filled to the brim with predictability, and that's what I wanted.

Predictability.

The predictability of a new Mercedes each year and a clothing allowance that supported my $5,000-a-week habit.

Massages.

Facials.

Jewelry.

Housekeepers.

Nannies.

The predictability bored me to tears, but it was something I counted on. I don't even know if I really looked forward to any of it anymore—I just knew that not *everyone* got the privilege of living like this.

I should have been more grateful.

Why wasn't I more grateful?

I trusted this world, as much as I hated it. The world beyond the gates of Hoffman Estates was wildly unpredictable.

I could end up poor.

I could end up poor.

You fucking whore! I just kept hearing him scream, over and over again, till several of the neighbors were lined up in front of our house, some on foot and others in cars, watching this production with mouths open.

It was more action than this quiet little community had ever seen.

How could life ever be the same again?

What could we possibly say to these onlookers, who at one time had thought us to be perfect? How could we have any self-respect and mingle with these self-righteous, highly successful, judgmental residents of Hoffman Estates and even fake an attempt at *normalcy* after this fiasco?

It really was *that* bad.

This was the end of it all.

The day my life fell to the ground, shattered to pieces, and burned to ash.

Holy.

Fucking.

Shit.

How would I ever live down this horror and shame? This was a sin for which there was *no* forgiveness—shaming Michael Keifer Cage in public and disgracing his family name. For there *are* places of shame from which there is no return, and by God, I had found one.

I don't know what possessed me, but I guess I was already

halfway out of my body and entirely out of my mind, so I picked up something sharp, at least from what I remember. It could have been a rock, or the end of my high heel, and threw it at him, nailing him dead center between the eyes.

"You bitch!" he screamed, grabbing his face, crying out in pain. And this is when he went for real blood.

He tackled me, put his arms around me, and began choking me.

Strangling me.

Cutting off my oxygen.

I couldn't breathe, and this is where I thought, for the first time, *I'm really going to die.*

Right here.

Right now.

At the entrance to the ivory castle. On top of granite, marble, and concrete. In front of a beautiful, sparkling fountain.

How ironic.

From the ground where I struggled, I looked up and saw the blazing rage which consumed all of Michael Keifer. There was a gash in the center of his forehead, blood dripping down his face. His lip was swollen and out of his mouth fell one of his front teeth.

Holy.

Fucking.

Shit.

I'll kill you!

I'll kill you!

It was all I could hear before the sounds of the sirens screamed into the background.

Michael's father, Alfred, rushed out and pulled Michael Keifer off me before the police arrived.

I couldn't believe that someone had actually called them. By now, the whole street was standing in front of our house, gawking.

Dear God.

Somewhere in this little world, this is going to make the papers.

A patrol car pulled boldly into our driveway and out stepped two officers. One tried to clear the crowd at the base of the entrance, and the other came to tend to Michael and me.

"What's going on?" the officer asked Michael.

"She's trespassing on private property," said Michael, hunched over, out of breath, and barely able to speak.

"I live here!" I screamed in my defense.

"Not anymore, she doesn't!" shouted Alfred from the sidelines.

"Sir, please," the police cautioned Alfred.

"This is my soon-to-be ex-wife," said Michael to the officer, rising to his feet. "She no longer lives here and is trespassing on private property."

I felt as though I were swallowed whole. My life went from color to black-and-white, from fast track to slow motion, and from real time to movie time.

Make-believe.

Science fiction.

Fantasy island.

What the hell?

This had to be somebody else's life.

It couldn't be my own world falling completely apart. In the blur, I looked down on the ground and noticed the intricate design in the custom tiles that Michael had installed at the entryway of our home.

It was a baby with angel wings flying, carrying a bow and arrow. I couldn't believe I had never noticed this before now, and I wondered if Michael had really ever noticed it.

The tiles were exquisite, and sadly, I had lived here for more than a decade and had never noticed them.

I was sinking into a trance-like state.

Everything began to slow down.

Words were muffled.

Faces intense.

Doom and gloom were imminent.

I was bleeding.

Michael was bleeding.

His tooth was gone.

My dignity was gone.

Jean stood petrified in the foyer, her face streaked with tears. Alfred looked horrified and appeared to have aged ten to fifteen years right in front of us, with his beautiful silver hair seeming to turn to a dull white.

I glanced up toward the sky, almost as if to ask God how I could have made such a mess of things, and just as I did, I saw Mayo in a second-story window, looking down on all of us.

Dear God.

I will never forget the expression on his face when he looked at me, covered in blood, standing in the reflection of the patrol car's flashing red lights, with the family, neighbors, and his school friends watching. I knew then that my relationship with Mayo was irreparable. I also knew that he would remember this for the rest of his life and he would hate me for at *least* that long, if not longer.

"She doesn't live here anymore," I heard Michael say again, repeating it over and over.

Doesn't live here anymore.

Anymore.

Anymore.

He gestured for the police officers to join him in a private huddle, which they did. It must have lasted about three minutes, but it felt like an eternity.

Thirteen years of nothing.

Gone.

Oh God.

The police turned away from Michael, and one of the officers gathered up the plastic trash bags. The other extended his arm to me, suggesting we go to my car.

I turned away, unable to hold my head up as I returned to my Mercedes with tears flowing from my eyes.

"Look, miss," said the officer, "we don't want to have to arrest you for trespassing."

"This is my house!" I cried out. "I live here!"

The officer cut me off.

"I understand that you're upset about the divorce, but..."
Then he stopped, seemingly afraid to continue.

"But what?" I asked. "But *what*?"

"But . . . but . . ." he said.

"But you cannot continue to stalk Mr. Cage and his family."
My eyes widened.

"What?"

"We understand that you've been going through a lot of
stress, but . . ."

"I'm not stalking anyone!" I screamed.

The officers shot each other a look. It was the kind that said
this lady's crazy, and cut me off from speaking.

"Listen," said one of the officers, "I won't press charges this
time."

"Press charges?" I asked, shocked.

"Mr. Cage doesn't want to press charges," said the first officer.

"For what?" I asked, horrified.

"Assault," said the second officer, "but he will if you return."

I was at a loss to contribute another word of conversation to
this absurdity. I glanced at Michael and Alfred and Jean, and the
neighbors, and their kids, and their dogs, and finally, at Mayo.

All of them.

It appeared in that moment that they had more knowledge,
education, resources, love, and support—connections with things
that really mattered in life.

And what did I have?

Direct access to a sewer line headed straight for Milwaukee,
Wisconsin.

I got in my car.

Sat there.

Numb.

Started it up and drove away.

Shattered.

Burned.

Ash.

Chapter 5

As I descended beyond the fifth floor, I remembered the day I showed up on his doorstep—homeless.

Scared to death, I went to the only place I felt it was safe to go.

I went to Anthem.

I arrived at his house just after sunset, and did a slow walk up to his front door, where I knocked.

He didn't answer.

I knocked again.

No answer.

Did he go out for the evening?

I knocked again.

I began to panic.

Where would I go?

I could get a hotel room but I didn't want to be alone.

Where would I go?

I didn't have real friends. I had acquaintances through my husband, and by now I'm sure *his* side of the story was well under way, and his side of the world all hated me.

I knocked again.

No answer.

I called out his name.

Anthem!

Anthem!

Anthem!

I slid down to the bottom of the door and sat still, quiet.

Shaken.

Frightened.

My body was starting to ache, and the bruises were settling in.

Painful.

The blood had dried on my shirt and on the inside of my nostrils.

It was hideous.

My delicate, expensive blouse was torn and my designer jeans were ripped and dirty from rolling on the ground. My lovely French manicure was peeling, and the back of my head felt as though someone had split it open with a two by four.

I put my head between my legs and started to cry.

Moments later, the commotion must have caught Anthem's attention because he opened the door. I rose to meet him as he stood in the doorway wearing a pair of half-zipped jeans with no shirt.

He had a look of panic on his face, eyes wide. He seemed uncomfortable, unprepared for all of this.

"Oh my God!" he said, extending a hand to help me inside. "Are you okay?"

I entered his apartment and noticed a different vibe in the room. I could smell candles burning and saw two wineglasses sitting on his counter.

The setting was romantic, and before I could even respond to his question, a very tall, elegant black woman emerged from his studio. Her dress was disheveled, as if she threw it on in a hurry, or had been interrupted in the process of taking it off.

She eyed me suspiciously and thoroughly. It was the kind of visual interrogation that a woman does when she is feeling territorial and threatened.

"I'm sorry," I said, my heart dropping to the floor.

"No," said Anthem. "It's cool."

But it *wasn't* cool.

It was anything but cool.

Cool was the understatement of the year.

There was a bruised, bleeding white woman standing in the middle of his living room with a beautiful black woman waiting in the wings, both competing for his attention.

So who gets it?

His attention.

The one who bleeds the most and begs the loudest, standing in the middle of the floor.

Dirtied.

Bloody.

Humiliated.

That's who gets it.

"I'm going to go," the woman said to Anthem.

"Okay," he said, obviously uncomfortable, trying to pretend that it was not as awkward as it was, but it *was* that awkward—and *more*.

He walked the elegant black woman to the door. It was easy to interpret the odd look she gave me, confirming that my unannounced arrival had interrupted their evening. And furthermore, she did *not* appreciate it.

I could hear him talking softly to the woman, almost whispering. He said something to the tune of, "I'll call you later."

"Okay," she said with a tone that suggested he had better not disappoint her.

They embraced weakly, so as not to give too much away. When she left, he faced the door for several beats with his back to me before turning around. Maybe he was trying to figure out *how* to face me.

"Who was that?" I asked.

"A bad habit," he said, looking at me. "What happened to you?"

My lips started to quiver and I broke down in tears. Anthem walked over to me and wrapped me in his arms, holding me tight.

"He threw me out of the house!" I said between sobs.

"Your old man threw you out of the house?" he exclaimed.

"He took pictures of you and me at the park this morning . . . and he threw me out of the house . . . in front of my son and the neighbors."

"The son of a bitch is rich!" said Anthem. "You're set. Don't even trip it!"

I pulled away from him and stared in disbelief.

"I just lost my entire family and all you can say is 'I'm set. Don't trip it?'"

Anthem's face froze—he looked like a scolded little boy.

"I'm . . . just trying to give you a different way to look at it!"

"There is no other way to look at it! I've lost everything! My son! My home! My husband!"

"You didn't know your son," said Anthem. "You didn't even like your husband, and you hated going home, so what have you really lost?"

"I'm somebody's mother and wife," I said. "I have responsibilities."

"Yeah," he said. "You've wasted the last decade of your life being something to somebody else and *nothing* to yourself. That's why you feel like you got nothing. You got the whole thing twisted."

"I don't know what to do," I said, sitting on his couch.

"Well," he said, taking a seat beside me. "Chill here a minute and go from there."

"Okay," I said calmly, trying to clear my head. "I'll file for custody of Mayo and I'll get child support and alimony . . . and I'll get a home . . . move far away from Hoffman Estates . . ."

"Slow your roll," said Anthem. "Tonight . . . just chill."

"Okay," I said.

"Come in the room."

"No," I said, shaking my head.

"Why?"

"You had that woman in there."

"Oh, please," he said. "It's not like we did anything."

"Who was she?"

"You jealous?"

"Please," I said. "I have a husband."

"*Had* a husband," he reminded me. "I don't get you, Adrian."

"What do you mean?"

"You were miserable there," he said. "Miserable!"

"And your point?"

He didn't say anything, just looked at me, shaking his head. I stared at the emptiness of Anthem's living room.

"Even though you were miserable, you would have stayed forever?"

"Yes," I responded again.

"Why?" he asked, struggling to understand.

"Because he took better care of me than I could ever have taken of myself."

"Have you ever taken care of yourself?"

"Not in the big, grown-up world, all by myself," I replied, sounding more like a little girl than a woman.

"Then how do you know you can't do it?"

"I don't."

"Then why don't you try?"

"Because I like *pretty* things," I said.

"You like *pretty* things?" he asked, almost in disbelief.

"When I was poor I couldn't buy pretty things," I said. "And I *really* like pretty things."

"What about your life?" he asked. "Was it *pretty*?"

"On the outside it was beautiful."

"What about the inside?"

That was a question I could not answer, though I knew the truth, so I dismissed myself from the conversation, and quietly shut down and refused to respond to more questions. But my unwillingness to answer did not stop Anthem from asking, and they just kept coming.

What do you want to do?

Where do you want to go?

What do you want to be now that it's all over?

His words fell heavily upon me, irritating and cumbersome.

I looked around Anthem's loft, which had seemed interesting and creative before, but suddenly it appeared small, empty.

What was my definition of life?

Something pretty.

Something expensive.

Something *pretty expensive*.

He lacked all of it.

Where were his fine art pieces and expensive antique rugs? Where was the cabinet filled with fine china? And where had all of his silverware gone? Where was his pool? Jacuzzi? Boat?

What kind of barbaric living situation was this?

Where were his luxuries?

Where was his life?

It seemed that he did not have a life because he had no luxuries.

He was poor.

Oh my God, I thought to myself. Thirteen years had changed me. I had become one of them, the people I disapproved of for disapproving of others.

I had become them when I wasn't looking.

Accidentally.

It could have happened in my sleep.

"I'm going to bed," he said, handing me a blanket.

"Thanks," I said.

He kissed me on the cheek and left me sitting on his couch.

I walked to the window, looked outside, and watched the stillness of the street.

Empty.

Downtown loft.

Concrete prison.

What happened to the trees and lawns? And where, dear God, had the countryside gone?

Nowhere to spread out.

In the tiny little world of poor Anthem Rogers, occupant of four walls and a roof, void of beauty and life.

I could have died. Instead, I closed my eyes and lay down on the couch and went to sleep.

Chapter 4

As I descended beyond the fourth floor, I remembered the day I tried to figure out how to make it all make sense.

I laid my head down on Anthem's couch and I do not remember much about the next four days.

I remember brief intervals of quiet conversation with Anthem sitting by my side, getting high, asking me so many questions my mind started to hurt.

I was in a deep depression, and somewhere around the fourth day, Anthem picked me up off the couch and carried me into the shower, removed my pajamas, and began to run the water. Listless, I allowed him to put me inside the shower where he began to bathe me, running his hands over my body. His touch felt so good that my weakened body started to awaken and respond.

He spread toothpaste on his finger, and put his fingers inside my mouth. I began to suck his fingers and soon we were kissing passionately, rubbing against each other.

It felt so good.

I was human and alive. He turned me around, bent me over, penetrated me from behind.

It was raw and honest.

It was skin against skin and it felt pure. There was nothing separating me from my pain, and I could feel a part of him absorbing some of it. Then he started getting rough and I started getting scared. I untangled myself and backed against the shower. He pushed me against the wall and began to make love to me, thrusting till he came.

I backed away and looked at him.

This beautiful black man.

I likcd him.

Liked him a lot.

The sex was less intoxicating than it was before, somehow diminished. Very strange, but the whole ordeal was more fascinating when it was forbidden.

Now that we were exposed and our misdeeds were out in the open, it was much less thrilling. Maybe because my whole life had just gone to hell in a handbasket and I needed to figure out a way to survive.

I realized in this moment that Anthem was a childhood fantasy and nothing more. This would never be the "great love" I hoped to experience someday.

No.

He would *never* be that.

In the end, as beautiful as he was, he just wasn't my type. At this point, I didn't even know what my type was anymore. Anthem rinsed off and got out of the shower, leaving me there. When he left the bathroom, I stared at the room, realizing where I was.

It was tiny and claustrophobic.

Common.

It wasn't opulent—the tub wasn't sunken into the floor. There were no beautifully lit candles, no thick towels. It was just a john.

It had only been a few days and I had already begun to miss Hoffman Estates.

I didn't miss the people.

I missed the *things*.

Something about that seemed immoral, but it was true. I missed porcelain and marble, dancing fountains and lush green acreage. I missed the shiny bumpers of beautiful cars and the look of freshly starched, crisp shirts. I missed the gold cuff links that Michael used to wear.

As I stood in the middle of his tiny bathroom, drying off with a worn, tattered towel, I looked in the mirror and felt so poor. I missed fine linen with a passion.

"I have to get my own place," I said quietly to myself. "And re-create what I used to have."

I quickly dressed and entered the living room where Anthem sat with his head lowered, staring at a bunch of envelopes and papers. I could see PAST DUE stamped on all the bills.

"What's going on?" I asked quietly as I dried my wet hair.

"What does it look like?" he snapped. "They're about to cut off all my shit!"

His face, so angry and bitter, seemed so different from the man I knew just minutes before.

I scanned the bills he had scattered over the table. "Why didn't you pay these, Anthem?"

"You don't have a clue, do you?" he asked, giving me a dirty look. "Obviously, if I had the *money* to pay these fucking bills, they woulda been paid!"

"What did you do with all of your money?" I asked. "Bad habits?"

"What do you want me to say?" he said, heated. "Studio's been fucking slow."

"Okay, listen," I said. "Let's go to the bank and I'll get you the money . . ."

"Yeah?" he asked, much relieved.

"Of course," I said. "You've been very kind to let me stay here, and honestly, it's not a big deal."

"Cool," he said, pulling out a cigarette as he sat back on the couch. "Cool."

I smiled as I watched his calm, unconcerned demeanor. It was much different from what I was accustomed to.

Michael was always in control of our money, and if he ever had any financial worries, he kept them to himself.

I didn't like giving Anthem money. I felt in many ways it diminished him as a man, but if he was willing to take it without shame, then I was willing to give it to him without having shame *for* him.

Like I said before, it was becoming increasingly obvious he was not my type.

Later that day we drove to the bank in silence.

I drove.

He rode.

"How much do you need?" I asked him.

"Five grand would straighten me out," he said without hesitation.

"Okay," I replied. In essence, I had no concept of five grand anymore. Michael spent that each month just keeping one of our many club memberships updated.

"It's really not a big deal to you, huh?"

"Not the amount," I said, slightly irritated.

"But in other ways it is?" he asked, because he could sense that I was not impressed by his financial irresponsibility. "What's up, Adrian?"

"What do you mean?"

"You're on your high horse," he accused.

"What do you mean, I'm on my high horse?"

"You can't believe that I don't have it, can you?"

I was silent.

"I didn't come from money," I said defensively. "I know what hard times are like."

"But you haven't had them in so long, you've forgotten."

"Are you judging me?" I asked, snapping at him. "You're the one with a fistful of bad habits!"

"Are you judging *me*?"

"Can we drop it?" I asked, much too tired to argue.

"Hell, yeah," he said. "It was a dead-end conversation anyway."

"Sometimes—" I started, then stopped.

"Sometimes what?"

"You can be harsh," I said. "I don't remember you being like that when we were kids."

"That's because we ain't kids no more."

I didn't respond to that, or anything else he had to say, for the rest of the ride.

It was tense.

When I got to the bank I stopped the car and looked over at him. "It's probably better if you stay here," I said. "They know me here."

"That's cool with me," he said, leaning back in the seat. In that moment, he looked a little slovenly. I opened the doors to the bank and I could smell the money. It smelled so good I took a deep breath.

I stood in the line that all the "special" members stood in for personal attention from Vivian, the branch manager.

When she looked up and saw me, she smiled and then quickly exited to a back room. A young woman motioned for me to have a seat at her desk.

"How can I help you?" asked the young professional woman with the blond hair.

"I would like to make a withdrawal," I said, pulling out one of my savings booklets. "From this account."

I gave her the withdrawal slip for $10,000 in cash. She accepted the slip, ran the numbers, and the computer beeped once loudly. She looked at me and smiled apologetically.

"I'm sorry, Mrs. Cage," she said, "but this account has been closed."

"What?" I asked, eyes wide with fear. "Try this one!" I quickly replied, giving her another account number.

"No," she said. "It's closed."

"Try this!" I said frantically.

"Closed."

I pulled out a stack of credit cards.

"Try these cards!"

She did and her regretful expression never changed.

"They're all . . ."

"Where's Vivian?" I asked frantically, standing up, looking around the bank in desperation. "Please get Vivian! Vivian!"

"Adrian," said Vivian in a soft, soothing voice, standing behind me in a beautiful deep purple suit. She looked like money in that suit.

She looked like *me* in that suit. I used to look like that effortlessly. Now there was a lot of effort involved just to look decent.

"Vivian," I said desperately.

"Come with me," she said with a serious tone.

"Okay," I said, following her to her private office, where she took me in and closed the door.

"Have a seat," she suggested.

I would rather have stood because I was coming out of my skin, but I sat because she offered and I didn't want to be rude.

"Michael came here three days ago," she began, "and he closed all of your accounts and transferred the money to another account."

"What?" I asked, ready to burst into tears.

"He also closed all your bank credit cards," she said. "Listen, you've always been one of our best customers, and you've always been so nice to me . . ."

"How much money do I have in this bank, Vivian?" I asked, cutting her off.

"Nothing," she said slowly. "Do you have any other credit cards or accounts anywhere else?"

"Michael controls them," I said quietly.

"Do you have any money?"

I opened my purse and poured the contents on her desk. All told, I was good for about twenty dollars. And I got that by putting together a couple of fives, some one-dollar bills, and a whole lot of change. I scooped all the money into my hands—I had never felt so poor in my life.

A single tear leaked down my cheek.

"Get a lawyer and get paid," said Vivian.

"I can't afford a lawyer."

"He owes you something," she said.

"He'd burn in hell before he'd give me a penny."

"It's the law," she said.

"When you're worth as much as he's worth, and you know as

much as he knows, and you're connected in the way that he is, you *are* the law."

I slowly turned and walked out of the bank. It felt like everyone was looking at me, staring at my poverty-stricken face.

When I got back into the car, Anthem had his hand out, ready to take my last dollar. I looked at him, void of all emotion, and whispered, "It's all gone."

"What?" he asked, coming straight to attention.

"He cleaned out the accounts," I said. "There's nothing left."

"Take his ass to court," ranted Anthem.

"It's not that easy," I said.

"Get a lawyer," he grumbled. "Go to court. How hard can it be?"

"You don't know him," I said, starting the car, pulling off.

Later, back at Anthem's loft, we sat in the middle of his living room, staring at the walls.

I looked distraught.

He looked lackadaisical.

He picked himself up and went into the studio, got a joint, and started getting high.

I just sat in the chair and stared at him.

"Are you kidding me?" I asked him.

"What?" he asked, inhaling.

"You're going to get *high* right now?"

"You got a better plan?"

"We need to figure out what to do, Anthem."

"Nothing to do."

I looked around his apartment and I suddenly began to feel imprisoned.

Who was this man?

Who was Anthem Rogers?

Had I thrown away my life for this?

It was not so much that I was worried about my marriage, or even my son. I just regretted losing my lifestyle. I felt guilty about not feeling the guilt I was supposed to be feeling.

Had I really walked away from the good life for this?

Cohabitation by default with Anthem Rogers, an unmotivated, joint-smoking musician who could not pay his rent and did not seem terribly concerned about it.

He was *so* different from Michael Keifer.

Very, very different.

Anthem disappeared into the studio, where he spent the night playing the guitar and getting high. I spent the evening sitting in his living room chair, staring at the walls, trying to figure out what I was going to do.

I stayed awake most of the night.

Couldn't sleep.

Couldn't stop thinking.

Could not stop reliving the horror of how it all ended in front of the whole damn world.

Couldn't sleep.

Couldn't stop thinking.

Couldn't stop reliving the horror. And when I would nod off, I would suddenly awaken again.

From sleep.

To think.

And relive the horror.

I stayed up what seemed like all night long, only to nod off for a single minute and wake up thirty seconds later to a changed world.

All over again.

Waking up wasn't easy today. At all.

I woke to the odd sound of gurgling noises coming from the bathroom.

"Anthem," I called. "Anthem."

I got off the chair and slowly eased my way to the bathroom, where I stood at the door and knocked.

"Anthem?" I called out again.

Gurgling.

Choking.

Gurgling.

"Anthem!" I called in a panic, banging on the door. "Anthem! Anthem! Anthem!"

Gurgling.

Choking.

Coughing.

I tried the door, but it was locked. In a panic, I began banging on the door.

"Anthem!"

But there was no answer.

Nothing.

I stood at the door, banging, knocking, and pleading.

"Anthem!" I screamed. "Open the door! Open the door!"

Eventually, I heard the lock give way and he finally unlocked it from the other side.

I stopped.

Looked at the door.

But he didn't come out.

"Anthem?" I called to him cautiously.

The gurgling stopped.

And the choking ceased.

Slowly, I opened the door and poked my head inside cautiously. Anthem was sitting on the toilet seat, fully clothed, with the lid down. He was wearing a pair of jeans and a tank top.

"Anthem?" I called to him. "Are you okay?"

"Why were you talking to them?" he asked, head lowered.

"Who?"

"*Them!*" he screamed. "You were talking to them about me!"

"Anthem," I said, extending my hands toward him, "I wasn't talking to anybody. What did you smoke last night?"

"Just don't put my shit out there like that!" he screamed. "Don't tell my business to everybody!"

"What did you smoke last night, Anthem!" I yelled.

"I heard you on the phone!" he accused.

"You're being irrational," I said. "What did you take?"

On the edge of those words, he jumped up from the toilet and punched the mirror with his fist.

It shattered.

I screamed.

I ran out of the apartment, and down to my car, where I jumped in and drove off.

Where was I going?
I had twenty dollars in my pocket.
Where was I going?
Hoffman Gated Estates?
Maybe I could buy property on the lower end of Hoffman Estates for twenty bucks, minus property taxes, and forget about a maidservant.
Where was I going?
Hoffman Gated Estates?
Anthem had gone mad.
I had almost gone mad.
I had twenty bucks.
Where was I going?
Hoffman Gated Estates?
Michael Keifer "Prick of the Year" Cage never did look so good as he did in this moment.
Where was I going?
Hoffman Gated Estates, where I would roll around in my lush backyard and sink into my plush furniture; kiss my gorgeous, marble-covered countertops; and take a birdbath in my elegant, flowing fountains. And maybe I would go into my state-of-the-art kitchen and prepare a feast, just because I could, but not because I could cook, because I couldn't cook a thing.
Where was I going?
Hoffman Gated Estates.
Where was I going?
To take my crazy, violent, psychopathic son to a water polo lesson. Oh, how I cherished the thought.
Where was I going?
To brunch with the uppity neighbor's wife with the bouffant hairdo and a poodle named Sophie.
Where was I going?
Hoffman Gated Estates.
To have tea with Jean and Alfred fucking Cage, and listen to their god-awful, warped opinions on the lower middle class.
Where was I going?
Hoffman Gated Estates.

Yet instead, I wound up at his job.

Across town.

Michael Keifer Cage's office.

The building never looked so good. As a matter of fact, it had never looked good at all, but it looked good today.

Where was I going?

Hoffman Gated Estates?

It was ten o'clock in the morning and I knew that he would be here, but I wasn't certain I would have the courage to go inside and face him.

But I did.

I had to.

Slowly, I entered the front lobby of his office, and saw Roxie, the receptionist. I could tell by the look on her face that she knew what had happened.

She looked very uncomfortable, and I looked like a wreck.

"Mrs. Cage," she said, acknowledging me.

Yes.

Yes.

I was still Mrs. Cage, wasn't I?

"Is Michael available?" I asked.

Her eyes widened and I could tell by her nervous twitch that it was killing her to spill the following sentence: "I was told to call security . . ."

Pause.

Pause.

Pause.

Breathe.

"By Mr. Cage!" she blurted.

"I need to speak with him," I insisted.

"I'll get in trouble," she pleaded.

"Roxie," I said sharply, "do you want me to blow through those doors and into his office?"

Her eyes shifted to the ground; then she slowly picked up the phone and dialed Michael Keifer's office.

"Mr. Cage," she said, "can you please come to the lobby?"

Why? I'm sure that was his response on the other end.

"It's important," she said.

Why?

"It's kind of an emergency," she said, before I snatched the phone out of her hand.

"I'm in the lobby, Michael," I said firmly into the phone. "Now, are you coming out here or am I going in there?"

There was silence on the other end, and within moments, he was in the lobby summoning me to a private conversation outdoors.

I noticed his appearance—elegant and exquisite. His suit was pristine, tailored, and expensive.

Yes.

This is what money looks like.

This is what it means to live well. I'd lived well for so many years I'd forgotten what it was to be common, and during this time of "desperate commonness," I began to understand, line by line and note by note, why it was that I stayed.

Everything's a trade.

You've got to make sure you get more than you give away. It's how we all balance our lives and make them make sense.

"I will have you arrested if you ever come here again," he said calmly, leading the way into the courtyard area in the back of his office.

"Michael," I pleaded, prepared to beg him to take me back. "I don't have any money."

He stopped, turned, looked at me with a blank stare. It was as if he never knew me at all, or even gave a damn. "Welcome to the rest of your life," he said.

"I need money, Michael," I said, quickly growing irritated.

"Then I suggest you look for employment," he said, with his back turned to me, staring at a bed of flowers.

I took a deep breath, and filled with anxiety, tears began to fall.

"I am your wife," I said.

"Divorce papers are forthcoming," he said. "I suggest you sign them without delay."

"What about my son?"

"The boy's filled with rage," he said. "He hates you, you know."

I lowered my head.

"What do you make of that?" he asked. "It's not natural for a child to hate a parent."

His comments hurt deeply, ripping me apart.

"I'm still his mother," I said. "I'll fight you in court."

"With what?" he asked, laughing. "Attorneys are expensive, but if you need a referral, I know someone who comes highly recommended."

I looked at him with contempt.

"I have eyewitnesses who saw you assault Mayo in your automobile, right out in front of his school."

"I didn't!"

"My mother witnessed it and so did several teachers," he said. "I have sworn affidavits on file. You could go to jail for abuse."

"I didn't abuse my son!" I stated emphatically.

"Sexual abuse," he said.

"What?" I asked, aghast.

"There have been accusations of sexual abuse."

"What are you talking about?"

"The nanny."

"Mrs. Brown?"

"She saw you . . . in his room one night."

"That's not true and you know it's not true!" I screamed.

"It doesn't matter what you know," he said with a smile. "It only matters what you can prove. And I can prove it happened, more than you can prove it didn't."

"You son of a bitch!"

"A child molester is a naughty, naughty thing to be. It's worse than being a murderer, don't you think?"

"Why are you doing this to me?" I asked, horrified.

"This is the bed you lay down in when you got under the sheets with a nigger."

He turned and walked back toward the office.

"Divorce papers are coming," he said. "Sign them immediately."

"And what if I don't, you motherfucker?"

"Well," he said calmly, turning back to look at me. "Right now you only *wish* you were dead. If you contest the divorce, attempt to see Mayo, or make a pathetic effort to get one dime from me . . . I will personally see to it that your *wish* comes true."

"How do you live with yourself?" I asked him, looking so deeply into his eyes that I could see the devil himself.

"I," he said with an evil smirk, "live *very, very* well. Always have. Always will."

And with that, he reentered his office.

I stood in the center of the courtyard, stunned to numbness by what had just happened, and no matter how I tried to wrap my head around it, I just couldn't.

Chapter 3

As I descended beyond the third floor, I remembered the day I learned the meaning of the words, "You dead, niggah. You dead."

I spent most of the day driving around the windy streets of Chicago, trying to figure out what to do, where to go, and who to be. I wasn't going to be Adrian Cage much longer. I would return to the world of Adrian Moses, fallen from grace.

I got on the expressway and made the eighty-eight-mile journey back to Milwaukee. I had not been to Milwaukee in thirteen years, and I didn't know what to expect, but I felt like I had noplace else to go.

I drove blind.

Numb.

And dumb, into the future by returning to the past.

Upon my arrival, I found the city still looked the same.

Home of the common man.

Center stage of America.

There were some refurbished buildings and then there were those buildings that were run-down beyond repair.

People still drove the same rusted cars with the dings in the side of the doors. The mail carriers looked like the same ones I remembered from childhood, just older with white hair. The grocery-store clerks and the coffee-shop waitresses looked like the same people, too, frozen in time.

I got turned around in the center of the city, but eventually made my way to the street where Reva Joe Moses lived. I had not spoken to her in thirteen years and knew she wouldn't be happy to see me.

I just came by to say hello, was how I imagined the awkward conversation would go. *After all this time.*

Who was I kidding? She probably wouldn't even remember me, and even if she did, she'd curse me for disappearing. Not that she really cared, but it was just the principle of the thing.

I turned onto her dumpy little street and ventured to the end where the road ran out. It always ran out down there. It hadn't changed much, except that it had gotten older, too.

I stopped in front of the house and sat out front for an hour, contemplating the miracle of *time*.

It looked like holy hell.

The bushes.

The weeds *(I remember those weeds)*.

A crumbling roof.

Peeling paint.

Eventually, I got out of the car and knocked on the door. I was nervous because I didn't know what to expect on the other side. Would I be embraced by a kinder, gentler woman or assaulted by the bitterness of her words?

No one answered.

I knocked again and anxiously waited. Eventually it opened, and a middle-aged woman stood on the other side. But it *wasn't* Reva Joe.

"Hi," I said quietly.

"Can I help you?" she asked, coming out onto the steps.

"Yes," I said. "I was looking for Reva Joe Moses."

"Who?"

"Reva Joe Moses," I said. "She lives here. I'm her grand-daughter."

"You talking 'bout the old, cantankerous woman who used to live here a couple years ago?"

"Yeah," I said.

"She died last summer," said the woman, the words rolling effortlessly from her mouth.

My heart dropped.

I had no idea.

"Oh," I mumbled quietly beneath my breath. "I see."

"I'm sorry," said the woman. "She was sick pretty bad, from what I hear . . ."

I nodded.

"How did you say you knew her?"

"Granddaughter," I said, almost embarrassed to utter the word.

"Guess ya'll wasn't real close, huh?"

"No," I said. "Guess not."

"You wanna come in for some iced tea?"

"No, thank you," I said with a smile.

The woman caught a glimpse of my car and then did a thorough inspection. "You from around here?"

"Kinda . . . sort of," I said.

"Looks like you done real good for yourself."

"Have a nice day," I said with a gentle smile, then stepped away from the property.

Got in my car.

Drove back to Chicago.

Lost.

Scared.

Confused.

I made my way down the only street I knew, Anthem's street. In a very strange way, he was the only friend I had in the world, though with the passing of each day, and the use of more and more drugs, he seemed to be losing his grip.

I got out of the car, hoping he would be himself upon my return.

I knocked on his door.

Slowly.

I almost wanted him not to answer, to turn away and force me to do something great with my life for a change. But he answered, and when he did, he looked like he was so relieved to see me.

"I've been worried sick all day!" he said, swooping me up into his arms.

"It wasn't a good scene here earlier, Anthem."

"I know, baby," he said. "And I'm sorry. That reefer's got me tripping. My boy laced that shit with something that made me paranoid."

"You scared me," I said.

"Oh, shit," he said. "It's just reefer. Where did you go today?"

"I went to see my grandmother."

"I remember her," he said with a smile. "The old lady with the bad attitude."

"Yeah."

"How is she?"

"Dead," I said without hesitation.

"Well," he said, "she's probably doing better than the rest of us. We're gonna have to be up outta here by the end of the week."

"Anthem," I said, exhausted.

"Eviction notice," he said, handing me the papers.

"Oh God," I said.

"Fucking sucks," he said, turning away.

"What are you gonna do?"

"I got a sister in Cincinnati," he said. "I'm going to go chill for a bit."

I nodded.

"And you?" he asked. "What're your plans?"

"Thought I'd spend the summer in the south of France," I said in jest. "I've been there enough times . . . maybe I could get a job as a tour guide."

"Really?" he asked, taking me more seriously than I intended him to.

"I'll be fine, Anthem."

"Get that rich motherfucker to give you some alimony and you will be fine for sure," he said.

"Yeah," I said, nodding. I didn't have the energy to discuss my earlier meeting with Michael.

"You know," he said, "you *can* come with me."

I was shocked at the invitation, and even more surprised that for about thirty seconds, I actually considered it. It wasn't like I had any better offers. It wasn't like I had any offers at all.

But I knew if I did go, it would be very short-term. As much as I liked Anthem, I knew our worlds would never mesh. He had never lived in the kind of world that I'd lived in, even as a visitor, and I had not lived in the kind of world he'd lived in for a very long time, and was trying like hell not to go back. And as beautiful as he was, I knew Anthem would never be anything more than he was now. And that just wasn't enough.

A flat-busted musician blowing in the wind without any real connection to anything. Funny thing—on many levels he and I were a lot alike.

I, too, had spent my life blowing in the wind. The only difference was that I was blowing in and out of million-dollar rooms where the breeze was much more gentle.

"I'm serious," he said. "I want you to come with me."

"To Cincinnati?"

"She's got a three-bedroom brick house, couple kids, family pet . . . backyard."

"Yeah?" I asked enthusiastically. It was wonderful to hear about a normal life.

"She's got a real family, you know," he said.

"Is she married?"

"Oh, yeah," he said. "Nice guy. Joey's a garbageman. Super-nice guy."

I nodded.

"Ever had a real family before?"

"I used to," I said.

"What happened to them all?"

"They died," I said with tears in my eyes.

"You know what happens when you die?" he asked, wiping a tear away from my eyes.

I shook my head.

"You get a chance to do it all over," he said. "Get a chance to come back and do the damn thing right."

"What's Cincinnati like?" I asked, holding his hand.

"It's like shit wrapped in silk," he said, laughing.

"What does that mean?"

"Ain't shit going on there," he said. "It's just a change of scenery till a new train comes back around."

I sat down on the couch.

"Anthem, I'm scared."

"Don't be scared," he said. "Just start over. Think about it. Think about Cincinnati."

"Okay."

He kissed me gently on the forehead.

It was a funny thing about Anthem.

He was beautiful in spite of himself. He wasn't as motivated and ambitious as I was accustomed to, yet there was something about him that was endearing.

"Start over, huh?" I asked him.

"Yeah," he said. "Start over."

"I gotta get ready."

"Ready for what?"

"Got a couple guys coming over tonight to play some cards."

"Really?"

"Yeah," he said. "Gotta earn some train fare to get up to Cincinnati."

"Anthem," I said. "We can just drive my car."

Even I was surprised when I said it. His face lit up.

"So you're coming?" he asked.

I paused.

Contemplated.

"Yeah," I said slowly. "I think so."

I couldn't believe my own agreeability.

Yeah, I think so.

What?

That was huge!

Yeah, I think so. I think I'm going to move with you to Cincinnati and leave my home, my husband, and my son.

My life.

The world as I knew it.

My home.

My husband.

My son.

Life as I knew it.

Then I realized, it was already over.

I was excommunicated from my home.

I was divorcing my husband, and my son hated me for sport.

It was already over.

I wasn't leaving anything.

Everything had already left me. In the process of trying to fathom the unfathomable, and understand the unexplainable, I saw Anthem's eyes light up.

"Right on!" he screamed, looking like a little boy in a grown-up body. "We'll leave at the end of the week!"

"Okay," I replied on auto-response.

"Okay, girl," he said, kissing me on the forehead, then each cheek, and the lips. "Gotta get ready. The guys are gonna be here soon."

"Who's coming?"

"Just some thug niggahs from the South Side," he said, laughing.

"Real thugs?"

"Musician thugs," he said in jest. "Not the kind of guys you're used to seeing in your neck of the woods, but they're harmless."

"Okay," I said. "Do you want me to make snacks for you guys?"

"Naw," he said. "Just chill out here and watch TV. We're gonna do our thing in the studio. We're playing for money so it can get kind of intense . . . it's best if you kinda lay low for the night. You know?"

"Okay," I said. "I'll just hang out here and watch some television."

"Cool," he said.

No sooner had I finalized my evening's plan than the doorbell rang. Automatically, I jumped to answer it, but Anthem stopped me.

"I got it," he said.

"Okay."

He opened the door and three of the largest black men I had ever seen were standing on the other side. They were big, black, and intimidating. All three had bald heads and some pretty intense tattoo art. Two of them had to be 300 pounds and at least six-five. The smallest one was about six-two and 250.

They all had a similar vibe and look. It was pretty scary.

In fact, they all looked like ex-cons, and I was nervous having them in the house. These guys didn't look like any musicians I had ever seen. These guys looked like bad news.

"Hey, motherfucker," said one of the guys to Anthem.

"What's up, niggah?" said Anthem, giving them five or whatever you call it.

"These are my partners," said the man who appeared to be the ringleader. He was the one with the big gut and a single gold tooth in the middle of his crooked smile. "These are my homies," he said. "KC and Mason."

"What's up, niggah?" said KC.

Oh my.

This was pretty intense for a blond-haired, blue-eyed, white girl from Saxon, Wisconsin, by way of Hoffman Estates, Illinois.

The man introduced as Mason didn't speak. He was the scariest one of all. He looked like he was on a weekend visa from hell, but that he would definitely be going back. And he also looked like he could be taking somebody with him.

He was pretty creepy.

"You ready to lose your shirt, niggah?" KC said to Anthem.

"Don't come in here talking that shit, man," said Anthem.

The guys entered the loft and all eyes immediately stopped on me. I felt like I was going to have a heart attack.

"This is my lady," said Anthem to the guys.

Whoa, I thought.

This was intense.

We had never discussed me being his *lady*.

I was still somebody's wife. Wasn't sure I was in a position to be someone else's *lady* right now.

"Snow White," said the ringleader, whose name I would soon discover was Tito. He was the big one with the gut and gold tooth.

"Damn," said KC with a frown, "that's the whitest bitch I ever seen."

I gasped, almost choking on my spit. *Did he just call me the whitest bitch he'd ever seen?*

How do you shake someone's hand after that kind of introduction?

"Squash that shit, niggah," Anthem said to Tito. "C'mon, let's do this thing."

"All right, bitch," Tito said, as he winked at me and they disappeared into the studio.

I was terribly uneasy with those guys in the house. It just felt like they were from the wrong side of the tracks and that anything could happen, especially with them gambling for money.

I sat in the living room and listened to the shouting, yelling, and moaning of the winners and the losers. I couldn't tell who was winning and who was losing, but there was a lot of commotion coming from the studio.

As the night progressed, the house was permeated with the scent of marijuana, strong and pungent. I could barely breathe. It was awful. Plus the shouting and all the hoopla.

It was all just too much.

I had to go for a walk.

I needed to breathe fresh air and clear my head.

I started to get dizzy from the fumes of the blunts.

"Motherfucker, you cheating!" I heard someone scream as I put on a light jacket.

"Fuck you, niggah!" I heard Anthem shout.

"Motherfucker, you were holdin' the ace on the side!"

"Yeah, the niggah was straight cheatin'!"

"Fuck all of you niggahs!" I heard Anthem say again.

"I'll bust a cap in your ass!"

"Chill with that shit!"

"Yeah," said Anthem. "Ain't gonna be no bullshit jumping off like that!"

Those were the last words I recall from that night. Everything else was more like a blur. And what I heard next was not human. It was the sound of savages waging war. Frozen stiff, I was holding one hand on the doorknob, listening intently to the escalating violence.

"You dead, niggah!"

"You dead!"

"What the fuck!" were Anthem's last words.

"You dead, niggah!"

Several rounds of gunfire echoed throughout the room, loud and thunderous.

It was final.

Armageddon.

Someone screamed and then the rest of the world went silent.

I stood at the door, petrified.

Horrified.

Completely in shock, I didn't know what to do or how to put one foot in front of the other. From the back there was movement and my eyes were fixated there, until I saw Mason emerge, covered in blood, holding a fistful of dollars in one hand and a gun in the other.

Our eyes locked and in that moment I didn't know if he was going to turn the weapon on me and blow me away.

I screamed, opened the door, and ran out into the cool night air, hysterical.

Screaming.

Shouting.

Crying.

And reliving the echoes of . . .

You dead, niggah!

You dead, niggah!

You dead, niggah!

You dead!

Chapter 2

As I descended beyond the second floor, I remembered death all over again.

2:47 A.M.

Kasey Walker Jones was pronounced dead.

2:48 A.M.

Tito Lynne Jackson was pronounced dead.

2:49 A.M.

Anthem Rence Rogers was pronounced dead.

I was found delirious in the middle of a Chicago street fifty-seven minutes prior to the gruesome discovery of their bodies in the back of Anthem's loft.

I was brought to the police station, where I was asked to make an official statement and identify Mason DeWilt James, who was picked up and charged two hours later for the triple homicide.

I don't remember what I said or how I said it. I was numb to the news when the police detective said, "Anthem Rogers is dead."

"He's not dead," I said.

"What?" asked the detective.

"He's not dead," I repeated. "He's just starting over."

He shook his head and had me sign my sworn statement.

I signed without blinking, thinking, or breathing.

"Don't leave town no time soon," he said. "We're gonna need your testimony in court."

I didn't blink.

Think.

Or feel.

I didn't say a word.

Agree.

Or disagree.

I didn't cry.

I wasn't quite an animal but I was a long way from being a human.

"Miss," I could hear the detective calling, "Miss . . . Miss . . ."

I looked at him with blank eyes.

"Is there anybody I should call?" he asked.

Mother's dead.

Father's dead.

Reva Joe is dead.

Michael Keifer wouldn't take the call.

And neither would Jean or Alfred.

Mayo hates me.

I have no friends.

And Anthem Rogers just died. So, "No . . . there's really no one to call."

I got up and slowly made my way to the exit door, and just then I saw Anthem's mother enter. She was the same as I remember, just older.

I recognized her behind those bloodshot eyes.

Devastated.

I knew that she and Anthem had stopped talking long ago, but I wasn't sure why. I knew they were close at one time.

So . . .

Why did they give up on one another?

Mothers always belong to their sons and sons belong to their mums.

Don't they?

All but me and Mayo, and her and Anthem.

She walked up to me and put her hands along the side of my face. "You were the heartbeat of American culture. You were everything from California dreaming to upstate New York royalty. You were the envy of every nation. You shoulda learned how to use what you had, but you ain't got it no more. You dumb motherfucker," she whispered into my ear. *"You were a real dumb motherfucker."*

Chapter 1

As I descended beyond the first floor, I remembered the day I flew.

After I left the station I spent the night walking the streets.
Lost.
Nowhere to go.
Nowhere to be.
No one to see.
No one to report to or wait to hear from.
One vast pool of nothing.
I looked at my life, and I was not fond of the part I was playing. I was ready to exit the stage.
Time to start over.
Like Juno.
Like me.
It was time.
Deep down inside, I always knew I would follow in the footsteps of my father.
Like Juno.
Like me.
It *was* time.
Time for a new assignment.
An awakening.

Unfolding.

My life, so upside down, needed to be put back together again.

Living people die when they no longer have the will to put themselves back together again, to smooth over the cracks, fill in the holes, and blend the uneven parts. Yes, living people die when they no longer have the determination and courage to put themselves back up on the shelf for display and public consumption.

Simply put, living people die when they no longer go on living.

When dawn broke the next morning I made my way to the twenty-eighth floor of the Landmark II building. This was the stage where I wanted to set my last scene. It only seemed fitting to stage my finale in the building that houses the prestigious Michael Keifer Cage law firm.

Meticulously.

Beautifully.

Brilliantly.

I climbed twenty-eight flights of stairs, gained access to the roof, walked to the edge.

Looked down.

Caught a rush, thrill, chill.

Took a deep breath.

Closed my eyes.

And I *flew*.

Chapter 0

This is the story of a dying woman who has twenty-eight floors to tell her side of the story and not a moment more. Time is of the essence, so let us not waste a page, a splotch of ink, or a breath.

This is not a suicide note; this is a suicide novel, and once I hit the concrete, the rest of this story will be written in my blood. But do not be alarmed— it is a fascinating story, *I promise*.

I hit the ground.

Upon impact, I was ripped apart by the concrete.

I died instantly.

Upon death, I learned being born and dying are synonymous. They are interchangeable. Birth is a guarantee of death and death is a guarantee of an eventual rebirth.

You never end.

Just start over.

You are as dead now as you will ever be.

I promise.

I know this for sure because I speak to you now from the other side.

I'm dead yet alive at the same time.

In fact, time does not exist on this side.

All time as we know it is simultaneous.

Past, present, and future all exist at once.

Earthly existence is governed by the laws of time and space, both of which are illusions. Perhaps it may be difficult to grasp this knowledge from the other side; however, every single word of it is truth.

The universe is *magical*.

Just you wait and see.

I chose to come back again.

I still had things to do, experience, and be.

I was rebirthed into a new body.

January 13, 2107, 8 pounds, 13 ounces.

African-American female, born to affluent parents, Paul and Marlene Washington, in Tucson, Arizona.

At birth, my parents named me AGAVNI.

It means *dove*.

I came back.

I'm here.

NAKED LOVE

Darnella Ford

The following questions are intended
to enhance your group's discussion of
this book.

Discussion Questions

1. Explore the nature of Adrian's relationship with her father, Juno.

2. Do you feel that Juno's sexuality had a dramatic impact on Adrian's childhood? If yes, please explain.

3. Explore the nature of Adrian's relationship with her grandmother, Reva Joe. Do you feel that Reva Joe's "negative" outlook on Juno, affected the way in which she also related to Adrian? Would you classify the grandmother as "abusive?"

4. Reva Joe's "breakdown" following the comments from the controversial radio show revealed a deeper, conflicted aspect of Reva Joe. What would you say was "revealed" through her emotional collapse following the program?

5. As children, how would you describe Anthem and Adrian's interaction? Should young people be allowed to explore dating "across the color line?"

6. How did life change for Adrian following her arrival at the school for girls in Tucson, Arizona? Would you categorize it as a "good change?"

7. Why didn't Adrian tell Dayglo's mother about the rape? And ultimately, did Dayglo's mother provide a "payoff" in terms of a scholarship, as a way to apologize for what had happened to Adrian?

8. What was the basis for Adrian's marriage to Michael Keifer Cage? Explore the nature of their relationship as husband and wife? And to their dysfunctional son?

9. Why did Adrian rekindle the "romance" with Anthem as an adult? Explore the consequences.

10. What did you connect with as the ultimate "theme" of the book? Was there any personal "themes" that resonated within you? If so, what were they?

11. What did you think of the unique storytelling style of this book, starting at Chapter 28 and descending in number down to Chapter 0?

12. What is the overall impression you were left with after reading the last page? Would you recommend this book to friends?